THE HEAD OF THE
SNAKE

THE HEAD OF THE SNAKE

Tim Conner

Three Towers Press

Milwaukee, Wisconsin

*This book is dedicated to my wife Elaine,
my two daughters Kerry and Kristi, my son Andrew,
my two sisters, Colleen and Katie,
the good people of Chicago,
and all United States Marines.*

Copyright © 2019 by Timothy Conner
All rights reserved.

This is a work of fiction. Names, characters, places, and events are either the products of the author's imagination or used in a fictitious manner. Any resemblance to actual persons, living or dead, or actual events, is purely coincidental.

Published by Three Towers Press,
An imprint of HenschelHAUS Publishing, Inc.
www.henschelHAUSbooks.com
Milwaukee, Wisconsin

ISBN: 978159598-724-2
E-ISBN: 978159598-725-9
LCCN: 2019945769

Printed in the United States of America

PROLOGUE

The street gangs of Chicago battle each other every day for power and control of drugs. Innocent people, including children, have died in the crossfire. City police, the Feds, politicians and neighborhood leaders have tried to fight and shut down the gangs in a variety of ways, but nothing has solved the problem. The inattention at all levels of government to the roots of the street violence is drawing wide criticism. Racially biased zoning laws, discriminatory lending and insurance policies, police discrimination and "ghettoized" communities generate a cycle of poverty and organized gang crime, rendering the neighborhoods dysfunctional. The gangs are just symptoms of a more serious social disease. The Disciples, Vice Lords, and P-Stones, who ravaged Cabrini Green and Robert Taylor Homes in the past, have been broken apart, only to be replaced by a hundred other gangs.

The five former Marines involved in this adventure served together in a Marine Huey Helicopter Squadron in Iraq and Afghanistan and are now back in civilian life in Chicago dedicating themselves to ridding the victimized neighborhoods of the savage gang leaders.

Creed ("Chief") Tsoodle returned to run his family's corn and soybean farm outside of Keokuk, Iowa in the far southeast corner of the state where the Mississippi and the Des Moines rivers converge. He is a descendent of the Sac and Fox Indians who were led by Chief Keokuk in the early nineteenth century. He has strong Native American features like his forefathers.

Nick "Guapo" Santos came back to Chicago to become a city police officer in the Gang Unit. He grew up being threatened by the gangs in the days of the brutal and crafty Larry Hoover and the Gangster Disciple Nation. But he escaped to the Marines. He's back now and has committed himself to ridding the neighborhoods of this scum.

Conor Cavanaugh thought about making a career out of the Marines as a helicopter pilot but returned to run his family's aviation charter business in Milwaukee after his father died. Conor also pilots the traffic 'copter for WTMJ-TV. He is still in the Marine Corps Reserves as a Captain.

Emma Scott was the only female in the Huey Helicopter Squadron. She now serves as a senior aircraft mechanic for United Airlines at O'Hare. Her grandfather came to the States from Ethiopia. She is beautiful like so many Ethiopians, shining face and glowing white teeth, like Haile Selasse looked when he was a boy.

Andrew ("Gunny") Franklin came back to Chicago after 25 years in the Corps. A gunnery sergeant is a highly regarded rank in the Corps. He is still in good shape and his tanned face and strong jaw would make for a colorful Marine Corps recruiting poster. He now works for a private security firm out in Rosemont. He meets fellow former Marines at the Marine Corps League bar almost every night.

The most harrowing event for the Marines was the Battle of Fallujah. It was a joint operation among American, British, and Iraqi forces against the Iraqi insurgency in November and December of 1994. Operation Al-Fajr (The Dawn) was the fiercest battle of the war, and for the US Marines, it was the heaviest urban conflict since the Battle of Hue City in Vietnam in 1968.

It was the second time the Marines entered Fallujah that year. In the spring, days after four American contractors were killed and their bodies strung up on a bridge, the Marines went in to clear the city of insurgents. They withdrew after a month of fighting, then reentered in November.

Creed, Nick, Conor, and Emma were members of Marine Light Attack Helicopter Squadron 169, part of Marine Air Group 39. The Group flew Super Cobras, Hueys, and CH-46 Sea Knights. They flew to transport and provide air support for several battalions of Marines.

The insurgents had people shooting from the rooftops, from the houses, from the sewers, or wherever they could take a shot. In the six-week battle, a hundred Americans died and 600 were injured. As a comparison or contrast, in the 1945 battle for Iwo Jima, 6,800 Marines died and 20,000 were injured in four weeks. Nevertheless, both battles left grieving Marine families with empty chairs at the dinner table forever.

Luckily, Creed, Nick, Conor, Emma, and Gunny Franklin came home safely. But their mental scars are still raw, and PTSD is always present to some degree. They all have flashbacks of bloody, badly injured and dead Marines whom they flew back to base. The former Marine squadron mates are brought back together by a tragic event and are dedicating themselves to the risky mission of bringing down the gangs and making the streets safe again for the people who have suffered so much. This is their daring story.

Plato said it best. "Only the dead have seen the end of war.

Semper Fidelis

CHAPTER ONE
A TRAGEDY AND DOWN THE BIG RIVER

The early evening call comes from Nick's mother Adoncia, who can hardly speak, as she spurts out broken sentences. "Come home, Nick, come home. It's Sammy."

"Slow down, Mom. What about Sammy?"

His mother, now sobbing, finally gets it out. "Sammy was shot by a gang on his way home from a track meet! Come home, Nick."

"Where's Sammy, Mom?"

"He's being taken to Rush."

"Mom, are you able to get there with Uncle Pete and Aunt Maria?"

"Yes, Guapo, yes."

"I'll meet you there." Nick switches on the blue rollers of his unmarked squad car, does a U-turn, and heads down the Ike toward Rush. His partner, Sherri Botkin, calls dispatch to give them the information. Sherri is Nick's attractive, young, police Gang Unit partner, who has only been a Chicago police officer for seven months. She recently graduated with a criminology degree from the University of Texas. Her father, an aerodynamics engineer, now works for Boeing in Chicago, having left NASA when the Shuttle program was shut down. Her mother, Patricia, is a professor of social psychology at the University of Chicago.

They arrive at the emergency room entrance at Rush just as Nick's mom, Uncle Pete and Aunt Maria are arriving. His aunt is sobbing and his mom is trying to console her sister. Uncle Pete is fuming, anxious, and not much emotional help to the women. Pete is tough, with a body like chiseled granite. He had worked as a construction foreman before he became a carpenter.

They all enter the emergency room together. Nick goes straight to the desk, shows his badge and very quickly gets the attention of the admittance people. "Do you have a Sammy Fernandez here?"

"Yes, Officer, he's in emergency surgery."

"He's my nephew. Can you give me his condition, please?"

The administrator, seeing the condition of Sammy's family, whispered to Nick. "Not very good, sir, not very good. He was shot in the upper chest and the doctors are working on him now."

"Thank you." Nick returns to the seating area where his mom, Aunt Maria, and Uncle Pete are sitting.

They look pitifully at Nick as he approaches.

"Admittance lady says Sammy is in surgery. Doctors are working on him now."

"Jesus, Mary, and Joseph!" cries Aunt Maria. "Is he going to die? Did she say?"

Nick sits down close to his aunt and puts his arm around her. "We'll just pray, Auntie, we'll just pray."

Sammy Fernandez is a great, seventeen-year-old kid with strong, handsome features, like his Uncle Nick. He lives with his parents, Pete and Maria, in the West Humboldt Park neighborhood of stone and brick apartment buildings tucked in among neat, single-family bungalows and well-kept lawns and gardens. His neighborhood borders East and West Garfield Parks. Traditionally, West Humboldt Park was mostly Hispanic, and now it is somewhat gentrified. Sammy's dad works as a fine carpenter at a woodworking shop in West Humboldt Park and has for twenty-five years. Sammy's mom takes care of the home and helps Sammy with his homework.

Sammy is entering his senior year at Marshall Metropolitan High School, an ethnically mixed school with some kids in gangs and many of their families designated by the Feds as low-income and underserved. Mothers and grandmothers try to provide a good home environment for their kids. But, it's hard with many fathers absent. These kids are vulnerable, and in many cases, lost. For them, a street gang gives them identity, a sense of belonging, and a surrogate family.

Sammy plays the trumpet in the high school band and he runs the 220- and 440-yard events for the track team. He quite often takes home blue and red ribbons for his team and is thinking about getting a field-and-track scholarship at one of the Big Ten universities. He's all a parent could ask for.

Saint Catherine's Catholic church is overflowing. The street animals had taken a young life away needlessly. Sammy's track team is here for the funeral. Hundreds of kids from Sammy's school are attending. As Father Seville speaks, there are few dry eyes in the church. Nick sits stone-faced with his family, Sherri and other police officer friends. In the pew behind Nick sit his Marine Corps buddies, Creed Tsoodle, Conor Cavanaugh, and Emma Scott. They've come to support their squadron mate.

After the gloomy ride to the cemetery and the graveside service, Nick invites his Marine friends and Sherri back to his Aunt Maria and Uncle Pete's home for lunch. The conversation is all about *why?* Why was a bright young man like Sammy gunned down before he could taste life? Why don't we do something about the gangs? Why aren't the Chicago police doing more? Why don't the mayor and the Feds do more? Doesn't it seem to be getting worse? There is grief and anger in the air. *Rightly so,* thinks Nick.

The crowd has thinned out and Nick asks Sherri and his Marine friends to stay a while. They, of course, agree. They sit down on the front porch to have a whisky and a cigar, a tradition they had shared as Marines and still do when they get together in civilian life.

Nick says to his friends, "We've got to do something. We can't let this go on. I need your help. I'm begging for your help, as my friends and Marine brothers. There's got to be something we can do. We've got to get these thugs off the streets, so that families can live without fear. It's too late for Sammy, but we can make some kind of difference."

They sit in silence for a while and then Creed speaks up. "I have a germ of an idea. But I don't think we should talk about it here. If you all can get a couple of days off and come to the farm, I'll lay out my proposed plan." They all agree. Conor suggests he pick up Nick and Emma at the Chicago Executive Airport, formerly Palwaukee, to fly to Creed's farm near Keokuk, Iowa, for the weekend. The "Chief" says he will have a country lunch ready for them. "And don't scare my chickens with that noisy whirlybird of yours."

The scenery along both sides of the Mississippi River is breathtaking as Conor flies his sleek, black Bell 429 Global Ranger south at 100 feet above the "Big River," just as he used to fly the Huey in Iraq. Only, over there it was over desert and he had M60 machine guns. This time it's a different kind of mission.

Conor decides to buzz one of the large barges making its way up the Mississippi. Nick and Emma just smile and hang on, as Conor takes the chopper to fifty feet on his altimeter and heads straight for the nose of a lumbering barge. At the last moment, Conor pulls up, giving the tug and barge crew a little haircut. What fun it is, knowing they aren't being shot at by Sunni militants.

They can see the families launching out for the weekend on riverboats. They watch boats going through the many locks that raise and lower the mighty river. Truly, a great feat by the Army Corps. They also discuss Sammy's death and wonder what Creed's idea is.

When they're about fifty miles north of Keokuk, Conor asks Emma to give Chief a call and tell him we should arrive at his farm in about twenty-five minutes. Just need some coordinates. Emma reports back with some longitude and latitude numbers and that Creed has lunch ready and a landing spot marked off with chalk in the barnyard.

"Chief hopes you can still make a safe landing."

Conor just smiles.

As he gets about five miles from Keokuk, he can see the magnificent Lock and Dam No. 19 and the Keokuk-Hamilton Bridge just beyond the dam. It is indeed a unique engineering accomplishment that helps keep trade active up and down the river. As they approach the dam, Conor turns his beautiful Ranger to the west and heads toward Creed's farm, reporting his position to the Keokuk Municipal Airport. As they get about five miles from Creed's, they're dashing over corn and bean fields as far as the eye can see. To the north, the south, the east, and west. This is great country, where farmers toil in all seasons, not knowing what next year will bring, both from the weather and the crop prices.

As they approach the Tsoodle Farm, they see Creed standing smack-dab in the middle of the landing circle. His bulldog Chesty is frantically dashing in circles around him. Chesty is named after famous Marine general Lewis "Chesty" Puller, the most decorated Marine in history. Chief's Chesty wears a silver-plated pendant around his neck with the Marine Corps emblem dangling at the end. For Conor, a Marine aviator, it isn't Puller he reveres.

It is Gregory "Pappy" Boyington, who led the famous Black Sheep squadron in the Pacific. He was a hard drinker, a talented aviator and a Medal of Honor recipient.

Conor finally lands safely and Creed meets them warmly, even though he gives Conor a good chewing out. They all laugh a lot as they head toward Creed's beautiful country home and some barbecued pork sandwiches, homemade rolls, cottage cheese, green salad, and cold Great River Redband Stout beers.

After lunch, Creed asks his buddies to take a walk with him. They stride in unison past the red barn and some green John Deere farm equipment, made just up the river in Moline, Illinois. They enter a quiet, green pasture that stretches 200 yards or so across the land before it ends at a cornfield. Bean fields border the pasture on each side.

"This is it," Creed says to his friends. "This is where my idea is going to be built. This is how we're going to solve the gang problems in Chicago. This is where Sammy is going to be avenged. Here's where we will build CAMP KEOKUK."

It's quiet for some time as Nick, Conor, and Emma look quizzically at each other. Camp Keokuk.

Nick whispers to Emma, "What the hell is Camp Keokuk and what does it have to do with the street gangs of Chicago?" He finally asks the question. "What do you mean, Chief?"

Creed hesitates and looks out at the pasture again.

"This is where we build a secret resort for special guests. The Camp will have cinder-block walls three feet thick and twenty-five feet high. The only way in is by helicopter through a huge, automatic roof. There is no way out. Once you're in, you're there forever." Chief surprises his audience by singing a few lines of *Hotel California*.

Creed's friends look at him as if he's taken leave of his senses.

Nick says, "Chief, you have to be more specific than the Eagles song. I'm not sure I understand. You're real bright, so I know your idea has merit."

"Actually, Nick, that song was written by Don Henley and Glenn Frey for Jethro Tull in 1972. Just thought you should know."

"Thanks, Chief."

"Now, walk with me to the barn. I'll show you what I mean," Creed says with confidence, as he motions to the big building. Nick, Emma, and Conor nod their heads and fall in line.

As they enter the huge, neatly kept barn, Creed's friends see that the Chief has been doing some homework. They look at the far end of the barn where he has hung large drawings. Creed has chairs lined up for his friends, a setup much like a pilot's ready room. He asks them to sit down, relax and have another Great River Redband Stout while he briefs them on his plans.

Creed begins. "These are drawings of Camp Keokuk I did this week after you asked for our help, Nick. Over here is the structure I told you about a minute ago. I will build it with money I got when my uncle died. I have a local supplier who will pledge to secrecy. The roof opens when Conor's bird comes to drop off the human cargo. The helicopter never lands. It just lowers the cargo via a cable and winch. Once it has dropped its cargo, it lifts off and the roof closes by remote control.

Inside, there are no windows, just light from the roof. There are 75 small single rooms with shower, toilet and bed. In the center is a large courtyard for exercise. In the winter the whole camp is heated. In the summer, ceiling fans cool it off. The structure will be camouflaged as a grain storage building. There will be four feet between an inner and outer wall all the way around. I will pour the corn and beans in by a conveyor, so that our secret will be kept from my neighbors. I will have video cameras and microphones put in place so that we can monitor the scum's every movements on our laptops. We may learn something valuable."

Creed's Marine squadron mates look on with admiration for the Chief's creativity. They ask no questions, but they're beginning to draw some conclusions, as Creed steps to his left and unveils another large graphic. It has at its center a map of Illinois and Iowa with a blue line drawn straight from Chicago to Camp Keokuk. On the top of the line, it reads, "271 nautical miles."

He goes on. "With your help and your gang knowledge, Nick, at night, every few weeks until we determine our mission is accomplished, we will scoop up a known gang leader or one or two of his lieutenants, cart them to Palwaukee Airport, put them aboard your 429, Conor, and fly them to Camp Keokuk. It takes approximately two hours there and two hours back with minimum time to drop the guests through the roof and let them each find their own cubicle. Everything that happens inside Camp Keokuk is up to the special guests.

"Food is dropped in the same way. The chopper that brings the scum also drops food. No utensils, no plates, just sandwiches and water. No metal, no glass.

"To avoid detection, we will have private discussions with security at Palwaukee and law enforcement here in Lee County. I know the people here. They're my friends.

"If there is a death at the camp, we tell the inmates to put the dead person on the gurney that is dropped from the chopper. Or, they can let the son-of-a-bitch rot and live with it. If there is a sickness, we will drop medicine. Nobody will come out and nobody will go in."

Nick begins to fidget and wants to ask questions. But he doesn't want to stop Creed, who's on a roll. "Chief, can I ask questions at this point?"

"Yes, of course, Nick."

"Are you telling me you want us to put a finger on gang leaders or their lieutenants, capture them, get them to Palwaukee, and have Conor fly them to Camp Keokuk to be lowered down into secret barracks in middle of the night without detection?"

"Yes, sir, that's what I'm asking. But you don't have to do it by yourself. You will have help from Conor, Emma, and me, your mission mates."

Emma, who's been silent all this time, has some serious concerns. "Chief, for Christ's sake, have you thought of the legal aspects of such a plan? Nick is a Chicago police officer and runs the risk of losing his job. Capturing people on the street and flying across state lines to illegally imprison them is totally unethical. Nick, you preach that people shouldn't take the law into their own hands—they should leave it to law enforcement and the courts to dole out justice. Conor could lose his business. And, United Airlines would ruin my life if they found out I was part of a human smuggling ring."

The entire group stops to ponder what Emma has said. Then Conor speaks up. "Emma, don't you think what the vile street gangs of Chicago are doing is unethical? When we were in Iraq, we sought to cut off the heads of the snake. Take out the leaders and you take out the problem. Remember?"

Emma is getting frustrated. "Do we really think we can solve entrenched social problems by dragging *some* of the leaders off the street and trapping them like animals in Camp Keokuk? I grew up in The Hood and saw drug addiction and bloodshed up close. That's why I escaped and joined the Corps."

Conor shoots back. "Fixing the social problems should be left up to the elected officials, families, and neighborhood groups. Besides, we said that we would help Nick in honor of Sammy. We agree that what is happening on Chicago's streets is very wrong. We agree that what happened to young Sammy was an awful tragedy. So, Chief has come up with a plan that could help. It's just very risky. Didn't we fight in a foreign land to help free the people of Iraq from oppression? Why shouldn't we fight to free people from horrible oppression in the neighborhoods of Chicago?"

Creed is passionate now. "What's the fucking difference? Is there a better idea than this? Huh? Is there? I'll build this camp, Conor will provide *his* helicopter, and Emma, you can help keep the helicopter flying, just like you did in Iraq. Nick and his partner Sherri can go after the scum. Besides, Emma, as you know, I'm Native American. So, don't lecture me about social issues and hardship."

Conor follows. "It may break me, but I'll do it in support of Nick and the people who have fallen victim to the savage gangs of Chicago."

There is silence, it seems for a long time, as Creed opens more beers for each of his squadron mates.

"I'm in," says Creed.

"I'm in," echoes Conor.

"I'm in, and grateful for your friendship," Nick says.

Emma tries one more time. "I'm dead set against this. But, because I'm your friend and a fellow Marine, I will support you any way I can. And, one more thing. You call them 'scum.' Do you know why they behave the way they do?"

Creed has the last word. "I don't give a shit."

"*Semper Fi,*" they all bellow as they raise their cans of Great River Redband Stout. "*Semper Fi.*"

CHAPTER 2
NOW FOR THE TOUGH PART

Back at work on Monday morning, the former Marines ponder their peculiar weekend trip down the Mississippi and into Iowa farm country. Was it a surreal dream, or stark reality?

Conor is back home in Milwaukee trying to find out how much it would cost him to fly his Global Ranger some 730 miles round trip, for who knows how many flights. He calculates that it would cost around $2,000 a flight in fuel. That doesn't count maintenance, even though Emma will be doing that. But she would need parts and the Ranger always required maintenance. Conor needs an angel before they can begin their mission. He starts his search.

Emma is still dizzy as she begins her Monday morning, managing maintenance on a 737 with brake problems. It's needed back in the fleet ASAP. *What's new?* she thinks.

Even though she agreed to participate in the gang eradication mission, and she believes that it could help, she's still skeptical about how they can pull it off without detection. She has seen her buddies in action and has no doubt about their skills and their commitment. However, this seems different with a wide range of risks and consequences. Nevertheless, she will talk to Conor and find out what kind of support he needs at Palwaukee or even at his base at Billy Mitchell Field south of Milwaukee. She doesn't live far from the Wisconsin line, so it won't be a big hassle going north. Palwaukee is just a few miles from her home in Glenview. She also has an idea of how they can get food for Camp Keokuk.

Nick is on the job with his Chicago Police Department Gang Unit rookie partner, Sherri Botkin, conducting a workshop for neighborhood people and offering tips on what can be done to stop or control gangs in their community. That is one of their jobs with the Gang Unit. He is telling them that the best defense against gangs begins in the home. Parents should be aware of the identifiers gangs use and notice if they begin to appear on their children's personal items.

Nick tells the anxious parents, "You should look for book bags, posters, and gang colors used to convey the gang messages. Be on the lookout that your homes are not being used by a gang to hide weapons or narcotics."

Those attending the workshop ask Nick about the death of his nephew, Sammy. Nick thanks them for their concern and tells them that the police are still interviewing witnesses, who so far haven't been very helpful because of their fear of retaliation from the gangs.

"One witness told me confidentially that the word on the street is it was a member of the Folk Nation gang, White Lightning. My unit is checking it out."

As Nick conducts the workshop, his mind is on "the mission" he and his Marine buddies decided on over the weekend. They have to wait until Creed gets Camp Keokuk built. Nick will make the call to him tonight. The whole team has to use caution in making their calls or sending texts and emails.

In the squad car after the meeting, Nick turns to Sherri. "We will have to set up a special code, as we did in Iraq. No problem. What mission code can we use? Sammy, that's it. We will use Sammy as a code. When will Sammy's house be built? When will the first Sammy acquisition be made? When will the first Sammy flight be made? How many Sammy acquisitions do we have? It will keep Sammy's memory alive."

Nick is also concerned about how to restrain and transport their scum cargo from the neighborhoods to Palwaukee. His Uncle Pete has a black Ford Expedition that he used to go camping with Sammy up in Wisconsin. *Will Pete join us? Will he be part of our mission?* Nick will make the call.

Back on the farm, Creed is taking action. He knows that nothing can happen until Camp Keokuk is finished. He also has the farm to take care of, like July corn and bean plowing to keep the weeds down. It looks like a good year if the rains keep coming every once in a while.

In the meantime, he has assessed the availability of cement blocks to begin the building. He calls on his old high school friend, Ronny Perkins, who now runs the lumberyard up in Argyle. Ronny tells Creed he can get the right number of blocks down the Mississippi in two weeks and then transported with cement to the farm. Ronny tells Creed that the new building will hold a "hellava" lot of corn and beans. Creed will tell everybody that he's going to store a lot of crops in order to hedge.

Then there is the crew to dig the foundation and the crew to build the rooms inside and a crew to build the special roof, a crew for plumbing and heating and a crew to construct the building itself. Creed thinks, *What have I gotten myself into?* He has the money, but the logistics are going to be a nightmare. So he asks Ronny if he can manage the whole thing, or knows someone who can. Ronny comes up with an out-of-work old friend who can probably do the job.

JJ Carter was always a hardworking boy. He worked at his father's construction company during high school and after he graduated. While Creed was overseas in Iraq, JJ's dad got killed in a gunfight at Paddy's, a local river saloon. JJ tried to take over the company but didn't have the business acumen to carry it off. He eventually filed for bankruptcy and lost the business.

Ronny makes the call and JJ meets with Creed in the barnyard to discuss the project. JJ is overwhelmed by Creed's offer. It saves his ass. The only stipulation is that he has to keep all plans confidential. JJ agrees and construction planning begins.

In a phone call the next day to Nick, Creed reports that Camp Keokuk would be ready by the end of September, guaranteed. That gives the team two and a half months to prepare for the first flight.

"Good work, Chief. Good work."

Emma takes the day off to ride her Harley-Davidson Fat Boy up to Billy Mitchell Field to have lunch with Conor and talk about the first mission. When she gets to his office, she is reminded that he is a true Cheesehead. Packers stuff all over his office, including three foam hats that look like Swiss cheese, is tucked among all the Marine Corps memorabilia. He also is a proud owner of Packers season tickets. They were handed down from his grandpa, who never missed Vince Lombardi coaching at Lambeau Field, no matter how cold it got. Packer fanaticism is more than a fever in Wisconsin; it's a full-blown, incurable virus.

Conor and Emma go over flight and maintenance plans for the Global Ranger. He gives Emma all the maintenance manuals to study and they do a walk around. From a flight-planning standpoint, it will take time to sort out Visual Flight Rules (VFR) and Instrument Flight Rules (IFR) plans; issues like if they can't fly for mechanical or weather situations, what would they do with the outgoing scum? What if they have to land somewhere else? How would they keep the fugitives hidden and quiet? Who was going to fly with them to guard the Camp Keokuk guests and lower them through the roof to the floor of the Camp?

Emma says that because the flights will happen at night, she can fly shotgun, guard the scum, and lower them into Camp Keokuk with the winch that Conor is having built. Since she is senior at United, she never works nights, so she could go on the night mission and be at work by eight the next morning.

CHAPTER 3
THE GANGS AND THE POLITICIANS

While the Marines make their final plans, the streets are still living hell for the neighborhoods, and gunplay like the old Wild West. The July summer heat is making the problem worse. Everybody is grouchy and they can't sleep inside because there is no air conditioning.

There seems to be no particular ethnicity to the violence: White gangs, Latino gangs, Black gangs, Asian gangs, and the new emergence of Islamic groups, all demanding respect, power and a piece of the meth, cocaine, heroin, and marijuana action. It's not pretty, even though the politicians claim progress is being made. Ask the mothers who are afraid to send their children to school. Ask the teachers who are afraid to send the kids home. Ask them if progress is being made. Ask Nick's Aunt Maria and Uncle Pete. They're still grieving the death of their son, Sammy.

One night, word comes to the Police Gang Unit that the Black Cobras are about to have a major rumble with the Latin Primera. Nick and Sherri are on duty and get the call to accompany the patrol and SWAT teams to the area on the Southwest Side. When they converge on the scene, the gangs are already at war. Handgun fire from the streets. AK-47 fire from upper floors of a grungy project building. Bottle bombs being hurled from every street corner.

It reminds Nick of the Battle of Fallujah, where his helicopter squadron launched to support the Marine Expeditionary Force in their efforts to retake the city. The Third Battalion Fifth Marines, Third Battalion First Marines, along with Eighth Marines, fought to gain the city back from the insurgents. Now, Nick is driven to take the streets back from the vicious gangs the only way he knows how.

But tonight about all they can do is watch the fireworks. Above the gunfire and bottle bombs, you can hear the mothers' screams, kids crying, the gangs cursing. "Motherfuckah, you gonna die, brothah, you gonna die." "Shoot me you honkie fuck, shoot me. I'll dumb you down fuckah."

For Nick, the language is different, but the hate and violence spring from the same core. Nothing has really changed. Bloody gang member bodies on the sidewalks. Grieving mothers. Young men taken out because they thought this was the way to gain respect and a way to get money to buy things for their families and their girlfriends. *This is the only way*, they think.

The Feds, in their infinite wisdom, try to do it with welfare checks to mothers, who are rewarded for having more babies. Welfare checks go to households that have no father, so fathers stay away from home. Then families crumble. The Feds have created a bad system. This creates fertile soil for street gangs, who create their own economy. Federal, State, and City money also created the Cabrini Green and Robert Taylor Homes. Gang- and rat-infested hells on earth. Places that smell of garbage and fear and death. Mayor Jane Byrne once tried to solve the problem by moving into Cabrini Green with hordes of police security. That lasted for two weeks, and the scourge continued when she moved back to her comfortable home. Nick thinks, as do others, that it was a stupid move that solved nothing.

Nick looks forward to the days ahead when "Operation Sammy" will be in full swing and gang leaders and their lieutenants are whisked away from the streets to a place called CAMP KEOKUK.

Back on Creed's farm, the construction of Camp Keokuk is going well. Almost half done. All inside work with the rooms and plumbing has to be done before they close up the building with the last cinder blocks. Constructing 75 rooms takes time. JJ Carter is doing a great job as general contractor. The floor has been laid with concrete. Cement trucks come and go and masons lay in the blocks.

At Gert's, the local restaurant two miles down the road, neighbors are asking Creed about the "huge grain storage building" they hear he is building. They also see a lot of truck traffic on the road leading to the Tsoodle farm. Creed tells them that he wants to store soybeans and corn until the price goes back up. He's hedging. They all think that this is a pretty smart idea and that his dad would have approved.

They all liked Creed's dad. He was a good neighbor. He had farmed the land for many years before he died in a road accident at the hand of a drunk driver. The neighbors and friends took care of the Tsoodle farm until Creed got back from Iraq. Creed is fond of Gert's and the people who go there. It's the center for news for the farmers around here. Best coffee, best eggs, best ham, best biscuits and gravy, best gossip. "Did you hear about Jenny Jennings's daughter, Peggy? Wow!"

Everybody at Gert's is proud of Creed for his service with the Marines. They hung a photograph taken of him in front of a Huey in Iraq. These are good, hardworking, patriotic, salt-of-the-earth people. They will never let you down.

Creed is about ready to give Nick, Emma and Conor a thumbs-up progress report. Camp Keokuk will be ready for its first prisoners on deadline, a month away. He has also had some private discussions with his old high school friend, Jack Boyd, who is now a Lee County Deputy Sheriff. Jack agrees to cover for them when they start flying their cargo down the Mighty Mississippi to the Camp.

The Chicago City Hall is a legendary place. It has marbled walls with Chicago and American flags and security guards standing on each side of the mayor, who is and always has been, one of the most powerful politicians in America. In this case, it's Sean Kelly's turn. His family is a historic piece of the Chicago political fabric.

He rules the city from his office and in the venerable City Council Chambers, with sworn allegiance from most of the aldermen of the fifty wards, and by controlling the microphones placed before each council member. He can shut them down with a wave of his hand to the sound booth, if one of the council members counters his wishes too many times.

This is where a special City Council session is being held to discuss gang activity after the death of Sammy Fernandez, Nick's nephew. Nick is there with his mom, Aunt Maria, and Uncle Pete. Also present are Nick's partner Sherri and their boss, Commander William Washington, the head of the Gang Unit.

Alderman Alberto Sariano of the Twelfth Ward is on his feet. "Your Honor, I stand before this Council on behalf of Peter and Maria Fernandez, who lost their son Sammy to gang violence in the Twelfth Ward just a few weeks ago. They are here today, and they are grieving, sir. Their son Sammy was gunned down on his way home from a track meet. He was a good boy with a bright future. He was a good student, a good athlete, and he loved his family. He is just one more young victim of the gangs that roam our streets and threaten our neighborhoods. I know we've tried a lot of things to stop this carnage. But nothing seems to be working."

Mayor Kelly is visibly upset that a loyal alderman would say that nothing is working. He interrupts the alderman. "Statistically, we have lowered the crime rate in the city and statistically the gang violence is limited to eight wards. That's a good percentage, I remind you. The Chicago Crime Commission has spent millions and done much to lower the crime rate and help the neighborhoods. You know that, Albert."

Sariano continues to challenge the mayor. "Sir, with all due respect, statistics don't bleed."

The mayor blanches. Sariano doesn't blink.

"We must do more. We simply must do more. This country is spending billions of dollars on fighting terrorists overseas. Why can't we spend more on fighting them on our own streets?

"I'm asking this council to double the number of Chicago cops in the Gang Unit commanded by Commander William Washington, who is here today. He will tell you that he needs more specially trained cops to work the streets. He needs more help to keep the neighborhoods safe from the gang hoodlums. I ask you to do this in the memory of Sammy Fernandez. Thank you, sir, and thanks to the council members for their support."

The gallery, packed with the friends and family of Pete and Maria, explodes with cheers and applause.

The mayor is now red-faced, like the first Richard Daley used to get when challenged. Sariano had called him out in public. That is not a good thing. He orders the sergeant-at-arms to remove the citizens from the gallery, except Pete and Maria, Nick's mom Adoncia, and Nick. They can stay.

Things quiet down.

The mayor speaks. "Mr. and Mrs. Fernandez, I am deeply sorry about your son. His death is inexcusable. No parent should have to endure this pain. I'm also concerned about the gangs in our city and have tried many things to diminish their threat to our city. It is a never-ending job for the members of this council and the police department. Alderman Sariano, I don't believe putting more Gang Unit cops in the neighborhoods will diminish gang activity. I wish there were another answer. So, I can't support a request for more cops. I'm sorry."

Alderman Sariano stands to speak again.

"Mr. Mayor. Would you reconsider on behalf of Mr. and Mrs. Fernandez?" he says with increasing passion. "Please, Mr. Mayor."

In about two seconds, Alderman Sariano's microphone goes dead and you can only slightly hear him, as Alderman Josh Levin stands, with the power of a full microphone, to ask the mayor if he would entertain a move to adjourn. And, there's a second. The mayor brings down his gavel and proclaims the special session over. You can still hear Alderman Sariano speaking, but to no avail. The mayor and aldermen exit the chambers.

Pete is still Latin-hot when he and Nick have coffee the next day at Jake's, their favorite greasy spoon on the West Side.

"That son-of-a-bitch," Pete grouses. "He hasn't done shit. With all his political wind and his Chicago Crime Commission bullshit, he's done nothing to stop the gang violence. City of the Big Shoulders, but no balls. That's what I would say. What would it take to add some cops to your unit? It could save lives. That fucking political hack. At least Sariano tried. He really challenged the mayor. That can't go well for him politically. What else can we possibly do, Nick? We can't wait for another child to be gunned down."

Nick sips his coffee and leans closer to his uncle. "I need your help, Uncle Pete. My Marine friends and I have an idea, a plan. And we need your assistance."

Pete leans forward attentively.

CHAPTER 4
MONEY AND A ROOF

Conor and Emma are meeting for lunch at the 94th Aero Squadron Restaurant at Palwaukee Airport to discuss flight logistics and special equipment needed on the Ranger to lower their human cargo and food into Camp Keokuk. Conor brings information from a supplier who can have a hoist custom-made for the Ranger that can be quickly attached to the door and detached and stored after each flight. They need to get it done and tested before the first mission.

Emma also has ideas on how to replenish food and water. She thinks about military C-Rations, the kind that troops use in the field. Conor thinks the essence of the idea is good. However, he is concerned about the metal containers they come in and how the scum might be able to use them to make weapons. Emma agrees.

"I also have another idea that may do the trick, Conor. I have a friend who makes box lunches for private pilots and their passengers flying in and out of Palwaukee, the Executive Airport. She has her business near here. What do you think?"

Conor agrees, and Emma will contact her friend Cali at LUNCHES TO FLY, just a half-mile down Milwaukee Avenue.

"I know Cali can do it, but I'm concerned about spoilage. If we fly only so often, we need to make sure the prisoners have enough until the next sortie. I don't want them dying of ptomaine. I want them to suffer." She grinned. "On my way home, I'll stop by and talk to Cali about it, without revealing our mission. I'm sure she has the answer."

"We can't stop it, Nick," Sherri says, as they turn into the South Side Community Center to conduct a workshop for the neighborhood. Nick and Sherri are discussing the mayor's decision not to fund more Gang Unit cops, and how that will negatively impact what is happening in the neighborhoods. Nick is now highly frustrated as he downloads on his pretty, young partner.

"What do we have to say to these good people about how we are helping them, when the mayor won't help? What the hell is he thinking? It wouldn't cost that much. Or, maybe he just doesn't give a fuck about these neighbor-hoods. Let the gangs kill themselves. But, what about innocent people like my wonderful nephew, Sammy? I guess he doesn't get that many votes from these victimized neighborhoods. The Feds have put some of them away, but they just operate their gangs from their cells."

"I'm sorry, Nick. My criminology books at Texas didn't cover this subject."

Nick thinks for a moment and opens himself up to Sherri, whom he trusts.

"We have a plan, Sherri. A real plan that will de-scum the neighborhoods, over time. It requires complete confidentiality, trust, your help, and most of all, balls. Are you willing to listen?"

"I am, Nick. What is it? Lay it out for me before we go to our workshop. Whatever it is, I'm in."

Creed is searching for companies that install retractable roofs on stadiums, like some in the NFL. He finds out that one company can customize an automatic roof that opens with a remote control so that scum and goods can be lowered through the roof and then closed once the cargo has been deposited. They can install it in two weeks, as soon as the building is ready.

In the barnyard just short of the old pasture, Creed admires the work of his friend JJ and his crews. JJ takes Creed for a walk through the inside of the Camp one more time before they close it up. Sure enough, everything inside is built according to plan. As they walk down the row of individual cubicles, he sees that each one has its own sink, shower, toilet, desk, and bed. There are no doors on the rooms. Lights inside of heavy mesh are bolted high on the wall above the bed. Some overhead lights are installed over the courtyard. A washing machine and dryer stand at the end of the courtyard. Video cameras are concealed in the walls and ceiling, unreachable by the guests. JJ and his crews have done an admirable job.

Now it's time to close it up, but not before Creed takes pictures of everything to send to his team members. It would take about three days for the roof people to come and finish the job.

"Close it up, JJ," Creed shouts! "Close it up!" JJ signals the crews to begin cementing the final blocks into place. Creed stands back in awe as he hands JJ a cold Great River Redband Stout. They toast the accomplishment, and JJ smiles, big time. Creed has saved his ass and he has finally built something that means something for an old friend. *Doesn't get better than this,* JJ thinks. He hugs Creed, who just grins and holds his stout high, as crews move the last blocks into place. "*Semper Fi, JJ, Semper Fi.*"

Up north at Billy Mitchell Field, Conor is working the phones from his hangar office. He desperately needs an angel to fund the operation for the Camp Keokuk flights. It's expensive and he can't fund it himself. He also can't divulge the nature of the mission to those who he's asking for money. Or, could he? There must be somebody with money who believes in the mission as much as he and his buddies and Uncle Pete do.

In the late afternoon, Conor receives a return call from a person of wealth in Chicago, whom he's known for years through a family connection.

"Hello, sir. How is your family? Yes, sir, I'm fine and the business is running well. We miss Dad, but I think he would be proud of how it's going. I just called to ask a very big favor. A few of my old Marine buddies and I are planning a special mission that is highly risky, strictly confidential, and very worthwhile. It also requires funding, which I don't have. It would all be anonymous. I was wondering if you would be willing to meet with me to discuss our project. I'll drive down to Chicago."

Conor listens.

"No, sir, there is no financial return. Just a helping hand for some needy people in Chicago." Conor listens again and smiles. "I can come down tomorrow. That would be great and I appreciate it. It will be good to see you again. Thank you, sir." Conor hangs up, claps his hands and shouts, "*Semper Fi!*" As he stares out at his Global Ranger, he says out loud, "Get ready to fly, baby. Get ready to fly."

Emma stops in to see her friend Cali at LUNCHES TO FLY to discuss the food requirements for Camp Keokuk. Cali had worked for Gate Gourmet at O'Hare and she and Emma became friends. Cali quit last year to start her own business. An authentic, hand-carved sign signaling her good taste hangs out front. Inside, Emma can't help but notice how orderly everything is as Cali's crews busily prepare a set of attractive red, white, and blue box lunches for the next private jet out of Palwaukee.

Emma speaks cryptically. She asks Cali if she can provide ongoing individual packets of food and water to Palwaukee airport late at night in increasing numbers over several months; food that contains no silverware or metal objects and could last a person for a few days until another delivery. Cali is very curious, but resists asking too many questions. She says she can do the job, whenever Emma pulls the trigger. She would just need a few hours lead-time.

"Thanks, Cali. It's for a good cause. I'll tell you someday. Just keep tabs on the cost, and I'll get you reimbursed."

Cali smiles and hugs Emma.

CHAPTER 5
GANG BATTLE TURNS TRAGIC

Gerald Tang, leader of the Bad Tigers, lounges in his makeshift office in his mom's basement in one of the hotbed gang neighborhoods on the Southwest Side. A thin, mean-looking Asian, he is becoming notorious. He's reading a tweet from a pissed-off community member after the mayor's decision not to fund more cops.

> U dumb cocksuckers stop gangbanging up
> the ass ruining ur hoods. The goal is to
> round up u subhuman trash and burn u.

Gerald chuckles, looks up at his gang's insignia on the wall—a growling tiger with a pistol in its teeth—and sits back to put in some calls.
Tang is twenty-two years old and has been living on the Southwest Side between Chinatown and Little Italy since his family moved from San Francisco to start a laundry business when he was sixteen. When the business failed, his father left him and his mother and went back to San Francisco. His mother stayed in Chicago to take in laundry and babysit for neighbor children. Gerald misses his father. His departure left a hole in young Gerald's heart. The senior Tang was a good dad and tried hard to influence Gerald in a positive way and adhere to the values of the Chinese culture, which is known for its ethic of hard work, discipline, and excellence, as well as its emphasis on family and ancestral traditions. So, when Mr. Tang went back to San Francisco, the anchor was gone and Gerald turned to the streets.
    Over the years, Gerald has risen to the top of the Bad Tigers with a reputation for toughness, violent behavior, and a knack for getting good drugs in from the West Coast. He has built a tough, take-no-prisoners organization of young men and women who are extremely loyal and frightened of Tang

at the same time. They have become serious competition with the spin-offs of the Gangster Disciples, including the Eight Ball Posse, Insane Gangster Disciples, and the Hellraisers.

"Billy, this is Tang. I need to talk to you as soon as possible about a potential rumble with the Hellraisers. They're poaching our business and I want it fucking stopped. Come to my office as soon as you can so we can talk without being detected. Come in the basement door as usual."

Billy White enters Tang's basement door and sits down across the desk from his boss. He is a refugee from the Roman Savages, who are now on the prowl for his head. White is a pugnacious Caucasian with thin, brownish hair that hangs in his eyes. He is about the same age as Tang, but a lot bigger and stronger. His tattoos are of fire-belching dragons and imprisoned maidens. He is a suburban boy who escaped to the city when he was eighteen.

Tang offers Billy a Mary Jane and a shot of Maker's Mark, as they sit back to talk about the looming battle with the Hellraisers. Tang places his .357 Magnum stainless-steel pistol on his desk and puts an extra few .38 Special rounds near the weapon. Billy glances down to admire the gun. He has his own Glock 42 tucked in his baggy pants.

"Billy, we've been ripped off by the Hellraisers and I'm pissed. They've been intercepting the good West Coast stuff on the way from O'Hare and reaping the benefits. Gomez needs to die. I mean seriously die. Do you hear me?"

"I do, Boss, and I'm happy to do the job. We just need to make the plans. He's a slippery motherfucker."

Tang turns and lifts a suitcase onto his desk. When he opens it, Billy smiles. There are kilos of good stuff.

"What Gomez doesn't know, Billy, is that we've been hijacking his stuff right back through a mole in his organization."

Billy stands up to admire the stash.

Tang says firmly, "We're gonna start bringing the West Coast stuff in by train: The California Zephyr. It takes longer, but it's safer and Gomez and his people know nothing about it."

At that moment, the basement door crashes open and all hell breaks loose. Gunfire shatters the basement walls and Tang's desk. Tang and Billy dive for cover. The quiet of the night is over. The Bad Tigers have been ambushed. A grenade explodes and the battle is on.

Nick is in his apartment on the near north side in Old Town, when he gets the call. It's midnight. Dispatch requests that he and Sherri join up at Central and head to the West Side. 911 had received a frantic call about a gun battle. It sounds like gang activity. As they head west, Sherri turns on the radio to WCOU, her favorite country station. She loves country music and sometimes drives Nick crazy with it. Nevertheless, the music breaks the tension. For the next two minutes, she sings along to a Carrie Underwood and Randy Travis song.

Nick has to admit to himself that it's a cool song and that Sherri has a pretty damn fine voice.

When they arrive at the scene, a small, single-story bungalow is ablaze. Chicago Fire Department trucks line the street and cop cars surround the trucks. Red and blue lights flicker on the rowhouse facades as neighbors watch the horror from the sidewalk across the street near Nick, Sherri, and their colleagues in blue. Nothing can be done until the firefighters finish their job. It will take a while. At least the late August night is warm.

When dawn comes and the CFD has struck the fire, the smoldering devastation is complete. There is nothing left but scorched ruins. Now, the grim task of recovering bodies commences. Yellow crime-scene tape surrounds the charred, blackened home. The Cook County Medical Examiner's van is parked near the walkway to the burnt-out home.

When Doctor Rod LaSage's van is present, nothing can be good, and families will be grieving. Crime scene investigators begin their tedious work. Homicide detectives are interviewing neighbors. Closest neighbors say they heard a lot of gunfire and an explosion from inside the home before the fire broke out.

Police data shows that the home is rented to a Mrs. Emma Tang. Gang Unit Commander William Washington joins Nick and Sherri. News vans from Channels 2, 5, 7, and 9 scout the scene for sound bites they can use on the morning news. High-profile incidents with casualties make assignment editors salivate. They canvas the neighborhood conducting interviews with anybody who will talk to them, while their videographers shoot B-roll of the police activity and the scorched home. Nick and Sherri protect Commander Washington from the reporters.

"Bloodthirsty assholes," the Commander whispers, not so quietly, to Nick and Sherri. "I bet none of them lives around here."

Soon, the body bags come out of LaSage's van and the forbidding chore of putting singed, blackened, human remains into the bags has started. Dr. LaSage has to pronounce them dead before they are loaded for the morgue, where autopsies and identification will take place.

Nick and Sherri see at least five bodies being removed from the house. At the end of the street, a young woman—in her thirties, they thought—is wailing at police to let her by. She weeps uncontrollably as she spurts out words. "My babies were in there! Please let me in! My babies were in that house. Let me see them!" she screams.

A police chaplain intercedes and holds onto the young woman, trying to calm her.

"Mrs. Tang was babysitting my babies. Are they alright?" she cries.

Nick and Sherri now realize the worst. Tang. Tang? Is she any relation to Gerald Tang, the notorious boss of the Bad Tigers, who rules in this neighborhood? They have to find out.

Emma is getting ready for work in her Glenview home when she turns on Channel 2 News and sees the live report from the Southwest Side. She stops and thinks about those poor people. She also sees the camera's recording the screaming mother. *Why do they have to record her?* she wonders angrily. She also catches a glimpse of Nick and Sherri in among the many police officers on the scene. *Why are they here?* They must think its gang-related. She would check in with them later. She also thinks about Creed on the farm and when Camp Keokuk will be ready. She is ready for the first operational flight down the Mississippi. Conor and his Ranger are also ready. His technicians have already rigged the bird with the special winch and hoist.

CHAPTER 6
AN ANGEL AND MORE ANGUISH

It's noon when Conor pulls his black 2010 XK8 up in front of Gene and Georgetti's restaurant on Franklin Street behind the Merchandise Mart. The valet takes his car and he enters the famous restaurant for his lunch date with a possible donor for their mission. This is a restaurant that has played host to celebrities, politicians, and priests since 1941. As Conor enters, he spots his dad's old friend Jon Difrisco sitting at the long, oak bar. Pictures of famous people—Sinatra, Lane, Martin, Avalon—hang behind the bar. "Hello, Jon."

Jon turns and hugs Conor. "It's been too long, Conor. You were just joining the Marines when I last saw you at your folk's home in Racine. It was a beautiful place on Lake Michigan. And, I'm glad you're home, out of harm's way."

Conor orders a scotch and soda and the two begin to talk. The conversation is barely underway when the old waiter invites them to be seated. They grab their drinks and head to a special booth just up the stairs. They can't go five feet without guests paying their respects to Jon, who stops to introduce his lunch friends to Conor and tells them he is a former Marine pilot. They thank him for his service.

If these booths could talk, Conor thinks to himself. *How many people would be outed? How many divorced? And how many would be in jail, if not dead?*

Jon DiFrisco is a plugged-in Chicago businessman whose construction company has done business with the city, including West Side and South Side projects, since the fifties. He won the job to build the new Navy Pier. That was a coup and he had to "pull some strings" to get the nod. Nevertheless, it turned out to be one of Chicago's greatest tourist attractions.

Jon is also one of the business leaders who sit on the Chicago Crime Commission. That could be touchy for the Camp Keokuk mission.

As the two men eat their steaks and sip their wine, Conor timidly requests $300,000 from Jon, who had loaned Conor's dad money for the start of the flight service. Conor's dad had paid back every cent. But Jon, rightly so, wants to know a little more about his investment and the charity.

Conor treads carefully. "Jon, it has to do with getting rid of the neighborhood gangs in Chicago's communities."

Jon looks at Conor for a moment and replies, "I don't think $300,000 is going to do that, Conor. The Commission has spent millions trying to rid the neighborhoods of these beasts. I know firsthand. What can you do with $300,000 that millions couldn't do?"

Conor feels comfortable about opening up a little. He looks around and speaks softly. "Jon, my Marine buddies and I have come up with a unique and bold idea on how to slowly, but surely, rid the neighborhoods of the scum. It is a bit militant, but with our good battle planning, it should work."

As Conor lays out the plan, Jon stares at him with puzzlement, astonishment, and a smile at the same time, not breaking eye contact. When Conor finishes. Jon sits back, looks around to see if anybody is listening and finally speaks. "Would half a million help, no strings attached?"

Creed has just finished his farm chores for the day and is cleaning up when a call comes from Nick. "What's up, Chief?" Nick then briefs his friend on this morning's tragedy on the West Side.

Creed hasn't seen the news. He doesn't have much time for it. Plus, he doesn't want to hear all the bad in the world. He'd seen enough in the Middle East. He is just happy farming, meeting his friends at Gert's, and planning for the Sammy Mission.

The news cuts Creed to the quick, along with the anger and frustration in Nick's voice. Nick tells him that the coroner has positively identified the dead: Mrs. Sarah Tang; two children she had been babysitting; five-year-old Tonya Rebald and her eight-year-old sister Ramona. A William White and a guy named Benito Gomez, leader of the Hellraisers, also died in the battle and fire. They had been riddled with gunshots and burned. Gerald Tang is nowhere to be found. The fire inspectors found a large stash of charred weapons in the makeshift basement headquarters of the Bad Tigers.

Creed shakes his head. "Kids, Nick, kids. I thought they were off limits to the gangs. They are collateral in the gang wars. I'll put a rush on everything, Buddy. We should be ready on or before schedule. I just have to get the roof in. I'm in the process now of finding a CH-47 Chinook to bring it in and set it in place. I think I've found one."

The CH-47 is a heavy-lifting cargo and troop-carrying chopper that the Marines and Army depend on for battlefield operations. It is called the 'Boeing Body Bag' for obvious reasons.

"I can try to expedite the delivery and move our deadline up. Everything else is ready out here. I know Conor and Emma are ready. Conor left a text this afternoon that he had secured some funding. A good amount, too. He didn't say where he got it. I'll make some calls and get back to you by morning. *Semper Fi.*"

When the news comes that Mrs. Tang and the two little Rebald girls were killed in the shooting and fire, the Internet lights up.

Lips: *This has to end now. We need to take our hoods back.*

linda moon: *innocent kids my God who's next?*

Pre:d *vigilantes, let's do it.*

sally t: *gun laws need to be stiffer.*

NickyName: *You nuts sally? Chicago has strict gun laws. Chicago isn't in a bubble. ATF says guns come from Indiana. Backward Hoosiers. Except in basketball.*

That night, almost all of the Police Gang Unit gathers in Commander Washington's conference room for an emergency meeting. The mood is somber and the cops are pissed.

Commander Washington is hot and the veins in his neck are bulging. "An innocent mother and two children died. Who gives a shit about White and Gomez? Good riddance. But, a harmless old lady and helpless children? First priority is to find Tang. I want all hands on deck in unison with the homicide boys. I want that son-of-a-bitch found and put away. I also want to put the heat on whoever has replaced Gomez as head of the Hellraisers. They are not going to get the best of us, you hear. Don't let up. We can do it without additional troops. So, let's get back to the neighborhoods. By the way, does anybody know how the young Rebald mother is doing? Can somebody check with the Family Support Unit?"

Nick and Sherri walk solemnly back to their squad car to head out. Nick breaks the silence. "I spoke to Creed on the farm this afternoon. He says in light of what happened early this morning, he's going to do all he can to expedite finishing Camp Keokuk."

"That's good. That's really good," Sherri replies. "I'd like to see Gerald Tang as our first guest at Camp Keokuk. And maybe one more snake to keep him company. Let's put out our feelers and try to track him down by the time the Chief gives the signal."

"I'm all for that, Sherri. I'm ready to work day and night to make this happen for Sammy, Mrs. Tang, and the two little girls. You would have made a good Marine, Sherri. I'll call my Uncle Pete and have him get his truck ready for our first mission."

Nick monitors Twitter: *W e comin for u mothafuker Tang. U broke the code you gook. U killed inocint children and a mother. U r dead.*

CHAPTER 7
A SHOWDOWN AT CITY HALL

Jon DiFrisco is having breakfast in his luxurious Lake Point Tower apartment with his wife, Jenny. They're watching the morning news, where there's still a lot of reporting on last night's tragedy. "This is terrible, Jon. Can't more be done?" she asks.

"I'm working on it, Jen."

The mayor is going to have a noon press conference on the matter. Jon is curious as to what Mayor Kelly is going to say. Commander Washington is interviewed on Channel 9 this morning and says that he is "redoubling my unit's efforts to clean the streets, even though new recruits are not authorized yet by the City Counsel."

Jon reflects on Conor's plan and wonders if it will work. At least it will be worth trying. With his contribution, it could. He had sent $500,000 to Conor's bank account yesterday after lunch. He is hoping that nothing would go wrong. It's highly risky, even for the four former Marines. Jon also begins to call in some chits to raise more money without revealing the nature of the confidential mission.

The trade unions are a good place to start. He has put many of their members to work over the years. The Navy Pier project alone sent many kids to college. Don Tracy, president of the local Electrical Workers Union, would be his first call. They had become good friends over the years and had negotiated in good faith. Not necessarily true with the Teamsters. But he would put the bite on Blasé Gravino anyway. It had to be couched as a contribution to a worthwhile charity. Jon would set up an account for the families of those who lost loved ones to street gang violence. His next call is to City Hall.

At noon, the City Hall Press Room is packed with reporters holding cell phones, pads, recorders, and cameras. No fewer than fifteen microphones are clamped to the lectern. A large City of Chicago seal hangs on a blue curtain behind the lectern. There is a hum in the room as reporters and crews set up. The mayor is always late, so there is no hurry. Reporters discuss in hushed voices the current tragedy and what had happened yesterday. Speculating is what reporters do until real answers come. This story would be over soon, only to be replaced by other mayhem or murder. That's the way it works. But, for the moment, this is the story. And it is sensational.

The mayor finally arrives, followed by Commander Washington and other uniformed police commanders, plus Special Agent Ronald Bartelme, head of the Chicago FBI office, and District Attorney Ben Samuels.

The mayor starts. "This is a sad day for Chicago. What's even sadder is the burden that families are carrying today because of what happened on Chicago's West Side yesterday. An innocent mother died in her fiery home. She was babysitting two young sisters, who also died. Their mother has been hospitalized with shock and it will never be the same for her. Two alleged street gang members, William White and Benito Gomez, also died in the home. According to the Medical Examiner, they died of gunshot wounds. There is also a gang leader who allegedly was in the building and is currently at large. His name is Gerald Tang. His mother is the one who died in the fire. She was a renter. Our homicide police are now searching for Tang. If you have information on him, please call 911. His profile is on the Chicago Crime Commission's website. He has just become the Chicago Crime Commission's most wanted criminal. He is armed and dangerous."

Veteran *Sun-Times* crime reporter, Jake Brennan, nephew of the late Ray Brennan, the famous, award-winning crime reporter, interrupts the mayor. Jake is just as tenacious, but not nearly as talented as his uncle. None of the reporters can carry a candle to venerable *Sun-Times* and *Daily News* reporters Georgie Anne Geyer, Peter Lisagor, Art Petacque, or Ed Rooney, who spent his journalistic career kicking down doors.

"Mr. Mayor, you said earlier in a council meeting that you would not recommend beefing up Commander Washington's organization. Now, have you changed your mind? How many more children will have to die for you to take some action? One, two, three, four, or more? How hard is it to rid the neighborhoods of savages? There's something fishy here."

"Jake, let me finish my statement and then I will take your questions."

Jake continues to hound the mayor. "Sir, just answer the question. How many?"

"Let me finish my remarks, Jake, and then I'll take questions." The mayor continues authoritatively: "We also cannot forget the tragic death of Sammy Fernandez, who died at the hands of street gangs just two weeks ago. I have asked Commander Washington to put more heat on the street gangs of this city. It must stop. I realize that I did not ask the council for additional funding for the Police Gang Unit, headed by Commander Washington, who is here today. The Chicago Crime Commission advised me that more officers would probably not help. That said, I'm beginning to rethink this and will make a recommendation to the City Council later this month. In the meantime, an anonymous donor, a friend of the city, has set up a website where people can contribute to families who have lost loved ones to street gang violence. The philanthropist has already contributed $100,000 to the fund as seed money. A portion of the money will also go to a foundation dedicated to ridding the streets of gangs. The site is www.takethestreetsback.com."

He continues, enjoying his time at the mic. "I have also made a special request of the FBI and Special Agent Bartelme and District Attorney Ben Samuels to help us turn up the heat on these savages, who prey on innocent people. I'll now take your questions."

The mayor recognizes Tom Fisher from WBBM-TV.

"Mr. Mayor, the Chicago Crime Commission was established in 1919. The Mafia has now been replaced by hundreds of street gangs. Chicago has become the laughing stock of the nation because of these gangs who sell drugs, and kill each other and innocent citizens, much like the days of Prohibition. Yet, no matter what you do, they still seem to ravage the neighborhoods. What if you legalize drugs? Would that help?"

"Tom, I don't believe that legalizing drugs will solve the problem. These gangs will find a reason to vie for position. Next question. Yes, Rita."

Rita Jackson is a tough veteran reporter for the *Chicago Defender*, a mostly African-American publication that has gained mainstream status over the years. She's covered stories since Jesse Jackson (no relation) was a pup, running Operation Breadbasket and Operation PUSH.

"Mr. Mayor. It seems that the gangs are predominant in poorer, underserved ghettos, where families are broken and jobs are not available. That's why kids turn to gang drug economics for survival of their families. If you agree with that fact, what is the city doing to provide a good education and job help for the kids, so they don't have to turn to the streets?"

"That's a good question, Rita. We have many programs in the city for young people: schools, after-school programs, job training and a lot more. We can't do it without parental guidance and community-based crime prevention programs, producing educational material and seminars. We can only do so much as a government body. The rest is up to parents and community activists."

Rita is not satisfied. "Sir, with all due respect, I know about these failed programs. Crime prevention needs to start with jobs. What is the city doing to get young people jobs?"

The mayor's Irish is up. "You obviously haven't done your homework, Rita. We do a lot to employ young people. I think you need to do more digging. You're a good reporter. Do some more research on what we're doing in the neighborhoods. You also should note that at least the MS-13 Los Zetas savages are not in Chicago. They're in the south suburbs and they own several gentlemen's clubs. Go write about them, why don't you? Or, don't they deliver good ratings and bolster circulation? Or, is it too dangerous for you to cover that? Next question."

Jake Brennan is still on the case. "Sir, who is the anonymous donor that set up the fundraising website?"

The mayor looks at Jake with bafflement. "Jake, you need to look up the definition of 'anonymous.'"

Turning back to the packed room, the mayor says, "Thank you for coming, ladies and gentlemen of the press, and don't forget the Cubs–White Sox game tonight at Wrigley Field. The Cubs still have a shot at the wild card. Maybe this year we can remove the Billy Goat Curse."

The mayor exits to the right with the police commanders, the FBI special agent, and the district attorney.

The reporters are surprised by the premature exit of the mayor. He usually stays longer to answer more questions. This is perplexing to the newsmen and women. The mayor was obviously upset by Rita's accusatory questions and Jake's stupidity. Now, they are all scrambling for their leads. What is the news here? The mayor reconsidering more funds for the Gang

Unit? The anonymous donor? The mayor's fracas with Rita? The apparent lack of progress by the Chicago Crime Commission, or his reference to MS-13? Who knows? Whatever it is, Sammy Fernandez and the grieving mother, Mrs. Rebald, would be part of every story.

Rosco Biggs, the fiery late-evening radio guy on WIND AM 560, is after the mayor, as he always is. And, his audience is large and loyal.

Rosco is enraged.

"This mayor once again has proven to us that he doesn't have a clue. Today at a special City Council meeting, Alderman Alberto Sariano of the Twelfth Ward made an impassioned plea for the mayor and his City Council hacks to set aside more funds for the Chicago Police Department's Gang Unit after two weeks of tragedy and shame in the neighborhoods. Rita Jackson of the Chicago Defender told the mayor that the Chicago Crime Commission and others aren't doing enough. The mayor basically told her to sit down and shut up. That's really a good way to deal with a serious problem, Mr. Mayor. I agree with Rita. Where are the jobs? And, since an election is coming up, you don't want to ask taxpayers to pay for a larger police department. Well, then, you can expect more innocent people, indeed children, to die before you do anything. I wonder if there's an impeachment process in this city. If there is, I want to call for it. I know Alderman Sariano would lead the effort. We'll take your phone calls.

"You're on the air with Rosco Biggs."

"Yes, sir. Thanks for taking my call. I have an idea. We need to form vigilante groups in these neighborhoods and take these urban terrorists out. I know enough people who will join. What do you think?"

"I would like to see that happen. Problem is, these gangs are shrewd, vicious, violent, cruel, nasty, brutal, sadistic barbarians. They have shown that they have no respect for human life, like children and moms."

Rosco is now shouting and spitting into his mic. "The CPD's Special Gang Unit has tried. I know several of them and they work hard at it. But, to no avail. You need an army. Wake up, Mr. Mayor, wake up. Just to remind you all that I'm beginning my podcast this week. Please tune in and I'll give you my real opinions and feelings. "Back in a moment with more of your calls here on the Rosco Biggs Program on AM 560, the Voice of Chicago."

CHAPTER 8
LEADING CAMP CANDIDATES

The Hellraisers had lost Gomez, their leader, in the gunfight and fire at Tang's mom's home. They are aggressively on the hunt for Tang, as are the Gang Unit and the homicide detectives. Nick has a paid mole inside the gang who will be sending secret messages to him. Nick has found that gang informants have discovered they can make more money being a police mole rather than selling drugs or shooting rival gang members. He just hopes that the Marines would get to Tang first.

They also want to find Sal Martinez, who reportedly has replaced Gomez as leader of the Hellraisers. They think Tang and Martinez would make good mates at Camp Keokuk. The mission now, for Nick and his Marines, is to find them and capture them at approximately the same time, so they can load them into Pete's Explorer to be transported to Palwaukee and then flown in Conor's Ranger to Camp Keokuk. It would be delicate and risky, but doable.

The last message from the Hellraiser infiltrator is that Tang was spotted coming out of an empty warehouse on South Halsted. He was surrounded by three of his Bad Tiger goons. They would have to somehow distract his thugs in order to capture Tang and get him into Pete's Explorer. It will require some heavy-handed work from Nick, Sherri, and Pete.

Martinez is another story. He is the new leader of the Hellraisers and his lieutenants would also protect him. The CPD Gang Unit knows his general whereabouts, but nothing specific. They will have to depend on their inside source for information. Nick is the contact for the source.

In In the meantime, Gerald Tang's father is making plans to return to Chicago from San Francisco for his wife's funeral. The services will be held at the Chinese Christian Union Church on South Wentworth, ironically only a short block from Gerald's favorite restaurant. Mrs. Tang was a member of the church.

Surely Gerald Tang would attend his mother's funeral, Nick thinks. He tells Commander Washington there should be added protection at the funeral. The Commander, now more dedicated than ever, agrees. The problem for Nick and his colleagues is, if CPD arrests Tang, they'll never be able to get their hands on him. Tang would be prosecuted and then operate his gang from his prison cell. Just like Larry Hoover had done before he was sent to Colorado.

"We have to capture Tang before the funeral services," Nick tells Sherri. "The funeral is in two days, so we have to operate fast. I'll make a call now to the Chief to see if Camp Keokuk is close to being ready."

Sherri is curious about what the mayor said in the final minute of his press conference. "Nick, what did the mayor mean when he said 'maybe the Cubs can beat the Billy Goat Curse'?"

Nick, being a bit of a baseball historian, gives Sherri his take. "There's the historic Billy Goat Tavern on lower Michigan Avenue. In 1945, the Cubs were playing the Detroit Tigers in the fourth game of the World Series at Wrigley Field. Billy Sianis, the owner of the tavern, brought his pet goat, Murphy, to the game. The goat smelled so bad that they threw Billy and Murphy out of Wrigley Field. He allegedly said as he was escorted out, 'them Cubs, they ain't gonna win no more.'

"That really sucks," Sherri replies.

"I don't give a damn. I'm a White Sox fan."

CHAPTER 9
THE FLYING LEATHERNECKS ARRIVE

You can hear the CH-47 Chinook coming from miles away. The hum of the huge engines and *whop, whop* of its giant rotors are unmistakable. Creed had heard it so many times in Iraq when the Big Bird was bringing in cargo and reinforcements and taking out dead brothers so they could be transported stateside to McGuire Air Force Base in flag-draped coffins and reunited with their grieving family members.

Creed leaves the barn with his remote radio and heads to the pasture and the huge Camp Keokuk structure looming above him. He can't help but notice that the corn is now chest high. Wouldn't be long now before the corn and soybeans would be picked, put into a John Deere conveyor, and lifted into the hollow walls of the Camp, which is now complete, except for a twenty-by-twenty-foot hole in the roof.

His radio crackles.

"Keokuk One, this is Chinook 22 inbound five miles northwest of Camp Keokuk with retractable roof hanging in place."

Creed replies. "Chinook 22, this is Keokuk One up on 121.5. I read you loud and clear."

"Keokuk One, Roger and *Semper Fi*."

Creed smiles. Brothers are flying the cargo in.

Soon the huge "Boeing Body Bag" hovers over the roof of Camp Keokuk. The sound is familiar and beautiful. A huge piece of glass and metal machinery reflects the chopper's lights about twenty-five feet below the Chinook. It's the automatic roof.

Just then, a county volunteer fire department hook-and-ladder truck pulls into the pasture. JJ is driving it with Harvey Swingley, one of the neighborhood farmers and a volunteer fireman, in the right seat. JJ, also a volunteer fireman, has "borrowed" the truck for the ladders, so he and

Harvey can get up on the roof and help guide the automatic roof into place and secure it.

"Chinook 22, this is Keokuk One, over."

"Keokuk One, this is Chinook 22. Go ahead."

"22, I've got two angels climbing onto the roof, now. They should be in place soon to help put the roof in. I've given one of my buddies up there a second radio. His call is Keokuk Two."

"Roger, Keokuk One. We're ready when they are, over."

JJ and Harvey are finally in place and ready for the Chinook to lower the large roof down into the opening. JJ is hoping that all the measurements are right. The huge helicopter hovers right over the opening and waits for contact with Keokuk Two.

"Keokuk Two, this is Chinook 22, over."

"Chinook 22, this is Keokuk Two. You are close to the opening. You can start lowering it now. Over." JJ feels like a Marine in battle with his own radio. The roof comes down inches at a time. Slowly, slowly as the two Textron Lycoming engines groan under the seven-ton load. The three-bladed rotors tear through the muggy afternoon air.

Creed catches a glimpse of Jack Boyd's sheriff's car parked out along County Road 322. He's standing watch in case somebody gets too snoopy. Creed is smart. He has invited some of his farmer friends into the barn lot to watch the spectacle. They would hear about it at Gert's anyway. Besides, it's tough to hide a Chinook. They don't come around very often. Watching the roof go on doesn't jeopardize the mission.

The Chinook now lowers the roof into the opening. *It fits, by gum! It fits!* JJ thinks as he and Harvey bolt on the new roof. It wouldn't take long. They had all the tools ready to go when the Chinook arrived. They just need to test the electronics and hydraulics that make the roof work.

The CH-47 pulls up and the cable and harness is retrieved into the back belly of the beast.

"Keokuk Two, how's it look? Over."

"Chinook 22. It looks terrific. You guys sure know what you're doing. Over."

"Keokuk Two. Thanks, sometimes we get lucky. Over." JJ smiles as he and Harvey finish bolting in the roof. They can't wait to try it.

"Chinook 22, this is Keokuk One. You get a thumbs up. Not bad for a bunch of leatherneck rotorheads. I owe you and your crew a big thanks. I'll talk to you when you get back home. *Semper Fi, Semper Fi.* Over."

"Keokuk One, this is Chinook 22. Takes one to know one. Happy to do it, Chief. We're out of here before the FAA catches up to us. *Semper Fi.* Over and out."

Creed watches, as the Chinook roars away from the structure and disappears over the tree line. The farmers in the barn lot applaud the operation. They would now have great stories at Gert's. JJ and Harvey are about to test the contraption. Creed holds the remote control. He can't wait to tell his mission buddies that Camp Keokuk is ready.

CHAPTER 10
TANG'S LOVER DISCOVERED

When fire inspectors search Tang's burnt office in his mother's basement, they find a partially charred picture of a young Asian woman. The inspectors don't know who she is, but they can tell she is beautiful. They turn the picture over to Homicide. When the detectives search through the facial recognition database, they find that the picture is of Louisa Chin, a confidant and girlfriend of Gerald Tang. She is also a member of the Bad Tigers. They provide that information to the CPD Gang Unit.

Nick and Sherri look at Chin's picture. "Find Chin and we might find Tang," Nick says to Sherri.

"We may have to take her too, depending on the circumstances when we take him."

"That's going to be touchy, because we don't want her going to camp with Gerald."

"We may have to drop her off on the way to Palwaukee. That puts her back on the street."

"Or, we can drop her in the middle of the Mississippi on our way to the Camp."

Nick thinks about this for a moment and considers what the downsides would be. "I'm not sure we want outright murder on our hands. Letting them rot in Camp Keokuk is quite a different situation, as I see it."

"You're probably right, Nick. But I have another idea."

"Shoot."

"I'll bet that the Hellraisers would like to get hold of her, since Tang is probably the one who took out their leader Gomez in the basement shootout."

"Now you're cookin'."

Conor's bank account has swelled by $500,000. Jon DiFrisco came through. *He saved our ass,* Conor thought. *I wonder if he had anything to do with the new website that the mayor announced in his press conference yesterday. Probably.*

Creed calls Nick from the farm and says he wants to have a conference call this evening with the entire team. He has good news. Nick is excited and thinks it means Camp Keokuk is ready for its first guests. He hopes so. But, if that's the case, Nick, Sherri, and Pete have to get their job done—find and capture Tang and Martinez. Time is running out, since Mrs. Tang's funeral is coming up in two days. They need to get Tang before he appears at the funeral and the Homicide guys get their hands on him. You can bet that Nick's buddies in Homicide will be all over the funeral looking for signs of Tang.

The mole inside the Hellraisers reports to Nick that the gang is hot after Tang and that they have discovered that he likes to dine with Chin at the Emperor's Choice restaurant in Chinatown on Wednesday evenings. If the information is good, Martinez is going to do the job himself. *What sweet revenge. He can take out Tang and Chin at the same time.* The plan is being completed now, according to the mole. So it appears that Martinez has the same idea as Nick, Sherri, Pete, and the Marines. Question is, who's going to get to them first?

Nick turns to Sherri in the squad car. "If we do it right, we can get all three of them at once. But I think we're going to need reinforcements. The three of us can't do it."

"Who can help?" Sherri replied.

"Who's got the balls to join us?"

Creed's conference call begins at nine. With his Marine buddies on the line, he reveals the good news.

"The new roof is in place and it's been tested. It works like a Swiss watch. It takes fifteen seconds to open and fifteen to close, and I have the remote control in my hot hand. Camp Keokuk is now open for business, ladies and gentlemen. *Semper Fi*. Where the hell are my new guests?"

Creed's Marine buddies are elated. They express it with a chorus of *Semper Fi*'s.

Nick speaks first.

"That's very good news, Chief. You and your farm buddies have done a great thing. Thanks a lot. Here's where we stand here in the city. We will have two guests within 48 hours, if everything goes as planned and my source is correct. Our plan now is to intercept Tang and Martinez at the same time. Our mole tells us that Martinez is going after Tang at a Chinese restaurant on Wednesday night to avenge the death of Gomez. Problem is that Tang will probably be with his girlfriend Chin, who is also a Bad Tiger. We also need to be sure there's no collateral when we do this. We have to take Tang, Chin, and Martinez without gunfire."

Emma weighs in. "I just don't want any of us to get hurt. We cheated death too many times in Iraq. In the meantime, I'm ready with the food and my toolbox for Conor's Ranger. I'll pick up the food on our way to Palwaukee. Just need a couple of hours lead time to alert Cali that we're coming."

Conor tells the team that the Ranger is ready to go, including the hoist and cable and a special harness to lower the guests in through the roof one at a time.

"All we have to do is snap the harness a couple of feet above the floor of the Camp and let our cargo fall to the deck." Emma and Conor had tested the customized device many times up at Conor's base at Billy Mitchell Field.

Nick gives everybody a cautionary warning.

"As we all know, most missions don't go as planned. So, we have to be ready to think on our feet and be ready to go to plan B or C or D."

They all agree. Nick adds, "We need one more person to help us capture Tang and Martinez, and drop Chin in the shark tank. Anybody got any suggestions?"

There is silence for a moment, then Emma offers up somebody.

"Do you remember Gunny Andrew Franklin? He's retired and works as a security guard at the Rosemont Convention Center. I've run into him a couple of times at a bar near O'Hare. Should I approach him? He's a combat-hardened, loyal patriot and a dedicated Marine, as you all know.

He proved that over his twenty-five years in the Corps."

They all agree that Gunny Franklin would be a good candidate for the job at hand. Emma will follow up ASAP.

CHAPTER 11
THE GUNNY AND SAMMY'S KILLER

Emma and Gunny Franklin sit at a table at Toby Keith's Bar and Grill in Rosemont. It's their favorite place to catch up. At lunchtime, it isn't so noisy. At night, it's a sports bar zoo with a lot of fed-up Bears and Cubs fans. "It's good to see you, Gunny. *Semper Fi*," Emma says warmly to her old squadron mate.

"It's good to see you, Gunny. *Semper Fi*," Emma says warmly to her old squadron mate.

"It's good to see you too, Emma. We should do this more often." The Gunny is as fit as he was on active duty. His rugged face still embraces a welcoming smile.

"You still drinking that rotgut PBR?" she chides.

"Can't get off it. The only thing is, these days, I can't have my cigarette or my Cuban with it. Fucking liberal weenies. I just have to run outside from time to time. At least they haven't outlawed cheeseburgers with fries. That's probably next."

"I'll walk out with you when you feel the urge."

"You still have your Hog?" Gunny asks.

"You bet, Gunny. I would never give it up."

Emma doesn't have a car. Instead, she rides her 2006 Harley Davidson special anniversary Fat Boy everywhere she goes. She also likes to take it up into hill country in northwestern Illinois.

Emma continues. "Gunny, you remember Creed "Chief" Tsoodle, Nick Santos, and Conor Cavanaugh from the squadron?"

"I do, Emma. Great guys. It's been a while since we had a reunion. What's happening with them?"

"Well, that's why I'm here and they send their best and *Semper Fi* to you. We need your help on a very special, serious, and risky mission. They're hoping you'll agree to join us."

"I'm listening, Emma."

After Emma's explanation of the mission, Gunny is intrigued and consents. "I'm really glad you've asked me. I'll join the team. Just have Nick tell me what my role will be. Now, I've got to go see Sally."

"Sally?"

"Yes, she's my manicurist over in Park Ridge."

"A manicurist, Gunny?"

"Yes, but she's more than that. She massages my feet. I swore when I got out of the Corps, I would never again cut my own nails. Sally is Japanese and she has long, strong fingers."

"That's great, Gunny. You deserve a little relaxation and fluffing. You earned it. Just as long as that's all she's massaging."

"You have to swear you won't tell the guys."

"I swear, Gunny. And, thanks for coming along with us on the mission. Everybody's going to be very happy."

Emma is back at work on her cell phone with Nick. "Gunny's in, Nick. He says he'll be ready when we call, and he knows the importance of the mission being secret. You just have to brief him on what role you want him to play."

Nick is delighted and can't wait to tell the others. Nick texts the team. *"Emma says the Gunny is ready to go."*

At police headquarters, Scott Green, the Homicide Commander is holding a briefing for other units, including members of the Gang Unit. "Ladies and gentlemen, we have it from a credible source that young Sammy Fernandez was killed by a member of the White Lightnings, a Rogers Park gang, as you Gang Unit members know. An informant gave us the tip this morning. The alleged gunman had mistaken Sammy for someone else. Her name is Alida Budreau and we have no idea why she was in Garfield Park. One of our sources says she was in the Twelfth Ward buying drugs and weapons. She's on the FBI's list. Here's a picture of her."

Nick whispers to Sherri, "She's a tough, ugly bitch with a pock-marked face and the Devil in her eyes."

Green gives a warning. "She is considered very dangerous, so be careful. Be advised that there are also plainclothes cops out there combing the neighborhoods for Budreau. I don't want anybody killed by friendly fire. Dismissed."

Nick turns to Sherri. "I never could understand the term 'friendly fire.' How could fire be friendly?" Sherri looks at Nick and giggles.

In their unmarked squad, Nick and Sherri talk. "I think we take out Gerald Tang and Sal Martinez first, then turn our attention to Budreau for our next flight to Camp Keokuk."

"I don't think we can manage capturing and transporting three at one time. And, we need to get Tang before his mom's funeral."

Sherri responds, "Goddamn, that's good. The only problem is that we run the risk of Homicide getting to Budreau first."

"I know what my Uncle Pete would want to do. He would want us to get to Budreau, since she's the one who, according to our informant, killed young Sammy. I'll have to convince him that we can get Budreau for the second flight. We just have to concentrate on Tang and Martinez. And, we haven't settled yet on what we're going to do with Tang's girlfriend, Louisa Chin."

Jon DiFrisco sits in a comfortable leather chair facing Mayor Kelly across the large walnut desk. This is not his first visit. The mayor smiles at Jon, whom he considers an old friend and a big campaign contributor.

"It's good to see you, Jon," says the mayor. "It's been a few months now. You and Jen doing okay? I suppose you're still paying for college for those two younger DiFriscos?"

"Yes, Your Honor, and I will probably be paying them off for a long time. How about the large Kelly clan?"

"They're doing great, Jon. I'm just trying to discourage them from going into politics."

"Good advice. I watched your press conference. It wasn't pretty."

"I know. Those goddamned reporters really got to me yesterday. They are all a pain in the ass. Necessary, but a pain in the ass. That Rita Jackson is a complete pest. She doesn't recognize all that we've done to build new housing to replace the Cabrini-Green and Robert Taylor gang-infested buildings. You certainly played a huge role in constructing new housing. But, she wants jobs, jobs, jobs. That's all she keeps demanding. I'm at my wit's end with her. Does she think that the gangs can make as much money working in legitimate jobs, when they can bring in thousands a week selling drugs? I don't think so."

"I know, Your Honor. You've done a lot for this city. And the Crime Commission has, too. Of course, that's good news and it's not a juicy story. Plus, Jake Brennan is trying to keep up with his Uncle Ray. Unfortunately, he doesn't even come close. I wish I could do more to help, Mr. Mayor. I'm working on some ideas to help rid the neighborhoods of the guns, the drugs, and the violence. I'm glad you mentioned our new website in your press conference. Maybe we can do something positive with the money we get in. I'll keep you posted."

"Thanks, Jon. I need to show some progress before the election, if they don't run me out of town before then. They threw Bilandic out for just fucking up during a blizzard in 1979. Then Mayor Byrne tried to stop the gang activity when she went to live at Cabrini-Green. I bet she wasn't sober the entire two weeks before she retreated to her home. I hope I can count on you for your support next year."

"You can bet on that. And, just one more thing, Your Honor. I'm bidding on a project to construct a new housing unit on the South Side sponsored by the Chicago Housing Authority and the Feds. The bids are out now."

"Don't worry, Jon, I'll call Sean Corrigan at the CHA today."

"Thanks for seeing me, Mr. Mayor. I appreciate your support."

"Sure, Jon, and say hi to Jen."

"Mr. Mayor, I forgot to ask you if you've made a decision on getting funding for more Gang Unit cops. I suppose people are wondering about that."

"I've talked to the City Comptroller and she says that we're way over budget for this year. She's afraid of a taxpayer revolt if we go further in the hole. My aides say that public opinion polls show that the majority of Chicagoans don't want to spend more money on what they consider an already bloated police department. And, I was elected by the majority."

TIM CONNER

Jon shakes hands with the mayor and departs between two well-built plainclothes cops outside Hizzoner's door. Jon thinks, *I bet they'd be fun at a party. But if I were threatened, I'd want them around.*

CHAPTER 12
THE FINAL PLAN AND TAPAS

Inside Nick's townhouse in the Old Town neighborhood, where notorious Alderman Paddy Bauler once held court with his ward heelers and Studs Terkel hung out, the Camp Keokuk crew sits around the dining room table. Creed is linked in via speakerphone. Emma brought sample Camp Keokuk box lunches from Cali's catering shop. She wants the team's approval before the meeting officially begins.

Nick's apartment is decked out in Marine everything. Pictures of their Huey squadron, including Nick, Conor, Creed, Emma, and the Gunny standing in front of the bird; shots of Nick getting his wings in Pensacola; models of the Huey; red and gold Marine Corps emblems; his uniform over in the corner on a coat rack. The Marines admire his adornments and then go to work.

From the conference phone comes, "Hey, Gunny, I'm glad you've agreed to join this motley crew. You sure you can hack it?"

"Listen, Cochise, I'm just glad you're not here in person. I'd kick your ass, just like I used to in Iraq."

"Is this shit edible?" Nick asks, looking at Emma. "You're lucky, Chief. You don't have to taste this."

"Thanks, Nick, I'm having chicken and dumplings with a salad with vegetables from my garden and a six pack of Great River Redband Stout out here on the farm. Besides, I don't care what kind of food you serve these barbarians. It better not be too fancy."

Emma chimes in as each team member opens the boxes and begins tasting the chow.

"If Cali fixed it, it's going to be fine. We're not looking for gourmet here. Just enough to keep our guests from starving."

Gunny pipes up. "Looks and tastes better than C-rations. We existed on them in the field. Why shouldn't this be fine for killers and thieves?"

Conor is on board with the Gunny. "But weren't we thieves, Gunny? I remember you pinching underwear and boots from 323."

Gunny grunts. "That was not pinching, Captain. That was appropriating combat goods for my troops for their survival. I resent the inference."

Conor retreats, but not much. "Sorry, Gunny. But, what about the Wild Turkey you confiscated from 323's lockers?"

"That was strictly medicinal. It was for the Chief's cold, if I remember right."

"That's exactly right, Gunny." Creed's voice comes in support of the Gunny. "Thanks, I was deathly ill."

Gunny smiles at Conor.

They all spend the next five minutes tasting Cali's food, grumbling but agreeing that it's good enough for the designated purpose.

In each box for one meal are a cheese sandwich on whole wheat, a peanut butter sandwich on white, a bag of salted potato chips, one large oatmeal cookie, a napkin, and two bottles of water. Each guest would need nine boxes to hold him for a few days, until a new batch came in the next delivery. Emma will tell Cali that she did a good job and will be getting the first order soon.

Gunny snorts, "This is too fucking good for these fuckers. Whole wheat bread?" They hear Creed laughing over the phone. "This chicken and dumplings I'm having sure is good."

Nick, with Emma's help, clears away the remains of Cali's box lunches and brings out plates and plates of tapas that his mom and Aunt Maria had prepared for the meeting. Uncle Pete had carted it all in this afternoon. Nick explains each plate as he places them on the table in front of the hungry Marines, Pete, and Sherri.

"These are *aceitunas*: Olives, with a filling of anchovies and red bell pepper; *pincho moruno*: a skewer with curried meat made of pork, lamb and chicken; *chorizo al vino*: Chorizo sausage slowly cooked in white Spanish wine; *chopitos*: battered and fried tiny squid, also known as *puntillitas*."

Nick has also fixed his special tequila drink for the group. There are no words, just moans of satisfaction.

"I am now jealous," Creed says loudly into the phone.

"Tough shit, Chief," Emma croaks.

As the crew chows down, it's time for the most serious and important part of the meeting: the plan to capture Tang and Martinez tomorrow night for the first flight to Camp Keokuk, and to put Chin where she can't harm anybody. Maybe just turn her over to the Hellraisers. That should end her involvement.

Nick leads the discussion. "Here we go, grunts. I have worked out a plan. See what you think and weigh in. Our informant inside the Hellraisers tells us that he can put a bug on Martinez's car sometime tomorrow afternoon. We can track him to the restaurant. Gunny, you and Pete are going to intercept our friend Martinez a block from the restaurant, put him in Pete's Explorer, and bring him around to the restaurant's back parking lot. I'll give you cuffs, silver tape for his mouth, and a fake badge, if you need it.

"Emma, you're going to be at a table inside the restaurant having dinner. Your job is to grab Chin when she goes to the ladies' room, clasp your hand around her mouth, and whisk her out the back door. Pete and Gunny will be waiting to help you tape her mouth, cuff her, and put her in the back of our squad. Pete will then pull his Explorer to the far back part of the lot."

Gunny speaks up. "Nick, pour me another margarita, please. This is getting exciting."

Nick gets up, goes to the kitchen, and comes out with his shaker. "There, that ought to keep you shitbirds satisfied for at least fifteen minutes."

"I'll just have another of Iowa's best beers," the Chief's voice booms from the speakerphone.

Nick continues. "As Gunny and Uncle Pete intercept Martinez on the street, Sherri and I will be directly across the street from the restaurant. As soon as we hear that Martinez has been captured and in Pete's Explorer, we will go in the front door of the restaurant and arrest Tang at his table. We won't do it before Chin goes to the ladies' room and Emma has taken her to the squad. It's going to take some precise timing."

Gunny intercedes. "How do we know that she'll go to the ladies' room?"

Pete follows up. "She's a woman, Gunny. You know that's inevitable."

Emma gives Pete an elbow to the ribs.

"We will all be wired so we can talk to each other as this goes down. In the parking lot, once we get Tang settled in the Explorer next to Martinez, it's up to you, Gunny, and Pete to get them to Palwaukee.

"Sherri, you, Emma and I will head out for a drop off. You two will unchain Chin in the squad and we'll drop her off in front of Temple Beth Israel in Skokie on our way to Palwaukee. Before we arrive at the Temple, we plant a Nazi flag on her and then call the Skokie Police Department to report anti-Semitic activity at the synagogue. Then we head out to Palwaukee before the Skokie PD guys get there."

"You are very creative, Nick," Gunny says.

"Emma, you call Cali tomorrow morning to order the box lunches and we can pick them up from her tomorrow evening on our way to Palwaukee. Can she stay open for us?"

"No problem, Nick."

Conor says, "Nick, I'll have the Ranger at Palwaukee and all gassed up by six or so. I've alerted airport security that we will be having late-night deliveries to the Ranger. I'll park it way out on the tarmac, where I'll be waiting for you."

"Great, Captain." Nick says.

Gunny has a question. "Nick, if Pete and I are to intercept Martinez down the street from the restaurant, what do you suggest we do if he's escorted by his armed protection?"

"Gunny, I would like to avoid bloodshed. So, that means we have to take out Martinez's protection without gunplay, which would summon CPD officers and that would fuck up our plan. I think that means we have to either make sure Martinez has no security or create some kind of distraction for his goons. Why don't you and Pete come up with something that can work? All we need to make sure of is that we make our first flight to Camp Keokuk tomorrow night, because Mrs. Tang's funeral is the next day."

Gunny says, "This is like old times. Pete and I will devise something inventive. We just need to huddle up tomorrow morning."

From the farm, Creed's voice comes over the conference phone. "Conor, I've put a red light on top of the camp roof, so you should be able to see it within a mile or so from the Camp. I'll also be on my radio. The weather is supposed to be okay and my buddy, the deputy, will patrol the road to keep neighbors from getting too close. If everything goes as planned, you should be here shortly after midnight."

"That's the plan now, Chief. But we have to be flexible, depending on how things go at Emperor's Choice."

"I'll be ready whenever you get here. I can't wait to see the first fuckers lowered into their new home."

Pete, who has been quiet most of the evening, chimes in for one last passionate word. "I can't wait to get our hands on that Budreau animal who killed Sammy. She's next." Tears well up in his eyes and his lip quivers.

"We'll get her, Unc. Don't worry." Nick reaches over to give his uncle a warm pat on his shoulder.

Sherri has something to say. "Lady and gentlemen, I know I'm not a Marine, but I am so proud to be part of this. And, thanks for including me. God bless you all. And, thanks for serving."

Nick acknowledges Sherri and wraps up the meeting. "I can't tell you how much this means to my family and the people of Chicago. We will slowly get rid of the garbage in the streets. We just have to do it slowly and carefully. *Semper Fi.*"

Nick's early-morning text reads: "*Good morning Mom. Can't thank u and Aunt Maria enuff for the tapas last nite. Crew went crazy over them. They want to make sure there's another occasion for a re-do. Hope u have a nice day. Be out of touch for 24 hours. Talk to u tomorrow morning.*" He texts his mom every morning. But this morning, it has more meaning.

Adoncia replies. "*Buenos dias Guapo u be safe today. I love u.*"

Nick smiles. She always calls him "Guapo," which means "handsome." She has also just learned to text. What a kick Guapo gets out of that.

It's time to check in with Gunny and Pete to see if they have a plan for tonight. Nick sends a text to both. "*u gents have a plan for tonite yet?*"

A brief and somewhat cryptic reply comes from Gunny almost immediately: "*Yes we do.*" That sounds just like Gunny—to the point and you don't question him.

A few seconds later comes Pete's reply. "*Yes we do.*" That also sounds like Gunny. In many ways, his Uncle Pete and Gunny are alike. They have obviously coordinated their responses. Nick won't ask questions. He just has to trust them.

A follow-up text from Gunny reads, *"We need u to get us two taser guns delivered to Pete's house."* Nick is curious and somewhat nervous about the request.

"Those things can be dangerous, Gunny. U know how to operate one?"

"I know and yes!" Once again, short and not so sweet.

"They'll be there this afternoon, Gunny. Be safe." Conversation over.

CHAPTER 13
THE SNAKES ALSO SCHEME

In a large apartment on one of the top floors of the sprawling Henry Horner public housing buildings, Sal Martinez, the new grand leader of the Hellraisers, sits on his fluffy pillows and smokes a large Dominican cigar as he prepares his lieutenants for this evening's mission. The apartment is adorned with Hellraiser insignias and anti-police signs and posters. There is a view east to the Loop that includes the Willis Towers and the Hancock building.

"Who needs those fuckahs downtown?" exclaims Martinez. "We have our own skybox right here, you mothah fuckahs." He reaches over to his red-haired, green-eyed girlfriend, Sopra Rojas.

"I will take you, KT, and Tre. Sopra, you'll be seated in the restaurant having dinner. You will signal us when Tang and his bitch are there. Me, KT, and Tre will walk slowly south on Wentworth. As we approach the door, KT, you and Tre will guard each side while I go in and blast the Chinese mothah fuckah to bits. I'll also take out his gook bitch. This is gonna be super revenge for killing Gomez, the mom, and the children. Fuck White."

Martinez then opens the old wooden cabinet and the large trunks where all the weapons are stored. There are AK-47s, Glocks, .357 Magnums, stun guns and tasers, leather billy clubs, pepper spray canisters, nunchucks, black jacks, brass knuckles, machetes, Lugers, RX-22s, M-15s, and a dozen more deadly tools of the trade.

Tonight, Martinez, KT, and Tre have to arm themselves with small weapons like Glocks and .357s. No shoulder-carried weapons. These are for apartment-to-apartment or apartment-to-street use. One had to know his tactical mission in order to select the right weapons.

"We are ready. We are ready for the fuckahs," Martinez spits. "We'll stay here until Sopra signals that Tang and his lover are having dinner. Then me and KT and Tre will head out to Chinatown. We'll park a block away and walk to the restaurant. When we get close, you two stay back and wait for me. I'll kill both the sons-a-bitches. Then I'll meet you back at the car."

Martinez takes out two handguns and loads them both. KT and Tre do the same. Martinez puts on his favorite sweater and sits back on his big pillow to wait for the time to come.

CHAPTER 14
A MOTHER'S PAIN PERSISTS

Two members of the Chicago Police Department Family Notification and Support Unit drive past the burnt-out Tang house to the humble home of Sarah Rebald two blocks away. The officers walk up the sidewalk through a corridor of pleasant flower bouquets, put there by caring people who want Mrs. Rebald to know that they are praying for her and have not forgotten the loss of her two beautiful daughters, Tanya and Ramona. The officers' hearts sink. They feel passionate about their work, but dealing with such tragic losses is always heartbreaking. They can't change the event, but maybe they can ease the burden.

When Mrs. Rebald opens the door, the officers notice that she is in deep pain. Her face is gaunt, and she is terribly thin.

"Hello, Mrs. Rebald, I'm Officer Jack Stuart and this is my colleague, Officer Dianne Scully. We met you at your daughters' funeral. We hope this is a good time for us to talk."

"Come in, officers. I've been expecting you."

The officers step in and take off their caps. Officer Stuart offers his condolences. "Mrs. Rebald, on behalf of the Chicago Police Department, we offer our sincere condolences for the loss of your daughters. We are very sorry and we're here to offer you support."

"Come and sit down, Officer Stuart and Officer Scully. Can I offer you something to drink?"

"No, thank you, ma'am. We're just fine," Officer Scully replies. "First of all, how are you doing?"

"I'm doing okay, but it's tough without my babies. It's hard to realize a world without them. People have been so sweet and that helps a lot. My brother and his wife are close by, which makes things easier.

I'm a single mom, and the house seems empty without the laughing and the playing. Do either of you have children?"

Officer Stuart replies. "Yes, ma'am, I have two children, a boy and a girl about the same ages as Tanya and Ramona. I can't imagine life without them either."

Officer Scully follows. "Yes, Mrs. Rebald, I have a young son. He's two. I'm so sorry for your loss. What can we do for you now?"

"I don't know. I've been getting money from that website that a kind soul set up. It's helped with my immediate expenses, including funeral costs. I haven't thought much beyond that."

"It's good you have close family and friends nearby. That surely is comforting."

"Yes, it is. Just one question, though. Do you know a good lawyer? I'm thinking about suing, but I don't know who to sue." The two officers look at each other.

"I will surely find out and I'll call you," Officer Scully says.

"I would appreciate that," Mrs. Rebald replies. "Also, I'm thinking of some way to honor my girls, like setting up a fund to fight these street gangs. We live in fear around here and in other neighborhoods. Can you tell me how I do that?"

Officer Stuart offers Mrs. Rebald some help. "I'm going to have a Police Department information technology technician call you and get something set up for you. In the meantime, the website set up for helping you is taking some of the contributions to help fight the gangs. That should do some good."

"Yes, it should. But it won't bring back my girls."

"No, ma'am, it won't. But it should keep other young children from dying."

Officer Scully puts her hand on Mrs. Rebald's knee. "Mrs. Rebald, do you have pastoral help?"

"Yes, I have a very fine minister."

"That's good."

Officer Stuart feels that it's time to go. "Mrs. Rebald, Officer Scully and I will leave now, if there's nothing else we can do right now. I'll have a lawyer and IT information for you this afternoon. I'll call you."

"Thank you, officers. You've been very kind. You would have loved my girls." Tears trickle down Mrs. Rebald's cheeks.

Officers Stuart and Scully say goodbye and walk again through the row of flowers lining the walkway. Officer Scully leans down, picks a yellow daisy and clasps it in her hand. As they depart, they pass Alderman Sariano going to Mrs. Rebald's door.

"He's a good man," Officer Stuart says. He and Officer Scully say nothing to each other for the next hour or so.

CHAPTER 15
D-DAY IS HERE AS MR. TANG RETURNS

Nick is texting his colleagues from his squad car.

"Team. I have set up a meeting place in Chinatown at an old friend's apartment. He's out of town and has offered his apartment for our pre-engagement summit. Make sure u gas up and bring everything u need. Conor, Chief, we'll hook up with u via phone. We should meet at 1800 hours sharp. The building is on the corner of 22nd Pl and Wentworth. Apt. 3A. U can park on the street."

The first text response comes from Emma. *"I've alerted Cali that we should be picking up the food at around midnite. She will have 18 lunches ready to go to Camp Keokuk. That should hold the first two until the next drop."*

Next comes a text from Creed. *"I'm at Gert's having coffee and will be at home for the call. The Camp is ready."*

Then Gunny: *"I'll be there with Pete."*

Conor checks in from Billy Mitchell Field. *"I'll be at Palwaukee and will be on the line for the call at 1800 hrs."*

Nick feels that everything sounds in order. He is still worried about the Gunny and Pete and what their plan is for intercepting Martinez and his goons, if they are with him. He thinks he has to go with the Gunny. *He was always good at planning. And, he has balls. So does Uncle Pete, for that matter. I just have to trust.*

Nick and Sherri sit down for a cup of coffee at their favorite diner to get ready for the evening's events. Sherri is pensive for a while and then speaks up. "I wonder what my mom, as a professor of Social Psychology, would say about Camp Keokuk. She would find it very intriguing and an interesting study on how the inmates behave in that unique environment. The cameras are already installed. I'd love to pose this to her in all confidentiality. She could study the videos. What do you think?"

Nick sips his coffee and takes a bite of his grilled cheese sandwich. He's thinking it over. *What good would it do? If authorities discover the videos, we could all go to jail. It would have to be highly secretive.*

He then replies. "I think it would be a truly distinctive study and would garner a lot of attention in social psych circles and among academicians. I'm not sure the rewards outweigh the risks."

Sherri thinks for a moment. "I think your concerns are legitimate. But maybe there would be something in studying our guests' conversations, thoughts, feelings, and behaviors that would help us understand the gang mentality more deeply and help us solve some of the problems neighborhoods are facing. I don't know, I'd have to ask my mom. I know she could keep our secret."

"I'm not concerned about that. I'm concerned with how long the study would take and what risks there are in taking the law into our own hands. I'm also not against taking risks. I've taken many, but somehow this seems super risky."

"Would you give me permission to at least talk to my mom in all confidentiality and see what her views are?"

Nick ponders again. "We will be recording and storing the activities inside the camp with the cameras Chief has installed. That would give your mom some time to think about this."

"I'll talk to her tomorrow after our first mission is accomplished."

Nick closes the conversation. "I think we ought to put this idea before our team before you talk to your mom. In the meantime, we ought to head out to South Wentworth for our meeting. We'll pick up some food for the guys and Emma on our way."

At O'Hare, CPD homicide detectives pick up Mr. Tang, Gerald's father, and escort him to headquarters. He has just arrived from San Francisco for Mrs. Tang's funeral tomorrow. They want to have a long talk with him about his son and whether he has talked to Gerald or not. And, if he has, what did the young murderer have to say?

In a headquarters briefing room, Detective Danny Ruble leads the conversation. "Mr. Tang, I'm sorry about your wife. I'm truly sorry. I understand from Mrs. Rebald that she was very good to her daughters."

"Thank you. She was a good woman."

"Mr. Tang, we won't keep you long and then we'll take you to your hotel, so you can get some rest before tomorrow's funeral. Do you know why we're questioning you?"

"Yes, I believe so."

"It's because your son is wanted for the murder of your wife, plus two little girls and two gang members. Do you understand that?"

"Yes, my son can be a defiant boy."

"Have you heard from your son?"

"Yes, once a couple of days ago. But it was a short talk."

"Can you tell me what he said?"

"Yes, he said he may or may not attend his mother's funeral."

"Did you record the number he was calling from?"

"No, he always has a blocked number."

"Sir, do you mind if we take a look at your cell phone?"

Mr. Tang resists. "That's my private property. You should get a warrant."

Ruble hesitates. "Mr. Tang, I can get a warrant. But that will take 24 hours. And it might mean you'd miss your wife's funeral.

Mr. Tang thinks for a moment and then hands his phone to Detective Ruble, who holds it out to his colleague.

Detective Ruble goes on. "Mr. Tang, do you know that your son is the leader of a notorious street gang and that his office was in the basement of Mrs. Tang's home?"

"No. All I know is that Gerald was running with bad people and that he lived in the basement. My wife said he never came upstairs and she never went downstairs. She was scared. I never asked why."

"Mr. Tang, did your son ever talk about his friends?"

"Only that he had close friends and that he made good money."

"Did he say how he made his money?"

"He said he was working at Sears."

"Did you believe him?"

"No. He always bent the truth, even when he was a boy."

Ruble's colleague comes back into the room, returning Mr. Tang's cell phone. "Mr. Tang, I guess that will be all for now. If you would, keep your cell phone on. We may want to talk to you further. Again, I'm sorry for your loss. Our boys will take you to your hotel."

"Thank you."

Detective Ruble asks one more question as Mr. Tang is leaving. "Mr. Tang, I'm curious, why did you leave Mrs. Tang and your son and move back to San Francisco?"

"I couldn't make a living here. She wouldn't move without our son. So I went without them. That was probably not a smart move. I may have been able to make a difference. I also might have died in the fire."

"Good point. Thank you, sir."

CHAPTER 16
THE MARINES FACE THE SNAKES

The crew is assembling at Nick's friend's apartment in Chinatown. One by one, Emma, Gunny and Pete join Nick and Sherri. They sit around a table and begin the conference with Creed from the farm and Conor from Palwaukee Airport on the speakerphone.

Nick once again leads the session. "Chief, you and Conor on?"

"Conor's on from Palwaukee. Bird is gassed and ready."

"Creed's on from Camp Keokuk. I'm ready to play host to our first guests."

"Sherri, Gunny, Pete, Emma, and I are here in the room just a few blocks from the target. First order of business is for us to check out our communications system. I have a Stingray wireless system for each of us. No need for you to have one, Chief. We'll communicate with you via cell as we go. And, Conor, the same for you."

"For us here in the room, we'll test this now and see how it works."

They all check out the lapel mics and the small earpieces.

"It works great," Gunny says.

Everybody agrees and clip their mics on their clothing and put the earpieces in their good ears.

Nick proceeds. "Sherri and I will be stationed directly across the street from Emperor's Choice. We'll be window-shopping at Oriental Art Imports and keep an eye out for Tang and Chin as they enter the restaurant. Emma will already be seated and ready to take Chin out the back door. What about you and Pete, Gunny?"

"Pete and I will be parked about a block away just north of the restaurant. Informant says that Martinez and his goons will be approaching from the north. Our plan is to intercept Martinez a block north of the target, so that you two can make your move on Tang and his bitch.

Martinez will be monitoring Tang's entrance into the restaurant, that's for sure. We'll make sure he never makes it to Emperor's Choice."

Nick is still concerned about Gunny and Pete's diversion plan. "You two all set with your plan to distract the goons?"

Gunny reassures Nick. "Don't worry, Trooper. Your uncle and I have everything under control."

Emma is next. "As Nick says, I will already be in the restaurant before Tang and his poontang enter." Emma has a great vocabulary, as well as a great sense of humor. "Get it? Poontang?"

On the conference phone, you can hear Creed chuckling from the farm and Conor laughing out loud from Palwaukee Airport, where he is having supper at the café after parking his Ranger out on the tarmac.

"As soon as Chin goes to the ladies' room, I'll make my move."

"Sherri and I will take Tang. That is, if Sherri doesn't want to stop and hear another Carrie Underwood tune."

Nick makes sure everybody is aware of the risks. "Ladies, gentlemen, this is it. This is where we begin to clean the garbage from the streets of Chicago. Stay alert and be ready for tactical shifts. Please stay in touch via your Stingray.

"This is the most important mission of my life. I thank you all for your support in the name of my nephew, Sammy, Tang's mom, and the two young Rebald sisters. And, remember what our hero Chesty Puller said: 'You don't hurt 'em if you don't hit 'em.'"

Conor replies, "Pappy Boyington would just bomb 'em."

"*Semper Fidelis.*"

Sal Martinez, formidable leader of the Hellraisers, is staring out the big window at the city lights just now coming on as he puts on his favorite sweatshirt and tucks his pistol in his waistband. His two lieutenants do the same. They would soon head to Emperor's Choice to take out Tang and his companion, Chin. He is particularly hyper and venomous.

"I want that son-of-a-bitch so fucking bad. Gomez was a good leader and I loved him. He brought us great respect from the other gangs. I don't give a fuck about White. I should have gone with him to Tang's office to help wipe the bastard out. But he said he wanted to do it himself. I should have insisted."

KT reassures his new boss, "Sal, we can't do anything about it now. You're doin' a great job as our leader. Let's just concentrate on our immediate mission. We will get him tonight and hopefully take down the Bad Tigers at the same time."

Martinez turns to KT. "You're a good lieutenant, KT. You're right. Only a few hours now and it will be over."

CHAPTER 17
H-HOUR - TIME TO SNAG SOME SNAKES

It's 8pm. Nick and Sherri stand on Wentworth looking into the windows of the store across the street from Emperor's Choice. Nick notices the tacky green awning bulging from an otherwise beautiful building with ornate columns framing a large balcony. There are several people on the streets enjoying the August evening and the bright, gaudy, multi-colored neon lights. The thick aroma of Chinese food fills the evening air. Nick and Sherri adjust their lapel mics and their earpieces on their Stingray equipment.

Then comes the check-in from Gunny. "This is Gunny with Pete. We're in place a block away, monitoring Martinez' movements from the bug."

Sherri responds, "Gotcha, Gunny. We're in place across the street from the restaurant."

"Check in, Emma. This is Sherri."

"Loud and clear, Sherri. I'm south of the restaurant about half a block down, on the same side of the street as you and Nick."

"Emma, why don't you go ahead in, get seated, and order?"

"Got it, Nick. I'm heading in now in case it gets too crowded. I did make reservations, though, for 8:30."

"Good. We'll see you soon. Stay safe."

The restaurant is now filling up. It's a popular place. What Nick and the crew don't know is that Sopra Rojas is already seated inside so that she can alert Martinez and his goons when Tang and Chin are seated. Nick's mole hadn't reported that. However, if everything went as planned, she would never see Martinez because Gunny and Pete would have taken him out. But if Rojas raises hell when Nick and Sherri arrest Tang, there would be another person to contend with. Hopefully, she will not be armed and will just leave quietly.

Emma is now seated inside ordering. "I'm in, everyone. Think I'll order the seaweed salad and crispy green beans, followed by the broiled whitefish with black bean sauce, then vegetable egg foo yung with brown rice. How does that sound?"

"That sounds absolutely awful," comes a gruff response from Gunny. "Why couldn't Tang hang out in a good Italian restaurant?"

"You're just an old grouchy grunt, Gunny. I'm going to enjoy this until the fireworks begin."

"By the way, Pete agrees with me," Gunny growls.

"Radio silence, troops, radio silence," comes a calm retort from Nick.

In Pete's Explorer, Gunny notices a blip on the screen that is tracking Martinez' movements. "Got a blip here that indicates Martinez is three blocks away from the restaurant, coming slowly south on Wentworth. We should get a visual on him momentarily."

"Roger, Gunny," Nick replies. "We haven't spotted Tang and Chin yet. Will let you know when we do."

In the next minute, Nick's voice comes through the Stingray. "Just what we fucking need. Two elderly bag ladies moving north on Wentworth and now near the entrance to the restaurant. Goddamnit. They're now begging people for handouts. We've got to get them out of here before they become collateral."

Without a word, Sherri dashes out across Wentworth to get the old ladies to move along. When she gets there, she discretely shows her badge to the old women and politely asks the ladies to move along up Wentworth, giving them each five dollars. The raggedy women slowly comply with the pleasant and kind young officer. Nick feels bad for the ladies but can't do anything about it now. Sherri has done her job and is now back at her partner's side across the street.

Emma is finishing her whitefish when the call comes from Nick.

"I've got Tang and Chin." The couple is unmistakable. Nick and Sherri had studied the mug shots over and over.

"They're walking towards the entrance to the restaurant now. You should spot them soon, Emma. Tang has on a blue jacket with jeans, a Cubs cap and sunglasses. As Nick and Sherri wait for Emma and Gunny to report their status, an impatient text comes in from Creed in Iowa.

"U guys on schedule?"

"Close to capture, Chief. Let u know when we're on our way," is Nick's reply.

"OK," comes the reply from Creed, who is sitting in his barn into his fourth beer. Nick hopes that the Chief will not be too shitfaced to handle the arrival of his first guests for Camp Keokuk.

Gunny reports that Martinez and his goons are on the move. Just waiting for Emma to report that she has Chin in hand and out the back door.

Then, Gunny reports that he and Pete are on the move. They are 100 feet away. Pete guns the Explorer and intercepts the three Hellraisers at the corner, a block from the restaurant. As they screech to a halt and exit the Explorer, the two bag ladies come running onto the scene. Gunny and Pete approach Martinez, while the two grungy ladies quickly move forward and begin tazing the two sidekicks. As the goons fall to the ground, Gunny and Pete grab Martinez, handcuff him, put silver tape over his mouth, and shove him none too gently into the Explorer. Martinez's two guards writhe on the ground as the two bag ladies stand over them, daring them to move. One of the bag ladies isn't finished. She tazes them again at close range, rendering them groaning and immobile.

"We've got our man and the goons are taken care of. We're heading for the parking lot," reports Gunny.

Inside the restaurant, Chin is heading for the ladies' room, as predicted. Emma puts down her chopsticks and follows Chin, who is dressed in a jacket with oriental markings and black slacks.

"I'm close behind target and will soon have her in hand," reports Emma.

Nick and Sherri walk quickly across the street and enter the restaurant to arrest Tang at his table. The restaurant is now packed.

Emma reports that Chin has been seized and taken out the back door.

Nick and Sherri approach Tang with caution. They don't know if he is armed or not. They assume so.

As they near Tang's table, Nick has one hand on his pistol and the other flashing his badge. Sherri goes to the other side of Tang's table.

"Gerald Tang, you're under arrest for murder. You have to come with us." Tang stands up and tries to resist. Sherri moves in, grabs his arm, and reads him his rights.

"Mr. Tang, you have the right to remain silent and the right to counsel."

Tang interrupts Sherri. "Yea, I know all that shit, bitch. You have no evidence and this is all a trumped-up charge."

Sherri continues. "Mr. Tang, we hope that you'll come with us without a struggle. We don't want innocent people getting hurt."

Nick frisks Tang for weapons. He finds a Glock inside Tang's pants and disarms him. Guests of the restaurant are now clamoring to get out. Nick reassures them. "Ladies and gentlemen, we're police officers. Please be calm. We have this situation under control."

Sherri now scoots Tang toward the back door while waiters and waitresses take cover in the kitchen. Customers are scampering out the front door and hiding under tables. Unnoticed, Rojas is dazed and scurries toward the front door, hoping to escape back to home base, not knowing what has happened to Martinez, KT, and Tre.

"Gunny, we're heading to the back door with Tang in hand."

"Roger, we're here and Chin is in the squad."

When Nick and Sherri get Tang to the Explorer, Martinez squirms in the back with Gunny and Pete, who are ready to secure both of them for the ride to Palwaukee. Nick and Sherri head for the squad, where Emma has Chin in the back cuffed with her mouth taped.

Some diners are heading for their cars. One customer, lobster napkin still wrapped around his neck, approaches the Explorer, wanting to know what's going on. Gunny flashes his fake badge and stares at the customer. "Get the fuck out of here, or I'll stuff a lobster up your ass." The customer takes off like a scared rabbit.

Nick's voice comes over the Stingray. "We're ready to roll, Gunny. After a stop in Skokie to dump Chin, we'll run by Cali's and then meet you at Palwaukee. You have Tang and Martinez secured?"

"No problem, Nick. Our scums are all buttoned down. I'm on top of them and we're heading toward the airport," comes the reassuring report from the Gunny.

"Roger, Gunny."

As the squad car and the Explorer head up the Dan Ryan and onto the Kennedy, Sherri texts Creed on the farm and Conor at the airport. *Scum in tow. Heading to airport.* She then texts Cali. *Heading your way to pick up the boxes. Should be there in about 30 minutes.*

In the squad, Emma tightly secures a Nazi flag to Chin's arm. Chin's dark-brown eyes glare at Emma. Emma quietly whispers, "Gonna give you some hell tonight, you gook bitch, and you're never gonna see your lover again. He's going to see Jesus."

As the squad turns north on the Eden's, Nick tunes to AM 560 to hear what Rosco Biggs is raging about tonight. He isn't disappointed.

"Well, ladies and gentlemen, good evening. First of all, I want to tell you that when you send mail to me, spell my damn name right. It's R-O-S-C-O. There is no E. Don't ask me why, there just isn't.

Well, it's happened again. A young student at the Jordan Academy up in Rogers Park was injured by a gang bullet as she was headed home from school today. She's now in fair condition at Northwestern Memorial. No neighborhood in Chicago is safe from the ravages of the street gangs. The mayor, as you know, has refused to give the Gang Unit funds for more officers. When are the mayor and the councilmen going to take more actions? I appealed earlier this week for an impeachment action for this mayor. I've got no response yet from City Hall. Probably won't. So, as one caller so aptly put it, we've got to form vigilante groups to take the law into our own hands to take our neighborhoods back. I'm not advocating for violence, but I am advocating for justice. I'll be back in a moment to discuss the Cubs and Sox. And, I'll take your calls. I'm Rosco Biggs on AM 560, the Voice of Chicago."

Nick turns down the volume. "Well, you see, Rosco's got it right. You hear that, Chin? You and your dirty friends are going to be wiped out. Your days are fucking numbered."

Chin in the backseat mutters through her silver tape as they turn off the Edens and head toward Temple Beth Israel for the drop off.

Conor is in the cockpit of his Ranger far out on the tarmac checking all the instruments for the first flight to Camp Keokuk. He feels the adrenaline building up in his body. He felt it before in Iraq and the Battle of Fallujah. It was the second-best thing to sex. No combat pilot could ignore it. The cockpit glows red as he goes through the pre-flight checklist waiting for the cargo to arrive. Nobody is in the tower after 10pm, so he files a Visual Flight Rules plan with the guys at the flight ops desk inside and checks the weather. Everything looks good for their first flight. He would just have to check in with various flight service stations along the way. The last one would be at Burlington, since he doesn't want them to track him after that.

Nick pulls the unmarked squad up to the front of the temple. Sherri gets out and lets Emma and Chin out. Emma takes the cuffs and silver tape off Chin; Nick calls the Skokie Police Department alerting them to anti-Semitic activity at the temple. Chin is angry, dazed, and confused as she sits down on the curb trying to untie the Nazi flag from around her arm, to no avail. Nick thinks, *I'd really like to hear her explanation to the Skokie officers.*

Nick is now back on the Edens heading north to Cali's to pick up the food. He's pleased with how things are going. They are half-way there.

A text from Pete chimes in. *"We're now pulling into Palwaukee. What's ur location?"*

"Sherri responds, *"Chin dropped. Heading for Cali's. Approx ETA Palwaukee, 20 mins. How is the cargo behaving?"*

"Gunny had to bring them in line a couple of times, but nothing they didn't deserve."

Sherri follows with a text to Conor and Creed. *"Cargo in hand. Things on schedule. Should be ready to depart Palwaukee in about 45 minutes. Keep u informed."*

Nick pulls the squad up to Cali's place where a light is still burning. Emma hops out and enters Cali's place. Soon she and Cali return with eighteen boxes. Emma introduces Cali to Nick and Sherri and puts the boxes in the trunk. Nick and Sherri thank Cali for her help and then are on their way. As they depart, Cali stands out front of her place, scratching her head. Emma will fill her in some day.

CHAPTER 18
COPS ON SCENE—THE BIRD IS READY

Back at Emperor's Choice, cop cars surround the place as patrolmen and detectives ask witnesses what they had seen. A Channel 9 news crew is there reporting live from the scene. Hundreds of people crowd up and down Wentworth to get a view. The cops have put yellow tape at each end of the block to keep them away while they investigate. Detective Ronny Gable is in charge. He's talking to the manager of Emperor's Choice.

"You say the people who took the Asian man were cops?"

The manager was visibly shaken. "Yes, they showed badges, disarmed, and handcuffed the Asian man before they escorted him out the back door. They were a male and female officer in plain clothes."

"What did they say to the Asian man?"

"They said he was under arrest for murder and then the lady officer read him his rights."

"Do you know who this Asian man is?"

"I don't know his name, but he comes in every once in a while."

"Did he pay by credit card?"

"No, he always pays cash and leaves big tips."

Out back, other officers interview eyewitnesses. They all have the same story. They say there was no cop car, just a black SUV and another plain car, a Chevy they thought. Men and women were putting a man and a woman in the SUV and the Chevy.

"Did anyone get a license plate number?"

A woman says she saw a Wisconsin plate on the SUV but couldn't get the number. It all happened so fast.

Detective Gable radios back to Dispatch.

"Was there a sting at Emperor's Choice restaurant on Wentworth tonight about 9:30?"

The dispatcher looks at the records. "Negative, there's nothing in the records."

Detective Gable thinks it might be an undercover operation that wouldn't have gone through Dispatch. He is right about that. Two blocks away, Rojas is surprised to find KT and Tre crumpled on the street, weapons gone, and no Martinez. They are still unsteady, recovering from being tazed by "two old bag ladies." They tell her that Martinez had been kidnapped and driven away by two men in a black SUV.

"You mean to tell me that two old ladies tazed you, took your guns and kidnapped Martinez? Are you dumb mothafuckahs kidding me?" She is dreadfully angry, and when she gets pissed, fire comes from her eyes, her jaw gets really taught, and you don't want to fuck with her. But there is no time to be mad right now. She has to get the two dazed idiots off the street, into her car, and back home before the cops come to question them.

Son-of-a-bitch, she thinks. *First Gomez and now Martinez.* The Hellraisers are fucked by two old bag ladies. Who in the hell has kidnapped Martinez? She knows Tang was captured by the cops in the restaurant and his babe Chin has disappeared. *But who's got Martinez?*

Nick, with Sherri, Emma, and a trunk full of box lunches aboard, pulls up to the security gate at Palwaukee. It's 11:30pm, 2330 military time. Nick and Sherri flash their badges, tell the Rent-a-cop about their special guest in the back and explain that they're heading for the black Ranger. The security guard gives them a salute and says, "Your colleagues are already out there."

Emma is halfway out the back door. "Hold on, Nick." She goes to the trunk, retrieves a box lunch, and hands it to the guard. "That's for you, my good man. Freshly made by Cali." The guard is surprised and pleased as he raises the gate and waves them through. The gate closes behind them as they head toward the Ranger. *Emma is very smart, there is just no doubt about it*, Nick thinks.

"Gotta feed the troops."

Conor is in the cockpit turning on external power and checking all the gauges and instruments. The external lights are illuminated. Gunny and Pete, along with Conor, struggle to get Tang and Martinez into the chopper, and finally get them secure inside by the time Nick, Emma, and Sherri arrive. Conor, Nick, Emma, and Gunny are going on the trip. Pete and Sherri will stay behind and get the squad and Pete's Explorer back to the city. Cali's lunches are loaded into the Ranger next to Tang and Martinez, who are now wide-eyed and frantic about their fate.

As Gunny and Emma take their places on either side of their special guests, Gunny can't help himself. "Hello, shitbirds. It's your Uncle Gunny, again. You ready for a nice flight with Captain Cavanaugh? You're going to enjoy your new digs. You'll no longer be able to hurt anyone, except each other. And we don't give a fuck about that."

Pete and Sherri close the Ranger door and move back toward their cars. Nick takes his place in the right seat to fly shotgun. Conor is strapped in the captain's seat. With the push of a few switches, the Ranger's two Pratt and Whitney engines begin to purr as Conor and Nick don their microphones and earpieces, as do Gunny and Emma. They all know the drill. Just a different place and a different time.

While Conor radios operations and advises them that Ranger One Zero One is ready for taxi, Nick texts Creed at Camp Keokuk. *"Chief. Departing Palwaukee in 5 minutes with Marines and two guests on board. Will call 10 minutes out."*

Almost immediately, *"Semper Fi, Nick. I'm ready."*

Conor gives Pete and Sherri the thumbs-up as he taxies away. They return the sign and the first cargo flight to Camp Keokuk is officially on its way. The smell of avgas and oil is heavy in the late evening air.

Conor opens his intercom to his colleagues, breathes deeply, and says, "Here we go, troops. Our first flight is about to begin. It looks like a good night for flying. I expect the journey to take one hour forty-five minutes direct to Camp. Is everything secure back there?"

"Everything's good back here, Captain," Gunny reports. "These two assholes are in for the surprise of their life."

"Roger, Gunny, here we go and *Semper* fucking *Fi*."

The large engines growl and the rotor blades chop through the air as Conor lifts off and begins his forward movement toward the southwest. Pete and Sherri watch the Ranger's lights disappear over the horizon and into the night.

"I'm praying Pete. I'm praying hard," Sherri says as she squeezes Pete's arm. "Me too, Sherri. We can stop at my church near our home and light a candle."

"I'd like that, Pete."

"Follow me, then, and we'll also get something to eat." As they pass back through the security gate at 12:30am, they notice that the guard is finishing the cookie from the box lunch Emma had given him on her way in. He smiles broadly and gives them a friendly wave.

Back on the road, Sherri calls her mom, who is always up at this hour doing lesson plans for her social psychology classes at U of C.

"Hi, Mom, it's your baby girl. You're still up, of course." She listens for a moment and then continues. "Listen, can you have lunch today at around noon? I have the day off and there's something important to talk to you about." Sherri smiles. "No, Mom, I'm not pregnant. You have to have action before that happens." Sherri loves it when her mom laughs. "I can drive down to campus to meet you. Super and I love you."

Nick's mom Adoncia and his Aunt Maria sit on Pete and Maria's back porch enjoying a midnight snack and a glass of Merlot. The two sisters love to do that on warm summer evenings. Maria gazes out at the basketball backboard and hoop that Pete had put up for Sammy. Sammy used to play there almost every night with his dad. There are no more sounds of the bouncing ball and the shouts, "You fouled me! That was no fair!" Maria and Adoncia sit quietly. Earlier tonight the two sisters had gotten some revenge.

They accomplished an important mission for the neighborhoods of Chicago and have cause to celebrate. Maria looks over at a stack of ugly clothes and wigs on a nearby chair. "You looked absolutely gorgeous, Dahling," she says to her sister. Adoncia giggles and reaches over and puts on a shaggy wig.

"I'm not only gorgeous, Señora, I'm a damned good shot."

She picks up a taser gun off the chair and fakes a shot into the back yard. "Those hoodlums were so shocked, so to speak, when we took them down. Two old bag ladies out of nowhere had them in pain. The tasers worked just like Pete told us. And, that Martinez guy's eyes were as wide as tortillas when Pete and Gunny snapped his butt up. I hope we didn't kill his little puppets."

"No, they'll be alright. But, they will be dazed for a while, thanks to your repeated shots, dear sister," Adoncia says. "Nick's partner sure was kind to us. I can't believe she gave us each five dollars. I wish I could meet her some day and tell her. All I know is that my Nick would be very angry at his Uncle Pete for putting us in danger."

"He never has to know."

"I haven't heard from Pete on how things are going. I'm worried, Adoncia. He left me a quick text when they were on their way to Palwaukee. That was around 10:30. But I don't know about Nick and the rest."

Adoncia reassures her sister. "We'll hear from them soon, Maria. Pete will call. In the meantime, we'll have another glass of wine and say a little prayer. The phone will ring."

CHAPTER 19
TWO SNAKES DESTINED FOR CAMP

"Ottawa Radio, this is Ranger One Zero One at Ottawa at one-five, 2500 feet, over." It's Conor checking in *en route* to Keokuk.

"Ranger "Ranger One Zero One. This is Ottawa Radio, loud and clear. Altimeter 2995— weather 10,000 feet light overcast. Surface temp is 74 Fahrenheit, over."

"Ranger One Zero One, thanks, Ottawa. Have a good evening."

"Ranger One Zero One, this is Ottawa Radio, over."

"Go ahead, Ottawa."

"Just thought you should know that three Medal of Honor recipients are from this small town. Their names are Richard Gage, Douglas Hapeman, and John Shapland. I pass that along to all the pilots I talk to."

"Ottawa Radio, that is a great honor, sir. Thanks for sharing. We have four former Marines aboard this flight."

"God bless you all and thanks for serving. Have a safe flight, Marines."

"Thank you, sir, good night."

What a great conversation, Conor thinks. Nick, Gunny, and Emma just smile.

The night is beautiful as the Ranger passes over Kankakee, and then Galesburg. The lights below are comforting and the moon above gives Conor enough light to make out white barns and country roads below. The folks down there have no idea about the mission passing over them.

Conor checks in. "Everybody okay back there? How's the temperature?"

Nick gives Conor a thumbs up from the right seat. "Like old times, Captain."

"Bird's running like a fine-tuned Rolls, thanks to the superb maintenance," comes from Emma in the back.

"Got that right, Emma, just like Iraq."

78

"Just keep us on time, skipper." The brusque voice of Gunny comes across the intercom. "I'm anxious to dump these two scabs and get back home to have my biscuits and gravy breakfast and a PBR. These two are beginning to dance on my very last nerve."

"And then a meeting with Sally, Gunny?"

"Perhaps."

"No problem, Gunny," the reassuring voice comes from the cockpit. And, who's Sally?"

Silence from the back.

Creed is in the barn sitting at his favorite table in his makeshift ready room with Chesty at his side. Before him is a plate of hot ham, green beans, fresh greens, a hearty portion of mashed potatoes, and a cold glass of beer. He spends most of the evening testing the automatic roof with his remote control. Up and down, up and down, the red light flashing. He gets a call from Deputy Sheriff Boyd. "Everything okay, Chief? I'm on the road."

"Good here, my friend. Thanks for your help. Looks as if the bird will be here in about 45 minutes."

"Okay, no worries."

Creed paces around the barn like a mad bull. This is the first of many missions. His Camp Keokuk is ready for its first two guests.

Back in Chicago, Pete and Sherri are almost to the church to light candles. He texts Maria to reassure her and Adoncia that everything is going as planned. *"Everything good. They're on their way to the Camp. Sherri and I going to light some candles and then have a sandwich at Jake's."*

"Thank you, darling. See you when you get home. My sister and I are getting loopy."

In the back of the Ranger, Martinez and Tang are getting restless. They're moving around trying to get comfortable being handcuffed and with silver tape on their mouths. Tang's nose is still bleeding from a Gunny blow during their ride to Palwaukee. But he will live. He'll have plenty of time to doctor his wound when he's inside Camp Keokuk.

Martinez is still dazed as he mumbles something from under the tape. Emma is beginning to get them rigged for the descent through the roof. The harness is an inventive contraption that hooks onto a snap-on belt that will be easily released when each scum reaches the floor of the Camp. They will be lowered one at a time and then the lunch boxes. It will be up to the scum to remove the silver tape and use the cuff key that is lowered with them. Amazing. They would have to help each other. That would make good video from Creed's cameras, and, for Sherri's mom, if she agrees to do the social psych study. Sherri would find out at lunch.

The Ranger reaches the Mississippi at Burlington. As Conor turns south to track the river, he reports in.

"Burlington Radio, this is Ranger One Zero One, at Burlington, 2500 feet turning to 180 degrees."

"Roger, Ranger One Zero One. Good evening, or good morning. What's your aircraft type?"

"Bell 429 Ranger."

Moment of quiet follows.

"Ranger One Zero One. Looked it up on the net. It's really a fine machine. Enjoy it. Altimeter is 2993. Have a good trip."

"Thank you, sir. You have a good morning, too. Ranger One Zero One out."

It is 1:30am when Pete and Sherri enter Saint Catherine's Chapel not far from where Pete and Maria live. Only a small lamp flickers behind the altar. They both light candles and place them in the wooden holder at the back of the chapel. Pete crosses himself and they proceed to the altar, where they kneel to say a little prayer.

"Make them safe, Lord," Sherri whispers.

"Bless their mission," Pete says as he crosses himself again. Sherri is a Methodist, so she doesn't do that, but she always liked the idea. She just bows her head. She also likes the fact that Catholics use real wine at communion, rather than Welch's grape juice.

They stay for another minute and then leave to get some breakfast at the 24-hour diner down the street.

They hadn't eaten in a while. They had been too busy capturing bad guys in Chinatown.

Conor turns the Ranger around the bend in the Mississippi and spots the lights on Dam 19 and the Keokuk-Hamilton Bridge. The green and white rotating light at the Keokuk airport is at his three o'clock. Soon they turn northwest and head up the Des Moines River toward Camp Keokuk. Their first mission is almost complete. But one more tricky part of the operation is yet to come; getting the two thugs lowered into the camp.

Conor opens his mic to talk to his passengers. "I think you can finish hooking up our two guests for the drop. Tang first, then Martinez, and then the lunches."

Conor then does a radio check with Creed at the farm. "Chief, this is Conor. We're now turning northwest toward Camp, over."

"Captain, this is Chief, loud and clear. I'm in the barnyard with remote control in hand. Deputy Boyd is on the road and the Camp cameras are working. Chesty's at my side."

"Roger. Pappy Boyington and Chesty Puller would be proud. Call you when we have the Camp in sight."

Conor descends to 500 feet and decreases his speed to 110 knots. The corn and soybean fields flash by under the Ranger and the Des Moines River sparkles off to the left. Nick watches for the red light on top of the building, which Chief is now calling "The Pig Pen."

In the back, Gunny and Emma fasten the special belt around Tang's waist, getting him ready to be hoisted into the prison. Martinez is still tethered to a seat awaiting his turn. They are both drenched with sweat and trembling. *Tough shit*, Gunny thinks, as he stands ready to open the Ranger's hatch and access the winch when Conor gives the signal.

Nick spots the red light on the Camp roof and lets Conor know that it is right on his nose about a mile away. "Roger, got it, Nick. thanks."

On the ground, Creed hears the Ranger coming. Then he sees it. "I got ya, Captain. Just keep it coming. I'm opening the roof now."

Conor slows the bird and prepares to hover over the roof. Gunny opens the hatch and pulls the cable in to latch it to Tang's belt. Emma has Tang standing close to the door, ready to push him out. Conor is now hovering the Ranger over the open roof.

"I'm in position. You can execute."

Gunny grabs Tang's shoulder and Emma gives him a huge push. Tang is screaming under his taped mouth. As soon as Tang is hanging beside the Ranger, Gunny starts the winch and the cable begins to lower Tang toward the roof. He is kicking as his body enters the building through the roof. Down, down, down he goes. From the barnyard, Creed watches the excitement from the live video on his computer.

"It is working. Goddamn, it is working."

As soon as Tang nears the floor of the Camp, Creed gives the signal and Emma flips a switch that electronically releases the latch from around his waist. Tang drops to the floor. Creed watches as Tang, now on his knees, looks around the expanse of concrete and cinder blocks.

"Beautiful, Marines, just fucking beautiful!" Creed yells into his radio.

As soon as he gets the signal, Gunny starts reeling in the cable. "One to go," he shouts. Up comes the cable with the latch in tow. Gunny pulls it into the Ranger and Emma then prepares Martinez for his trip into the Camp. Martinez is now trembling with fear, as his neighborhood victims once did. Conor holds the Ranger steady over the roof. His skills are still sharp.

Once Martinez is hooked up, Emma tucks a handcuff key into his sweater pocket and gives him a swift kick out of the hatch. As soon as he is clear, Gunny starts the winch again and Martinez begins his trip down into the Camp.

Still watching the operation on his laptop, Creed observes their next guest being lowered. Tang is still on his knees looking up at his enemy coming toward him. As soon as Martinez is a couple of feet from the camp floor, on a signal from Creed, Emma releases the latch and Martinez falls to the floor not four feet from Tang.

Creed radios the Ranger, "He's free. He's now dazed and he's looking at Tang."

Gunny begins to bring the latch and cable up and it's soon free of the roof. Gunny brings it in and Emma closes the Ranger's hatch. "Goddamnit, Marines, you have done it," Gunny shouts as he slaps Emma on the back and then gives her a big hug. She gives him a warm smile.

"You can close it up, Chief," Conor radios.

"With pleasure, Captain. You are terrific. I'm proud of all of you jarheads."

"You too, Chief. You did all the heavy lifting. We're heading back to Palwaukee now. We'll call you when we get back. See you in a couple of days."

"I'm going in to have a couple of beers and watch these two on my laptop. It's better than the World Series. *Semper Fi.*"

"*Semper Fi*, Chief."

Nick looks at Conor from the right seat, smiles, and gives him a thumbs up.

Conor pulls the bird up and heads east.

"Hold it, Marines," Emma shouts on the intercom. "We forgot to drop the fucking box lunches. Shit."

"Chief," Conor radios Creed. "Open the roof again. We forgot to drop the box lunches. Don't want the scum to go hungry."

"Roger." Creed pushes the 'open' button on his remote control and the roof starts spreading.

Conor brings the Ranger back around.

"Conor, I'll get the winch and cable ready again. Just give me a second."

"Never mind, Emma. I'm going to come down about five feet over the roof and hover just to the side of the open roof. On my signal, just open the hatch and toss the boxes down through the roof. Gunny, hold on to Emma. We don't want her down there having an early morning breakfast with the boys."

Conor maneuvers the Ranger into place. On the ground, Creed opens his laptop again to watch this episode on the cameras.

"Okay, Emma, I'm close enough. Kick the lunches out."

Creed sees the boxes fall through the roof and crash to the floor of the camp, sending Tang and Martinez scampering and spreading sandwiches, water, and cookies everywhere.

Creed is laughing uncontrollably as he reports the scene on his radio.

"Jesus Christ, Emma, that's a bullseye." Creed can hardly get his breath, he is laughing so hard. "This is going to be fun as our two guests try to get their chow sorted out."

"Close the roof, Chief," Conor chuckles on the radio.

Creed is still laughing, "Roger, Captain."

Creed watches as Conor lifts the Ranger away from the Camp and steams for the river and back to Palwaukee, where they will have accomplished their first mission. Hopefully, there will be many more.

CHAPTER 20
BACK HOME - WHO'S NEXT?

It's 5am when Conor lands the Ranger at Palwaukee and taxies it to his tarmac parking space. Pete is here to pick up Nick, Gunny, and Emma and get them back to Chicago. Conor will gas up and be back at Mitchell Field in time for his morning traffic reports on WTMJ. They are all exhausted as they exit the Ranger. Pete walks out to meet them.

"Welcome home, troops." Pete says, with hardy handshakes for all of them. "Did it go as planned?"

Nick replies proudly. "Uncle Pete, It did. These colleagues of mine, including you and Sherri, have gotten us started on our mission on behalf of Sammy and the others who have suffered. Next guest is Budreau, as I promised you."

"Thank you, Nick. I'm ready."

Conor hugs his colleagues and starts walking toward Operations. "I'll see you guys soon. Keep me posted. Nice job and *Semper Fi*."

As Conor gets about ten feet away, Gunny speaks. "Captain, you've still got it. That was a fine bit of aviating for a kid. You're tired. Be careful going home."

"Thanks, Gunny, I appreciate it."

As Pete drives his Explorer toward Glenview to drop off Emma, Nick texts Creed back on the farm. *"Back home safely, Chief. First mission accomplished. Semper Fi."*

Chicago's WBBM News Radio is reporting about the activities last night in Chinatown. Morning newswoman Jackie Thompson anchors, with reports from Todd Jamison in Chinatown and Kerry Langford at Police

Headquarters. Todd says that the Emperor's Choice manager, Gingwen Cho, and other witnesses can't shed much light on what happened in and outside the restaurant. All Cho knows is that he saw two plainclothes officers, one male and one female, capture the Asian man and cart him out the back door. Also, one customer says that a woman was taken out back and put into a car. Todd speculates that it was a covert operation by the Gang Unit under the leadership of Commander William Washington.

Kerry Langford at police headquarters says that she has just talked to Commander Washington and he assured her that the Gang Unit had not been a part of this. Also, Kerry had talked to her homicide sources and they deny any role in what happened at the restaurant. Besides, there was no homicide that they know of. She also says that credible sources tell her that the Asian man is a gang leader.

Back on the mic, Jackie is reporting another story out of Skokie. Late last night, Skokie police arrested a woman wearing a Nazi flag for anti-Semitic activity outside Temple Israel. Jackie says that an insider at the Skokie PD told one of their reporters that the woman is a known gang member.

Pete, Nick, Gunny, and Emma say nothing as Pete nears Emma's home. She has to get to work at United.

"Thanks, guys, I appreciate it. I better not be working on anything intricate today."

"Talk to you soon, Emma. Thanks for everything and *Semper Fi*," Nick says.

As Pete heads to Rosemont to deliver the Gunny, Nick is curious. "I'm still wondering how you guys took out Martinez's thugs and captured Martinez at the same time. And, what happened to them? Did you use the tasers I got for you?"

Gunny replies first. "We didn't have to use the tasers. It was just luck that two old bag ladies came along and distracted the two goons. They approached the three scumbags and asked for money. When the two protectors went to give them money to get rid of them, we snatched Martinez. The two ladies were just enough distraction. As we drove away with Martinez, the two ladies were beating up on the goons as they tried to get away."

"We were lucky. Real lucky," echoes Pete.

———————

Creed gets Nick's text as he enters Gert's for his morning breakfast of biscuits and gravy with fresh ham. The café is already buzzing. Everybody greets Creed. As Creed sits down at the big circular table, Hop Hardy doesn't waste any time. "Jesus, Chief, what was all the commotion at your place early this morning? Sounded like a helicopter attack."

"I've given my old squadron permission to carry out some night training missions over the farm. It's part of my patriotic duty. Did it keep you awake, Hop?"

"No, I was up anyway. Couldn't sleep with this goddamned gout."

"I'm sorry, my friend. Did Doc Shepherd give you medicine? And I suppose you're still smoking a pack of Luckies and drinking a pint every day?"

"I am. No fuckin doctor's gonna spoil my fun." The table of farmers just laughs.

Gert herself has a question. "Chief, I saw Deputy Boyd along the road last night outside your house. What was that about?"

"The deputy volunteered to stand by while the helo operations took place, in case we needed him."

Hop is wondering. "Chief, do you have any old Indian remedies that might help my gout?"

"Yes, my grandma said if you piss on your feet every morning, that should clear up the gout in about a month or two. But you have to do it every morning. Then, you can't take a shower until midnight."

"I'm not gonna piss on my own feet," Hop growls.

"Grandma also said if you didn't want to do that, you could have someone else do it."

"I'm not gonna let anybody piss on my feet. I'd rather be crippled."

By now, the whole table has erupted. Hop gives Creed a shot to the shoulder.

"You're pulling my leg, you bastard, Chief."

"Is there anything else hurting, Hop?" Gert asks.

"No. And if there was, I wouldn't tell the Chief." The conversation then inevitably turns to the weather and how the crops are doing. It's not long before harvest and the soybeans and corn look good. Now, it's a question of how much they can get for their crops at market. Creed doesn't have to worry.

CHAPTER 21
THE MONGOOSE IS LOOSE

At the Chinatown Hotel on West 22nd Place, homicide detective Jerry Fernwell is sitting in Mr. Tang's room, where Mr. Tang is getting ready for his wife's funeral this afternoon in Chinatown.

"Mr. Tang, I don't want to bother you. I know you have to get ready for the funeral. I just have a couple of questions. Have you heard from your son in the past few hours?"

"No, I haven't, officer, but that's not unusual. I suppose he will show up for his mother's funeral this afternoon, don't you think?"

"I don't know, sir. I would hope so. Do you know if Gerald has a girlfriend?"

"He was once going with a girl named Louisa. I think her last name is Chin."

"That's very helpful, Mr. Tang. Do you happen to know where she lives?"

"No, sir, I don't."

"Okay, Mr. Tang, we'll probably see each other at the funeral. I hope things go okay. In the meantime, if you hear from your son, will you contact me? My cell phone number is on this card."

"Thank you, Officer Fernwell."

Fernwell heads north to the Skokie Police Station to see if he can get any information from the woman they had arrested last night outside Temple Israel. Police intelligence and the Gang Unit say she is a gang member and reports her name as Chin. She doesn't have any ID. They don't have much more information than that. But they think she is connected to a gang.

Fernwell enters the station and asks for Detective Friedkin, his contact there. Shortly, the two are discussing the situation. Indeed, Chin is still being held and she is an "ornery inmate."

Friedkin gives Fernwell permission to interview her. "Go in here and I'll have officers bring her to you."

Fernwell enters a briefing room, sits down, and waits for Chin. Soon, two uniformed police officers enter the room escorting a thin Asian woman about thirty years old, a little weary and worn, but still beautiful. The officers sit her down across from Fernwell and move back to stand in the corner of the briefing room.

"My name is Detective Fernwell with the Chicago Police Department. I just want to ask you a couple of questions. That okay?"

"And if I say no, would that make any difference?"

"Probably not. Is your last name Chin?

"A lot of people are named Chin."

"Is your first name Louisa?"

"Maybe."

"Okay, do you know a Gerald Tang?"

"I don't know him."

"Did you have dinner at Emperor's Choice Restaurant last night?"

"I may have. I can't remember."

"How did you end up in front of Temple Israel late last night with a Nazi flag on your arm?"

"All I know is that I was kidnapped by a man and two women and dropped off there. They put a Nazi flag on my arm and threw me out of the car. Then the Skokie pigs arrested me."

"Where did the man and two women pick you up, Chin?"

"In Chinatown."

"Where in Chinatown?"

"On the street."

"What street?"

"I don't remember."

"You don't remember?"

"No. Can I have a cigarette?"

"Sure." Fernwell takes a pack of Camels out of his pocket, hands her one, and lights it.

"Do you belong to a street gang?"

"I think I should get a lawyer."

"That's up to you."

"I have nothing else to say."

"Thank you, Ms. Chin."

The two Skokie officers escort Chin back to her cell. Outside, Fernwell thanks Detective Friedkin and asks him for a mug shot of the woman.

Sherri heads south to Hyde Park, she reflects on Nick's early morning text saying everything had gone well. She is anxiously anticipating lunch with her mom, whom she adores. She is also looking forward to sharing the team's scheme and asking her if she'd be interested in conducting a social psychology study of Camp Keokuk. Sherri has been on the computer this morning watching the two inmates wander around the Camp, still perplexed by it all. They have finally gotten out of the cuffs and taken the silver tape off their mouths. They've reassembled most of the lunch boxes and found rooms for themselves far away from each other.

Sherri is proud of her mother, who is a prominent professor of social psychology at the venerable private research institute founded by John. D. Rockefeller and John Dewey. But her mom isn't an elitist, as most of the professors here are. She is a smart, down-to-earth Texan, is worshiped by her students, and recognized for her good teaching style. Sherri inherited her striking good looks.

During World War II, social psychologists studied persuasion and propaganda for the U.S. military. After the war, researchers became interested in a variety of social problems, including gender issues and racial prejudice. In the sixties, there was growing interest in new topics, such as cognitive dissonance, bystander intervention, and aggression.

Sherri meets her mom at Medici's Restaurant, a U of C hangout known for its pizza and burgers. She makes sure that they have a semi-private table so they can discuss the project without big ears listening. That wouldn't be too hard since the customers are busy discussing their latest physics or economics projects and tapping messages on their cell phones.

Sherri hugs her mom, sits down, and they both order some comfort food.

"How is police work going, darling?"

"It's fine, Mom. I'm learning a lot and have a great partner in Nick Santos. He's taught me a lot. I like him. And he's very protective. How about you and Dad?"

"We don't see a lot of each other by the time we get home. He's got some exciting projects with the new Boeing space program. He loves it, even though he misses the Shuttle program. I'm busy nights trying to get ready for the next day. We do have some time together on Sundays, though. Would love to see you more often. We miss you."

"I miss you too, Mom."

"What's this you want to talk to me about?"

Sherri takes out her laptop and opens it to live shots from inside of Camp Keokuk. "Mom, what I'm about to show you is super secret and may be illegal. Not even Dad can know. But I think you, as a social psychology expert, will find it compelling." She slides the computer in front of her mother.

"I promise that this is between you and me. You have my word," her mom assures her. As her mom intently watches the activity inside Camp Keokuk, Sherri tells her the whole story with minute details and finally asks her mom if she is interested.

They barely eat their food. It's already 2 o'clock.

"Jesus Christ, Sherri. Have you guys taken leave of your senses? You could all get hurt, or even worse, killed. You could also get arrested and lose your jobs. You and your Marine buddies have bitten off a huge chunk."

"I know, Mom, but if we can make a difference for the people of the neighborhoods, we think it's worth it. Are you interested in going along with us, Mom? With your expertise, we think you can help us make a difference by studying the behaviors of the Camp guests."

Sherri's mom sits back and takes a deep breath as she pushes aside her cold, half-eaten hamburger. She can't keep herself from glancing at the live video as she considers.

Sherri quietly sips her espresso and Sambuca, which she carries in her purse, since the restaurant is a BYOB.

A text comes from Nick. *"How's it goin?"*

"Still at lunch. Jury still out. Will call U on my way home. U OK?"

"I'm fine. Got some shuteye. Talk to U soon."

Sherri's mother finally looks at her daughter and speaks softly. "Can I give it some thought tonight and get back to you tomorrow? I need to reflect on the principle of the mission and the possible methodology and potential use for the outcome of the project."

"That's just fine, Mom. I want you to be comfortable with it."

"I'll never be comfortable with it. That said, pioneers run risks, and that's what you and your Marines are doing. Your dad worked with astronauts in the Shuttle program. They took risks on every mission. And sometimes they paid the ultimate price."

Sherri closes her computer and gives her mother the password for getting into the Camp video. They get up to leave, and give each other a hug. This time it's an especially long, tight hug.

Detective Fernwell of Homicide wades slowly through the Tang funeral procession on Wentworth to get to Emperor's Choice after his interview with Chin at the Skokie Police Station. He wants to show her mug shot to the manager. His police colleagues are on the street in great numbers, hoping to arrest Gerald Tang, not knowing that the former gang leader is tucked away, all pissed off, in Camp Keokuk, being observed by the whole team on their personal laptops. Fernwell has a front-row seat to this very colorful parade coming up Wentworth from the Chinese Christian Union church. He pulls his squad up onto the sidewalk to let it pass.

Even though he is anxious to show the mug shot, he's enjoying the parade and the music. It's sort of like a mini-Rose Bowl parade on New Year's Day. A casket, all adorned with vivid red and white flowers and bright red banners on ten-foot-high batons, is carried by men in white robes. There's a band, mostly brass, that follows Mrs. Tang's casket. It's indeed a wonderful tribute to Mrs. Tang, who lost her life in the fiery clash between her son Gerald and Gomez.

Fernwell is saddened and at that moment, rededicates himself to finding Gerald Tang, as he slowly moves his squad car toward Emperor's Choice. Inside the restaurant, he confronts Gingwen Cho to show him the mug shot of Chin. "Sir, sorry to bother you, but would you give me a minute and look at a picture?"

"Of course," says Cho, who is obviously upset over the procession, which is now passing his establishment.

"This is very upsetting. And, it's hurting my business. We depend on tourist traffic this time of year, and they're not coming close. This is real trouble."

"Yes, sir, I'm sorry, but would you look at this picture, and then I'll be on my way?

The manager stares for a moment at the mug shot of Chin. He thinks and then says, "Yes, this is the person with the Asian fellow. I'm sure."

"Thank you, sir. I appreciate your time and I'll recommend your restaurant to all of my family and friends once this is over."

CHAPTER 22
ROJAS IS PISSED -- A BUG IN THE PLAN

In Martinez's apartment, Sopra Rojas and the Hellraisers are licking their wounds after last night's blunder in Chinatown. Rojas is furious and is pacing back and forth. KT and Tre are still dazed from the sting of the tasers, but more afraid of Rojas's rage.

"Goddamnit, you poor bastards. How could you let two old ladies get the best of you? Now, we've lost another leader. Who the hell took Martinez? Did you see them? Were they cops? Give me something to go on, you motherfuckers."

KT dares to speak up. "All we saw were two guys in a black SUV. They grabbed Martinez real fast and tossed him in the back. I blacked out after that."

"Me, too," Tre says.

Rojas is raging. "Another fucking thing. How the hell did those two guys and the bag ladies know Martinez and you two were coming? There must be a leak somewhere in this organization. If I find out who it is, I'll cut his balls off and stick them in his mouth."

Rojas then sets the record straight. "Since Gomez is dead and Martinez is missing, it looks like I'm your new leader. Our first goddamn job is to find Martinez and Tang. Tang is still out there, as far as we know. All of you in this room, start searching. At the same time, I want the rest of you fucking weaklings to keep buying and selling. We've got to show the Bad Tigers who's in charge. So, let's hit the streets tonight and make some fucking progress. I want answers by morning."

Jon and Jen DiFrisco are watching the evening news while they have dessert in their posh Lake Point Tower condo. They comment on the police pursuit of Gerald Tang and Mrs. Tang's funeral in Chinatown.

Jon is quietly texting Conor Cavanaugh up in Wisconsin. *"Evening Conor. Has operation started yet?"*

Jon waits for a response while the news continues. Reporters have been interviewing Commander Washington and other police department leaders about the disappearance of Gerald Tang and the arrest of Louisa Chin in Skokie. Commander Washington continues to deny that the Chicago PD is involved in the disappearance of Gerald Tang. However, he does say that homicide detectives have confirmed that Louisa Chin, a member of Tang's gang and the person the Skokie Police are holding, was with Tang at Emperor's Choice last night when he was allegedly taken from the restaurant. The restaurant manager has confirmed that.

Conor's text came. *"Jon. First mission complete with two snakes in custody in the Camp. Thank U for your very kind support."*

Jon sits back, takes a deep breath and another sip of his Grey Goose. He's proud that he's able to be part of it all. He's happy that the operation has started, and that the two union leaders had unknowingly coughed up money for the "mission."

Patricia Botkin, Sherri's mother, is in her home office in Hyde Park burning the midnight oil. She can't take her eyes off the live video playing on her laptop from inside the Camp. Creed had rigged the cameras so that viewers can switch from camera to camera. Microphones were also hung from the ceiling of the Camp so that any conversations can be heard.

Patricia first notices that Martinez has taken to his cubicle in the far corner of the Camp, putting the lunch boxes neatly in one corner. When she switches cameras, she sees Tang at the other far corner of the camp, roaming outside his cubicle like a tiger in the Lincoln Park Zoo. Some lunch boxes are still strewn outside.

So far, Patricia has heard no verbal communications between the two opposing gang members. Just stares. She thinks this project could be very compelling and seems an extremely worthwhile venture on several levels. She is still sorting out the empirical method of investigation, how much time it would take to study the inmates, and how the results could help rid the neighborhoods of the gangs. She had promised Sherri an answer by morning. Her fertile mind keeps her awake, and she has early classes.

THE HEAD OF THE SNAKE

Nick and Sherri are having a late dinner at the Twin Anchors Restaurant in Old Town, not far from Nick's apartment. It's known for its barbecued babyback ribs and onion rings. The Anchors was a Sinatra favorite. It's also a place where Nick can get a cold Budweiser and not be ashamed of it. The two sit in one of their favorite booths and relax. It's been a stressful week. Sherri orders an Argentinean Malbec. She says that Malbecs have robust tannins. They peruse the inviting menu and order. Nick is curious about Sherri's discussion with her mom.

"Did your mom seem to like the offer of doing a study?"

"She found it intriguing but has to think hard about it. She's afraid for us."

"I don't blame her; her daughter getting mixed up with a bunch of crazy Marines. I'm glad she is taking some time to think it through."

"Most of the time during our lunch, she was glued to the live feed from the Camp, watching Martinez and Tang move around at each end."

"I watched it today, too. At least they're not killing each other yet."

"We'll see what happens," Sherri said

They sit silently for a moment, sipping on their drinks. Then Nick reveals an interesting development. "You know, I've been going through Gerald Tang's cell phone.

"I find it curious that there were three calls yesterday morning to a 415 area code. That's San Francisco. Isn't that where Tang's dad lives?"

"Yes, it is. And, according to Homicide, Tang's dad said he hadn't heard from Tang. Did you call the number?"

"No, not yet. I'm afraid Homicide is tapping Mr. Tang's phone."

"Maybe we don't have to. Can we run down the cell phone number and see if it's Mr. Tang's?" Sherri says.

"I think so. Let me try. If it works and it's Mr. Tang's number, we have a big issue. In the meantime, let's have another drink and enjoy the ribs. Then we have to talk about our next Camp Keokuk guests. I know one of them has to be Alida Budreau. I promised Uncle Pete. And, if we can get our hands on Louisa Chin, then those two can travel in comfort together."

"Good," Sherri replies. "Only, I just thought of one thing."

"What's that?"

"You going to put two women in with Tang and Martinez?"
"Holy shit."

Professor Patricia Botkin is putting the finishing touches on her makeup in preparation for her first class, *Human Behavior in Crisis Situations*. It was a sleepless night. She has become obsessed with the Camp Keokuk video feed. Throughout the night, she kept switching from camera to camera. But, it's time to respond to Sherri. Patricia picks up her phone and begins to text. *"Good morning sunshine. Hope U got some sleep. I didn't sleep all night. Just watched video. After a lot of thought, I'm saying yes and I've already begun the framework of the methodology. Gotta go to class. Talk to U this PM. Love ya."*

Sherri responds, *"GO MOM!!!!"*

Sherri texts Nick. *"MOM'S IN. SHE'S ALREADY BEGUN THE STUDY!"*

Nick's text comes back within seconds. *"Happy to hear that. It should do some good. Thank ur mom for me. U are very persuasive. See you at work."*

"Semper Fi," comes a response.

Sherri had never used that term before. It means something special to Nick and his Marine buddies. So she's adopted it, too. *Always Faithful.* Sherri has become an honorary Marine. And a good-looking one at that. In the old days, female Marines were called BAMs—Broad-Ass Marines. *Better not go there today*, Nick thinks to himself.

Nick texts Conor, Creed, Emma, Gunny, and Pete.

"Everything fine. Hope u'v all got some rest. Have a little problem. Sherri has a good point. If Chin and Budreau are the next guests, we haven't thought about what to do with them. Are we actually going to put the women down there with the two thugs?"

It took a while for a response. The first comes from Creed on the farm. *"I didn't think about it. That's my mistake. But, let me talk to JJ this morning and see if there's a way to divide the Camp into halves at this point; one for men and one for women. It will be difficult and risky, but maybe it can be done."*

Then from Gunny. *"Why don't we just let them fuck each other and die from VD?"*

Pete echoes Gunny, as usual. *"Good idea, Gunny."* They have become quite a duo.

Then Emma. *"Gentlemen, I think the Chief has the best idea. Let's see what he and JJ come up with. We sure don't want any babies in Camp. No procreation. Meanwhile, U Marines b'have. And U 2 Pete."*

Conor weighs in from Wisconsin. *"I don't want any of my brothers or their agents going down into that Camp to build a wall. It's too dangerous with those two killers down there. It's our fault for making a chauvinistic assumption that the gangs have no women. That was a false assumption."*

"Let me work it out, brothers. I'll get back to U soon," comes the text from the farm.

They all agree to wait for the report from the Chief.

CHAPTER 23
THE HUNT FOR SAMMY'S KILLER

Commander Washington, Nick and Sherri's boss, calls a staff meeting for his Gang Unit at 3pm. He doesn't do that very often, so it must be important. He thinks staff meetings are bullshit. So do his men and women. When he does call one, then you'd better have a death in the family to miss it.

The plainclothes officers sit down in the CPD's large auditorium and wait for the commander. PowerPoint projector is on, which means the commander will have visuals.

The commander enters. His officers stand for him out of respect. He doesn't mind this part of it. "Please sit, ladies and gentlemen," Washington orders. "I appreciate you all being here. I won't take long, because you're needed in the neighborhoods. I called this meeting to bring you up to date on the Tang, Chin, and Budreau cases." Washington clicks the remote control and there's Tang's mug shot from a while back.

"Two nights ago, somebody snatched Tang from Emperor's Choice Restaurant on South Wentworth. The manager said that two police officers came in and arrested him. Witnesses say that his girlfriend Louise Chin was also carted away. The commissioner is demanding to know what unit did it and where Tang is. He has disappeared. No one in this unit had any authority to make an arrest. Homicide says they had nothing to do with it. Well, then, who the fuck took those two?"

Washington clicks his remote. Up comes a picture of Louisa Chin. "His girlfriend, also a Bad Tiger, ended up being arrested in Skokie for being a Nazi. Under questioning, she said she was snatched off the streets of Chinatown and dropped off at Temple Israel in Skokie. She's being tightlipped and has asked for counsel. I'm tempted to keep Ms. Chin on ice so she can help us find Tang, her lover. An inside informant also confirms that Sal Martinez, new leader of the Hellraisers, went missing after Gomez was killed.

Washington clicks the remote control again. Up comes an ugly Facebook picture of Alida Budreau. "In addition, we're after this scag, Alida Budreau, a member of White Lightning up in Rogers Park. She's suspected of killing young Sammy Fernandez, Nick's nephew. I want the heat turned up on these three. Nick, you and Sherri lead this effort and coordinate with Homicide. Get all the resources you need. The rest of us will continue our efforts in the other neighborhoods. I know we're thin, but we have to do this. It's our job. In the meantime, I have two Cubs tickets for tonight. Anybody want 'em? This meeting is adjourned."

Creed and JJ are standing in the barnyard talking about what could be done to retrofit the structure to divide it in two, one half for male scum and one half for the hags. It would take a lot of thought.

"There's one thing for sure, JJ. We don't want anybody down below near Tang and Martinez. That means we have to do everything from above. Shit."

"How about this, Chief?" JJ offered. "Graphene. It would be the solution to our problem."

"Graphene, JJ? What the fuck is graphene?"

"You remember Mac Jeffery in high school?"

"Yeah."

"He was a close friend of mine, and remember, he was the smartest kid in school? We ran track together. Well, he went on to MIT and then the University of Manchester."

Now Creed is intrigued. The two men sit down on a bench outside the barn with bottles of Great River Redband Stout in hand.

JJ continues. "According to the *Daily Gate City* story, at Manchester, Mac met two professors named Gelm and Novoselov who came up with graphene. I don't know much about it, but Mac is somehow involved with the breakthrough development. They won a Nobel Prize for it."

"That's impressive, JJ. How does graphene help us?"

"In an email to me last spring, Mac said that this material is tougher than diamond and 200 times stronger than steel. He said that it's virtually transparent and so strong that a sheet of it is as thin as clingwrap and could support an elephant."

"Where are we gonna get an elephant?"

"Funny, Chief, funny. Mac says that the material stretches like rubber and conducts electricity and heat better than any copper wire and that it weighs next to nothing."

"What are you getting to?"

"Mac asked me recently if I could think of any construction job he could use as a pilot for graphene, to please let him know. This could be it, Chief."

"You mean use rolls of graphene as a wall to split the Camp in two?"

"Yes. No cement, no cranes, no driving of piles, no wood, no nails, no noise, just a thin Graphene wall the length of the structure that we could lower into the Camp to keep the boys separate from the girls. Do you want me to contact Mac?"

"This is really risky, JJ. If Mac were to use it as a pilot, he could never show it to potential customers. He would have to disguise it. That is, if he agrees to do it. Besides, we don't know if Mac has enough Graphene to stretch 100 feet long and 25 feet high."

"At least we could get the discussion started," JJ says, leaning forward.

"The other thing is timing. We have to do it pretty quickly. Hopefully, our Chicago crew will have some more guests ready for delivery soon."

"I'm going to email Mac and see if it's possible. No worries, I won't reveal what the structure is for."

"Okay. In the meantime, we better come up with something more practical. Let's have another stout."

Back in Chicago, Nick discovers that the 415 number on Gerald Tang's phone is that of his father. "So, they *did* talk before we captured Gerald. That is very curious," Nick tells Sherri.

"Yes, it is. I wonder where the elder Tang is now. I know that Homicide interviewed him before Mrs. Tang's funeral. I'll give them a call and see if they're still tracking him."

"We also have to get a plan together to extract Chin from the Skokie PD. That's going to take some thought. I'm curious too about what the Chief and JJ are going to do to retrofit the Camp and how long it will take."

Nick turns the squad into the Rogers Park area to see if they can get some leads on the whereabouts of Alida Budreau. They have some street contacts here. Sherri tunes the radio into her favorite country station. The DJ is playing the Vince Gill-Patty Loveless duet at George Jones's funeral. She hums along with it as Vince hardly makes it through. He and George had been good friends.

Sherri actually has tears in her eyes. Nick looks at her with some qualms. "You love this county shit, don't you?"

"I do. Country music has soul and I'm sad that George Jones isn't still around."

"What about the Stones or the Beatles?"

"Nothing compared to country."

Nick shuts up as they pull up to the curb to talk to a street person. "Harpo," Nick yells to the man on the street. "Come over and talk to me."

The man knows Nick. "What you need, bro?"

"You know an Alida Budreau with White Lightning?"

"I may."

"You owe me, Harpo. You know that, don't you?"

"Yeah, you always remind me."

"Can you give me some information about where she hangs out?"

"She has lunch at the Little Bad Wolf on Bryn Mawr. That's all I got."

"Thanks for your help, Harpo. I won't forget this."

As Harpo walks away, he mutters, "Better bring your thick cop wallet."

As they pull away from the curb, Nick says, "I wonder if Uncle Pete would accept this special assignment of spotting Budreau, since she's the one who killed Sammy."

"I think he would go for it."

Patricia Botkin is back in her home office making notes as she watches and listens to the live video from inside the Camp. She has put together a research methodology based on her deep experience in social psychology. She will specifically observe the feelings and behaviors of the two men toward each other. She will also plot their habits to see how they cope with this strange and lonely environment.

As she watches, Martinez sits on the ground in front of his cubicle. From time to time, he looks over to see what Tang is doing. Still no words. They both have gone through six of their box lunches; the empty ones are stacked outside their rooms. Since the incinerator is in the center of the Camp, neither of them has used it yet.

From time to time, Tang sits at his desk and stares at the wall. Then he washes his hands and face and comes back out to see where his enemy is.

Martinez is learning how to use the washer and dryer. They both look as if they want to say something to each other. But, not yet. Tang, after all, had killed his leader Gomez and burnt up his own mother and two kids. Talking is not in the cards for Martinez.

Patricia is taking copious notes in her logbook. She writes under the heading of Feelings; *suspicion, anger, hate, frustration, mistrust, confusion and anxiety.* Ironically, some of the same feelings the gang leaders have caused people to have in the neighborhoods where they savagely rule. *Interesting,* she thinks, as she rewinds the video to review it again.

Homicide reports back to Sherri that they had indeed tracked Mr. Tang this morning to Union Station and onto the California Zephyr train.

"Strange" Sherri says. "Why didn't he fly back, instead of taking the two-day trip by train? Maybe he wants to relax after burying his wife. But, why did he lie to Homicide?"

"Maybe we ought to ask Homicide to contact the San Francisco police and have them put a tail on Mr. Tang for a few days. Also monitor his cell phone."

"I'll request it."

Nick nods in agreement.

A text then comes in from Creed on the farm. *"All: JJ and I have made some progress. There are a couple of options. But, we need to shake them down before we begin work retrofitting the Camp. I know the deadline is crucial. Give us 24 hours."*

Nick replies. *"Thanks Chief. Appreciate it."*

That night Rosco Biggs is enraged again about a lot of things. But, once again he is centering on the gangs.

"Ladies and gentlemen, I hate to sound like a broken record about the gang filth in this city. But I'm not giving up. I'm going to use these 50,000 watts to campaign for justice. This afternoon, I talked to Mrs. Rebald who lost her two daughters in that awful fire. It is known now that a gang leader by the name of Gerald Tang was living hoosin the basement of his mom's home and running his ruthless operation from there. His mom and two other gang members died in the fire. Tang is now missing and I'm told by my sources that CPD Homicide and the Gang Unit are turning up the pressure not only to find Tang, but Alida Budreau, who allegedly killed

young Sammy Fernandez. But, as you know, they are doing it without additional officers, which the mayor has denied them. Mr. Mayor, you said you were going to reconsider your decision. Have you done that? The people of the neighborhoods want your answer.

"On the saddest note of all, as I said, I talked this afternoon with Mrs. Rebald who lost her two daughters in the Tang fire. Here's some of what she had to say. Play cut two, Mr. Producer."

"Thank you Rosco for taking on this fight. It means a lot to me and the memory of my two beautiful daughters who died at the hands of the gangs. I don't know why the mayor won't budget more for fighting the gangs. I guess election time is coming up."

"Mrs. Rebald, how are you doing?"

"I'm pulling through it with the help of my family and kind neighbors. I have had some help setting up a website to raise money. It's TanyaRamona.com. I have a friend who is taking care of that. Also, through an angel, I've retained counsel so that I can sue the city."

"I hope that you're successful. I wish you could sue the mayor. But that will go nowhere. How else can Chicagoans help?"

"I think they should listen to you and maybe something good will happen so we can get rid of the gangs."

"I will sure keep on trying, Mrs. Rebald. In the meantime, I'll pray for you. Thanks for talking to me."

"You're welcome and God bless you."

"Mr. Mayor, you've heard it from a brave woman. Now do something! You and your predecessors built the ghettos, where all of this is happening. You and they should be ashamed."

"Just want to remind you that after tonight's program, I'll meet you over at my new podcast, where I will tell you what I really think and how I really feel.

"I'm Rosco Biggs and we'll be back in a moment to take your calls."

After Rosco goes off the air, he starts his podcast for his loyal subscribers.

"This is Rosco Biggs over here on Radio Free Chicago. The mayor and his gutless City Hall cronies are flaming assholes. Folks, they don't give a shit. They are pathetic bastards who only think about the re-election chances. The fuckers won't cough up the funds to add more Gang Unit officers to the force. Of course, the mayor gets his votes from the middle- and upper-class neighborhoods, not from the threatened neighborhoods where the gangs are. I think we need to organize a protest in front of City Hall and raise some hell.

"This is Rosco Biggs on Radio Free Chicago."

CHAPTER 24
UNCLE PETE FACES SAMMY'S KILLER

Nick drops off Sherri at her apartment and heads to Uncle Pete's to show him a mug shot of Alida Budreau and to discuss Pete's possible assignment of going to the Little Bad Wolf up in Rogers Park for lunch. He hopes his uncle will accept. As he approaches Uncle Pete's and Aunt Maria's home, he gets a call from a number he doesn't recognize. He takes it.

"This is Nick Santos."

From the other end: "Officer Santos?"

"Yes."

"This is Jake Brennan from the *Sun-Times*. Do you have time to talk to me?"

"Jake, is this on or off the record? You know I'm not authorized to talk to reporters, even though I respect your work."

"It can be off the record if you wish. That means I can't attribute this conversation to you. Would that be okay?"

Nick knows that what he says to Jake could make its way back to him. He decides to go ahead anyway. It may help his cause. "Yes, that will be okay."

"I understand that you and your partner have been assigned by Commander Washington to head up the search for Gerald Tang, Sal Martinez, and Alida Budreau. Is that right?"

"Our mission at the Gang Unit is to halt the gangs from terrorizing our neighborhoods. That goes for all gangs and their leaders."

"I'm asking if you and your partner, Sherri Botkin, are assigned specifically to find Tang, Martinez, and Budreau," Jake says.

"Many of our operations are protected, since it's important that we not signal our intentions to those we hunt."

"Do you have any idea where the hoodlums are?"

"If we did, they would be in custody. We will find them. In the meantime, we ask all Chicago citizens to be vigilant and if they see anything suspicious, call us."

"Are you upset that the mayor won't fund more officers for the Gang Unit?"

"I'm upset over the scum running through our neighborhoods threatening our good citizens and killing our kids."

"Some of my sources say that your unit wants the Skokie Police to release Louisa Chin, Tang's girlfriend, to the CPD. Is that right?"

"I don't control those things. That's up to the department. I'm on assignment, Jake. I've got to go now."

"Thanks for your time, Officer Santos."

Nick hangs up and thinks he has avoided any traps. He just hopes that Brennan will honor the "off the record" agreement. But he knows not to say anything he wouldn't want printed. Now to convince Uncle Pete to help them catch a glimpse of Alida Budreau.

At Gert's the next morning, Creed is having breakfast with the regular crowd. They are discussing the USDA's prediction of record crop production this year, especially corn and soybeans.

Hop is the first to comment, as usual. "You know what that means for us, don't you? That means there will be a flooding of the market, sending prices tumbling and pinching our wallets."

Brad Wheatley joins the conversation as they all sip on Gert's thick, black coffee.

"Looks like you got the right idea, Chief; stockpiling it in your new monster silo until prices get back in line."

"Well, we'll see, gents. You know how unpredictable the weather can be. The *Farmer's Almanac* says it's going to be favorable to us. Depends too on what the government says about ethanol requirements in gasoline. You know how those sons-a-bitches are. I may get screwed by hedging or I may have to expand the barn."

Hop jumps in to defend Gert. "Watch your tongue, Chief. Gert's here."

Gert is ready to join the conversation. "Screw you, Hop, you big, fat farmer. Go piss on your feet like Chief's grandma said to do."

The table is still laughing when JJ comes in to get a cup-to-go and head back to the farm. "See you back there, Chief."

"Be there in five minutes, JJ. Got to set these hicks straight first."

Pete enters the Little Bad Wolf restaurant at noon. It is a true gastro pub with wooden stools and tables, a good-looking bar, globe chandeliers and some kind of abstract painting on one wall. Perfect for Cubs fans, not White Sox fans. The aroma is mouthwatering. He asks if he can sit and have lunch at the bar. The waitress happily consents and escorts him there.

As he walks to the bar, he looks around for any signs of Alida Budreau. She won't be hard to spot as ugly as her mug shot is. Nothing yet. Just thin, shapely thirty-year-olds who could use a cheeseburger, fries, and a shake.

He sits down, greets the bartender, orders a Dos Equis and peruses the menu. He likes the looks of jumbo fried shrimp. And, it's only $14 for a half pound. *Jesus*, he thinks. Pete keeps his eye on the large mirror behind the bar as he and the bartender discuss the Cubs and the Sox, and the Cubs' chances for a wildcard. Pete assures him that the Cork and Kerry Pub near US Cellular Field on the South Side is the greatest.

"Their meatballs and Irish Fries with a shake are the best. My son and I used to go there after Sox games. He loved it, no matter what the outcome of the game. It was a good thing." Pete chokes up with the memory and has to turn away. He then remembers his mission and concentrates again on the mirror. The bartender notices and thinks that something sad has happened. He is right, but he doesn't push it.

While Pete is finishing his second beer, he sees someone come through the door who could be Budreau. He watches her as she comes toward the bar. *Holy shit*, he thinks to himself. At a yard away she greets the bartender. "Hi, Ted, how's things?"

The bartender says, "Hello, Alida. How you doin'?"

"Just fine. Nice August day. I'll have the same."

Pete is stunned but tries not to show it. He watches her in the mirror as she sits down three stools from him. He can't believe it. Sammy's killer not six feet away. *Be cool*, he thinks, *be cool*. He looks at her once again in the mirror. She isn't as bad as her Facebook shot. She's really buff with evil-looking tattoos on her biceps. She orders a Wild Turkey straight up, glances at her cell phone, and begins texting.

Pete does the same. *"Nick. She's here at the bar not six feet away. What U want me to do????"*

"Just stay with her while she's there. Listen for clues. Then, let me know what time she leaves. Just stay cool Unc. We're not far away."

"OK."

Then Pete hears a "Hello" from his left. When he turns, it's Budreau greeting him.

Pete returns the greeting. "Good afternoon. Nice afternoon."

"Yes, it is. You're new here, aren't you?"

Pete has to think fast. "I'm just passing through on my way to Evanston."

"You a salesman or somethin'?"

Pete takes a slug of his beer, while he thinks.

"No, I'm retired and going to see my old friend up at North Shore Hospital."

"What's wrong with him?"

Shit, think fast Pete, think fast. "He's got some kind of infection in his bladder."

"I'm sorry. How did you find this place?"

"I Googled it and it sounded nice."

Pete thinks that he will start asking the questions, since he's running out of answers. "What about you? Sounds like you're a regular here."

"Yeah, I live here in Rogers Park. I like comin' here. Ted is a good bartender, sometimes. And I like the food."

"I guess you can walk to the restaurant?"

"Yeah, it's very convenient."

"That's nice. You have your business here?"

"Yes, I'm a freelance designer. Do mostly graphic design."

Yeah, thinks Pete. *You design different kinds of violence and terror for the neighborhoods.* Now he is getting angry. *I'm actually talking to my son's killer.* Again, he reminds himself to stay cool. She would get hers when she's taken to Camp Keokuk.

Budreau turns again to her cell phone and begins texting again.

Pete does the same. *"Nick, she lives in the neighborhood within walking distance of this restaurant."*

"Good Unc. Time to get out of there."

"OK." Pete pays Ted and says goodbye to Budreau. "Gotta go now. Hope you have a nice day."

"You too, and I hope your friend is okay."

"Thanks."

As Pete leaves the restaurant, he passes a gnarly, tattooed-covered character entering. He thinks that this guy doesn't look like a typical customer of this restaurant. He glances back to see the man at the bar hugging Budreau. Another clue, maybe. He sees Nick and Sherri drive by in their beat-up Chevy with Florida plates. They just glance at him and keep on moving. They would talk later.

CHAPTER 25
A TAIL ON MR. TANG - A NEW FENCE

The San Francisco Police have been alerted by CPD that Mr. Tang is a person of interest in their investigation into young Tang's activities. Two plainclothes agents from the SFPD meet the California Zephyr from Chicago to put a tail on Mr. Tang. They know he was lying when he said he hadn't talked to his son. There are a lot of unanswered questions.

The two detectives spot Mr. Tang as he exits the Ferry Building train station with a single, small suitcase. A late-model Mercedes picks him up. He deposits his suitcase in the backseat and climbs into the front passenger seat. The detectives record the license plate number and follow the Mercedes into Chinatown, just a few blocks away. The Mercedes moves into Waverly Street and stops at a small, well-kept apartment building next to a modest Chinese restaurant.

The two occupants talk for a short time. Then Mr. Tang gets out and enters the building, waving at some people on the street. As the Mercedes drives away, the two officers receive information on their computer that the car is registered to a Chi Chen. He is the overlord of the notorious Waverly Street Boyz, an Asian-American street gang and successor to the Wo Hop To Triad. The SFPD relay the information to the Chicago Gang Unit and order the two detectives to stay on station across the street from where Tang entered the building.

On the farm, Creed and JJ have ruled out the use of graphene, the new high-tech fiber. JJ's high school friend, Mac Jeffery, had emailed from the University of Manchester that there isn't enough of the product to experiment with. So, they decide to go with a high-voltage electric fence to divide the camp in two.

"Problem is, JJ, we need to get enough electric fence to place down the center of the Camp and find a way to install it as fast as possible for the next drop."

JJ thinks for a moment as he gazes at the huge cement block structure. "I can get the electric fence in a couple of days, but we'll need a crane and some help installing it. That means we have to take a couple more guys into our confidence."

"You order the fence and the crane, and I'll think about who we can get to help us and keep the secret. We don't have a lot of choices, JJ. I'll text Nick and tell him that we can be ready to go in a week. Do you think that can happen?"

Once again, JJ thinks, scratching his head, as he paces back and forth looking up at the structure. "Yes," he finally replies. "I'll make it happen."

"In the meantime, we may need some more food for the scum."

Nick's mother Adoncia and her sister Maria are holding a private meeting at Maria's home while Pete is at work. They are formulating secret plans to take on the gangs themselves to avenge Sammy's death. Their bag lady disguises, used when they tasered Martinez's thugs on the street in Chinatown, are tucked in one of Maria's closets. Their first target would be Budreau. Maria is concerned. She wrings her hands and stares out the window. Dark circles under her eyes are showing her distress at the loss of her son.

"I'm worried about Nick and his Marines finding out what we're up to. That would really upset them and their plans."

"We'll just have to be very, very careful."

Maria follows up. "If we can only find a way of luring Budreau out in the open and then letting Nick and his crew capture her for the helicopter trip to Iowa. Pete and Gunny could help. But we can't let them know that we're involved. It's getting complicated, sister."

Adoncia is thinking as she and Maria sip on their glasses of Tres Valles cabernet. "Better yet, we could capture her ourselves and put her somewhere secure so they could find her. That way they never have to see us."

Maria thinks that to be a good idea. "You were always smarter than me. I do think we're prepared. We've got our disguises, the tasers, and our grocery cart.

"Also, I wonder who replaced Martinez as head of the Hellraisers? If we find out, we can also take him or her. I have an idea. Remember, Pete and Gunny somehow tracked Martinez the evening they captured him, and Nick and Sherri took Tang and his girlfriend Chin from the restaurant?"

"I wonder how they did that. If we find that out, maybe we can trace it to where the Hellraisers are."

Maria takes another sip of her wine. "But, when do we get Budreau? I want her to be in Camp Keokuk."

CHAPTER 26
SHERRI SINGS AND HER MOM WATCHES

Nick and Sherri are about to call it a day as they cruise the West Side. Sherri has her favorite country radio station on and is listening to an old George Jones ballad, *He Stopped Loving Her Today.*

Nick waits for the song to end. "Is George Jones your favorite artist?"

"Yes, he is. He's gone now. And, the world is poorer for that. Who's your favorite?"

"The guy who wrote the Marine Corps Hymn." Then Nick begins to sing.

From the Halls of Montezuma, to the shores of Tripoli.
We fight our country's battles...In the air, on land and sea.
First to fight for right and freedom and to keep our honor clean...
We are proud to claim the title of United States Marine.

Sherri turns to Nick and claps.

"You have a great voice, Nick, and that's a great song."

Silence for a moment as the partners continue to cruise the West Side.

Nick breaks the silence. "You know, Sherri, I've been wondering who the hell replaced Tang as head of the Bad Tigers. It can't be Louisa Chin. She's still in the Skokie jail. We ought to find out, because the San Francisco Police Department indicates that Tang's dad may be involved in gang and drug activity in San Francisco. They're tailing him now."

"You're a regular Sherlock Holmes, Nick. You find connections where most people don't."

"Maybe my senses are keener these days since Sammy was killed and I'm really bothered by the sadness it has caused Uncle Pete and Aunt Maria."

"That makes sense. Let's find out more when we hit the bricks tomorrow."

"You want some dinner? I'll buy," Sherri asks.

"That would really be nice. I appreciate the invitation. Got someplace in mind?"

"Yeah, let's go to Old Town Social. The Cubs play the Mets tonight. We can watch two bad teams earn millions playing pro ball."

"I can't wait to have a cool Bud. I also need to text Creed to see how he and JJ are doing with the renovation of Camp Keokuk. Have you heard from your mom on how her research is going?"

"I talked to her late last night. She was still watching the live Camp Keokuk video and taking lots of notes. I'll call her again tonight."

Patricia Botkin is in her study again watching and listening to the Camp Keokuk video to see how her subjects are behaving. They are still staying far apart, going about their own business. They don't sleep much, probably afraid that the other will pounce. From time to time, they stare at each other, but there's no verbal exchange. Patricia has notebooks on her desk. She has already filled one. She continues to monitor the Camp and write.

The two men remain separated. Staying away from each other. Haven't conversed yet. Frequently staring at each other. They still seem dazed. Running out of food soon. Tang paces a lot in front of his cubicle and from time to time puts empty food boxes into incinerator. Martinez sits at his desk, mumbling to himself. Can't make out words.

Then to Patricia's surprise, Martinez exits his compartment and turns toward Tang at the other end of the Camp.

"Hey, Tang, you mothafuckah. You killed Gomez, you son-of-a-bitch. I'll get your fucking ass. Don't turn your back and don't go to sleep, you fuckah."

Patricia writes furiously, but she knows all of this is being recorded, so she can go back and review it. For the moment, she is glued to the computer screen.

Tang stares back at Martinez but says nothing. There is still no movement toward each other. Martinez's verbalizing his feelings toward Tang is an important part of Patricia's study. Martinez's thoughts and feelings are now being expressed, but there's no physical behavioral change. They are beginning to be influenced by each other's presence, just as she had predicted. Patricia can't sleep. This is too important and too exhilarating.

Gang Unit Commander William Washington and Homicide Commander Scott Green are having a private morning meeting trying to sort out the latest events. Commander Washington leads the conversation. "Scott, we've got an operational, as well as a public relations problem. None of my people and none of your people seem to know how Gerald Tang disappeared."

"I've combed all the records, Bill, and I found nothing. It's very perplexing. Could it be that another gang captured Tang? There's also a confidential report that Sal Martinez, head of the Hellraisers, has disappeared. "

"I wish I knew. All I know for sure is that they're gone, and the Commissioner and the mayor want some answers. They're being hounded by the fucking press, especially Jake Brennan, Rita Jackson, and that nut on the radio, Rosco Biggs."

"Is there something we're missing? Plus, we have other fish to fry."

They both sit for a moment, thinking about the question and some other options.

Commander Washington offers an idea. "Even though the City Council hasn't coughed up funds for additional Gang Unit officers, I have two of my best people turning up the heat in the neighborhoods. They're working long hours. I'll meet with them this morning and see what they've discovered."

"And I'll talk to our San Francisco colleagues this morning to see if they've found out any additional information on their trail of Mr. Tang. They have uncovered some interesting information so far and are still tracking Tang."

CHAPTER 27
IT'S PICKIN' TIME AND GERT'S IS HOPPIN'

It's a beautiful fall morning on Creed's farm. The aroma of pine trees, fresh cornhusks, and soybeans fills the air. The oaks and maples are beginning to show color. It's corn and bean picking time and the bright green John Deere pickers and shuckers are moving through the fields like giant, motorized praying mantises. The pickers and the shellers grind away, getting ready to put the crops into Creed's giant, new "silo."

In the meantime, Creed and JJ have found two trustworthy friends to help them put an electric fence down the middle of the huge Camp and secure it. The fence has been delivered and a giant crane is moving into place to lift the fence to the roof. The crane operator will also lift the workers onto the roof.

JJ's face is contorted and he chews his lip raw. He says through gritted teeth, "Chief, I just hope that the workers don't fall into the Camp. They have to be very careful and work slowly as they string the fence down into place. I know the scum would love some fresh meat. Our guys need to wear safety harnesses."

"I agree, JJ. We'll be able to test the fence and alert our guests not to go near it. If they can read, they'll be able to see the high-voltage signs strung along the length of the fence. If they get electrocuted, that's their goddamned problem. I'm sure St. Peter will have some harsh words for them before he sends them to Hell to pay for their awful crimes."

JJ has one more concern. "I'm also worried that the workers will get suspicious when they see our two captives down there. We'll have to take them into our confidence. That worries me. The more people who know about our mission, the higher the risk of a leak."

The crane hooks onto the huge roll of fence and is beginning to lift it to the roof. They would lower the fence a length at a time through the motorized roof. It's a tricky operation. Loyal Deputy Jack Boyd is parked along the road watching the operation and keeping Creed's nosey neighbors from getting too close.

Creed is curious about how long it will take to install the fence, so he can text his Marine buddies back in Chicago and Billy Mitchell Field. "What do you think, JJ? If everything goes as planned, how long do you think it'll take to make it operational?"

"I'm guessing a couple of days, Chief. It's not only placing the fence but also hooking up the electricity."

"I understand. I'll alert the troops. In the meantime, if you're okay here, I'm going to Gert's for breakfast. You want anything?"

"Just coffee and a roll. Thanks."

The same old crew is at Gert's talking about the big crop yield the USDA has predicted for this year. Creed orders ham and eggs and coffee from Gert, glances at the picture of him and his squadron mates, then sits down at the big, round table to a series of greetings from his good friends.

Hop is still grousing about his feet. "Doctor said my gout is better. So, I can help with harvesting this year."

Clyde chimes in. "Did you piss on your feet like Chief's grandma said to do?"

"No, goddamnit, Clyde, I told you I wouldn't do that."

"You wouldn't tell us if you did, you old geezer."

Emory Shively, the most well-read of the group, has a suggestion for Hop. "Hop, a long time ago a kid by the name of Edgar Cayce was born on a farm in Kentucky. He turned out to be quite famous, because he could see things that other people couldn't see. He became a controversial psychic. He recommended castor oil for all sores. And, it's still recommended by naturopaths."

"Castor oil? I thought you drank that?"

"You can. But, for your sore feet, it might work to rub it on."

"I'll try it."

Creed changes the subject. "The USDA said Mother Nature is going to be good to us as far as the yield is concerned this year, gentlemen."

Lloyd Spears has his own take on it. "Which means, my friends, that there will be a big supply, which means the price per bushel will be down. I guess it's six a one and half dozen of another."

"Chief's got the right idea," Hop replies. "Store the crops 'til ADM wants to pay more for their production of ethanol. You're not as dumb as you look, Chief."

Creed just smiles, sips on his coffee, and orders a couple of cups and a roll to go for JJ.

Then Hop asks Creed the big question. "Drove by your place this morning, Chief and saw a huge crane next to your silo. What the hell are you doing now?"

Creed is ready for the question. "I had to retrofit the silo to separate the corn from the beans. Didn't expect this big of a yield. Should be finished in a couple of days."

———————————

CHAPTER 28
NEW THREAT UNCOVERED

Nick and Sherri head to another community meeting to talk about how they can help combat gang activity. Sherri is doubtful that the meetings help much. "I think the meetings are worth holding, but I'm not sure how much good they actually do. The people are up against a bunch of brutes."

"I tend to agree with you, in part. I feel awareness of how they can help is the most useful and at least alert us to the activity and know that we're working on eradicating the gangs. I also think that having them keep an eye on their kids to detect any strange behavior can also help."

"I agree. We need to remind them to alert us immediately through the hotline if they see any gang behavior. I also believe they're scared of gang reprisals if they squeal."

"That's true."

After the meeting, they are approached by a handsome, young, African-American man who is in his senior year at U of I Circle campus. His name is Woody Archibald. He tells the two Gang Unit officers that his senior thesis is about breaking the cycle of recidivism, a relapse into criminal behavior, in the ghetto. Woody tells them that his thesis examines this depressing issue and concentrates on fourteen- to eighteen-year-olds, who have been in detention centers at their early ages. Doctor Twila Reese, his Social Work professor, is guiding him.

"Here's the problem," Woody tells them. "They can only stay in a detention center for two weeks and then they're back on the street. Some commit crimes again and go back in. The fact is, inside the detention center, there's a better life than outside. A clean bed, three meals a day, warm in the winter, cool in the summer, and activities. That's the truth."

Nick and Sherri see that young Woody is passionate about this subject. Nick asks Woody what solutions he's come up with.

"Jobs. Get them jobs so that they can make money and gain self-worth. Problem here is that the fourteen- and fifteen-year-olds are legally too young to get jobs. So, we have to have help provide them with worthwhile activities."

Sherri asks Woody about how he's going to bring his thesis to life when he graduates. "Who's going to help put it all together with you?"

"I have an angel who promises to help me. She's Rita Jackson, a reporter for the *Chicago Defender*."

Nick and Sherri share a glance.

"That's terrific, Woody. She's been a solid proponent of jobs for kids for a long time. How can we help you going forward?"

"If you could help me find a place for an office and some funding, that would help my cause a lot."

"Woody, Officer Botkin and I will start pulling some strings. We think your idea has merit. Will it have a name?"

"I'm still thinking about it, but nothing yet, unless you have some ideas."

"Officer Santos and I will give it some thought and give you a call," Sherri says.

"Thanks for listening and for offering to help me."

A text comes into both of them from Commander Washington. *"the heat is on operationally and politically. What additional resources do u need to find Tang and Martinez, as well as Ms. Budreau?"*

They need to buy some time before they reply to their commander. Sherri texts back: *"in community mtg. back to u after."*

"OK," comes from the Commander.

"This puts us in a pickle, Nick."

"Not if we give it some serious thought. We'll talk about it and get back to Commander Washington."

"We've got to get to Louisa Chin and Alida Budreau before anybody else does. Have you heard from the Chief about any progress on the installation of the divider?"

"No. But he said he'd keep me informed. I hear from him every night. Remember, it's harvest time and that may be slowing down the work on Camp Keokuk."

The mayor is holding a special meeting with Commander Washington, DA Ben Samuels, and Chicago FBI Office Chief Ron Bartelme. Commander Washington leads the briefing with support from Bartelme and Samuels. The mayor is alarmed at what he's hearing.

"Mr. Mayor, we have credible information that there is now a radical Islamic street gang in operation. They call themselves the Windy City Jihadists and according to trusted sources, they are led by a Mr. Hanbal Haniff Muhammad. They are purportedly operating in the Englewood area."

"That's all we need, gentlemen!" The mayor exclaims. "Just what we fucking need, another street gang and this one tied to Islamic terrorism. They will be operating in one of the most dangerous neighborhoods in Chicago."

FBI's Bartelme tries to ease the mayor's anxiety. "Mr. Mayor, we don't have enough evidence yet to collar this group. What my colleagues in the counter-terrorism unit know, at this point, is that Muhammad is building a group here. Two of the unit's plainclothes agents are working the case and are coordinating with Commander Washington's office."

The mayor twists his wedding ring until he gets a burn from it on his finger. On the surface he looks stoic, but inside he's a boiling pot of soup. The political fallout if the people find out that they have terrorists in their midst would crush him. It's a dread he's been feeling for years, but now it's at its most suffocating. He paces around his office, back and forth, back and forth.

"Gentlemen, this is a political hot potato and could be a huge public relations problem for the Office of the Mayor. Ron, can we get more help from the FBI to get to the bottom of this?"

"I'll try, Mr. Mayor, but we're running thin on resources right now with so much extremist activity, and Commander Washington could use more Gang Unit detectives. They're running thin, also."

"Maybe I ought to go back to the City Council and ask for more budget for our own Gang Unit. I know that would please you, Bill."

"Yes, Your Honor, that would be very helpful."

"How many people will you need and what will it cost us?"

"Ten more detectives would give us a boost. It would cost around a million, which would include recruiting, training, salaries, and desks. It will take some time, sir."

"I'm going to start on it today without the City Council's approval. It's not nearly as bad a political hit as extremists in our midst. Why don't you start the process? Bill, I'll talk to Commissioner Baldwin when he gets back from rehab. And, Ron, maybe you can put pressure on the director for more resources. You want me to call him?"

"If you don't mind, sir, it could expedite things. He's a big supporter of yours."

CHAPTER 29
ROSCO AND RITA GO AT IT

Nick and Sherri are cruising the West Side in their beat-up unmarked car after a community meeting when a text comes from Commander Washington. *"Good news Nick. I just left the mayor's office. He'll fund 10 more people. Start looking. Got a new problem. U and Botkin come in before the day is over and I will discuss."*

"That's good news sir, thanks. We'll see you this pm."

"Jesus, that's great, Sherri. Got anybody in mind who we can recruit?"

"I guess we're going to have to go external. We don't want to scavenge other departments. Know anybody who is qualified, who has just entered retirement, and may want to come back?

"I'll have to think about it. We can also reach out to suburban cops who want to do this. We need some very tough, experienced people."

Sherri thinks for a moment and then is curious. "I wonder what's on the Commander's mind. Sounds ominous."

"Our whole life is ominous."

Rabbi Chaim Perkovich, head of the Chicago chapter of the Anti-Defamation League, is leading a demonstration in front of the Skokie Police Station where Chin is still being held for wearing a swastika in front of the Skokie synagogue the night the first flight to Camp Keokuk took place.

Perkovich wants her kept in Skokie. He hears that she is to be transferred to Chicago. The Village of Skokie is an enclave for a sizeable Jewish community, and Perkovich thinks Chin should be left there as a symbol of anti-Semitism until her trial, if there is one. He claims that Chin's actions are a hate crime, even though no one was harmed and the Synagogue was not defaced.

Skokie Police Chief Daryl Jernigan says on the record that he believes Chin should stay in Skokie custody until charges are reviewed by Cook County DA Ben Samuels. He says that so far there is no evidence that Louisa Chin broke any laws, although he thinks her story about being kidnapped and dropped off at the synagogue is a little far-fetched.

Professor Patricia Botkin is now ensconced in her home office after a long day in the classroom. She rewinds the video of the day from Camp Keokuk. She watches as JJ's crew installs the electric fence. She observes Tang and Martinez watching the operation from outside their cubicles. She notices they are tense and curious at the same time. But they don't move a muscle. They just stare and chew on whatever is left in Cali's box lunches.

She always takes notes. She is looking for emotional responses and behaviors in reaction to what is going on. The crane operations distract them from concentrating on each other. She also notes something else that compels her to zoom the camera in. Tang is using his teeth to cut up the used lunch boxes into small one-inch pieces and storing them in neat piles on his desk. *What is that all about?* she wonders.

Patricia switches cameras to observe Martinez. He just sits there outside his cubicle watching JJ's crew place the electric fence into place. He suddenly gets up and walks toward the fence. She hopes he sees the "High Voltage" signs along the fence, warning anybody that they could be electrocuted if they touch it. He comes closer and then backs off. He stares at the roof where the crane is lowering the fence.

Creed and JJ watch from the barnyard as the crew finishes putting in the high-voltage fence. The Camp is now divided into two parts, one for the female guests and one for the males. Minutes later, as the huge crane moves away from the Camp structure, Creed closes the roof with his hand-held remote control and turns on the voltage.

"Nice job, JJ. You are amazing, my man."

"Thanks, Chief. I think we're ready for our next guests."

Creed puts his arm around JJ. "I'll buy you chow at Gert's. But first, I have to alert Nick that everything's ready for the next Operation Sammy scum flight."

Rita Jackson, the venerable, crusty, and dogged reporter for the *Chicago Defender*, is following a tip from one of her "reliable" sources. She calls Rosco Biggs' producer and says she has new information on the disappearance of Tang and Martinez and would only reveal it on his show before the full story goes digital, since there's no more paper. The producer salivates and tells her she can appear tonight live in the studio, when Rosco has his largest audience at 9:05 after the news. Rita's digital editor loves it. They can tease it all day and tonight before she files her story overnight on *Digital Defender*.

Nick and Sherri cruise the North Side, looking for more clues on the whereabouts of Budreau. They tune in WIND only to hear the station promoting the fact that Rita Jackson will appear tonight on the Rosco Biggs Show. The promotion said that Rita has some exclusive news about the mysterious disappearance of Gerald Tang and Sal Martinez.

Nick is anxious as he shifts in his seat. "Sherri, what the hell could she have that would implicate us? We have been so careful in our mission to rid the streets. Is there a leak somewhere?"

There's a protracted silence as Sherri ponders what Nick has said. "There's no way there's a leak. Our crew is sworn to silence. I can't imagine anyone leaking our secret intentionally."

Nick thinks and then replies. "The operative word is 'intentionally.' One of our crew or one of those we've taken into our confidence could have inadvertently spilled something. The best thing we can do now is listen to Biggs tonight and see what Rita has to say, and then be ready to deal with it."

"I'm hungry."

"Okay, let's stop and get some chow."

Jon and Jen DiFrisco are having dinner in their Lake Point Tower apartment. They're waiting to hear the Rosco Biggs Show, where Rita Jackson promised to reveal exclusive information on the disappearance of gang leaders Gerald Tang and Sal Martinez.

Jon can't sit down. He paces back and forth, staring out across the Chicago skyline, martini in hand.

Jen speaks first. "You seem particularly anxious tonight, my dear."

"I am. I don't like Rita Jackson. She's really annoying and a flaming liberal."

"But, Jon, she may have something new about the disappearance of the two thugs."

"Who gives a damn, as long as they're off the streets?" Jon has invested heavily in the Marine expedition to Camp Keokuk. He doesn't want anything happen to spoil the mission and to harm the Marines on their worthwhile venture. "I don't trust her." He goes on. "She's a close friend of Jesse Jackson. And I've never liked him."

"Well, let's see what she has to say. Come back and finish your dinner."

Then Rosco Biggs opens his program.

"Good evening, Chicago. It's Rosco Biggs and this is the Voice of Chicago. What a night we have for you. A blockbuster. A huge blockbuster. As you know, two gang leaders have disappeared from the radar. That's good riddance. But, nobody knows the whereabouts of Gerald Tang of the Bad Tigers and Sal Martinez of the Hellraisers, who disappeared a few days ago in some kind of ambush at a Chinese restaurant. The Chicago Police Department denies any involvement. Yeah, sure.

"But, tonight we have new information. Our guest is veteran 'Chicago Defender' reporter Rita Jackson. No relation to Jesse. She is here in the studio to tell Chicago what it's all about and what will be further revealed in the 'Digital Defender' overnight."

Nick is fidgety as he and Sherri listen intently from their squad. Conor listens from Milwaukee. Gunny and Emma listen from her Glenview apartment, where they're having dinner. Pete, Maria, and Adoncia listen from Pete and Maria's back porch. Patricia Botkin listens from her Hyde Park home. Creed listens online from the farm. Mayor Kelly listens from his home Back of the Yards. Commander Washington listens from Headquarters with Homicide Commander Green.

Rosco continues. *"Rita, thanks for being with me tonight to talk about what you've found out about the mysterious disappearance of Gerald Tang and Sal Martinez."*

"Thanks, Rosco. It's a pleasure being here and I look forward to sharing my full article in the 'Digital Defender' overnight."

"Everybody's waiting to hear what you have."

Rita pauses and goes on. *"I've been a reporter for many years and have many credible sources throughout the city. On this issue, I have two sources who shall* remain anonymous because they fear for their lives. Both sources confirm that two plainclothes police officers, a man and a woman, kidnapped Gerald Tang and his girlfriend, Louisa Chin from the Chinese restaurant.

"A source at the restaurant confirms that the officers came in, showed their badges and read Tang his rights. The girl had left the table and was apprehended and put into an unmarked car in the back parking lot. Witnesses out back couldn't get license plate numbers. One of my most credible sources has confirmed that the unmarked car drove Tang's girlfriend to Skokie, put a swastika on her clothes and dumped her in front of a synagogue. As you know, the Skokie police arrested her and she's in the Skokie jail now."

Rosco weighs in. "How do you know all of this? Tell us who your sources are, so that we can believe you."

"I can't reveal my sources. That's not journalistically ethical."

Jon, on his third martini, says to Jen, "Yeah, what does she know about ethics?"

"But you must either have an inside source at the police department or have talked to Louisa Chin, who's locked up in a Skokie jail."

"Rosco, I don't reveal my sources. I told you that."

"So, do you reveal your sources in your article in the 'Defender' tomorrow morning?"

"No, I don't."

Rosco is persistent. "Your informants, you say, can confirm that Tang was abducted from the Chinese restaurant by two officers, and his friend Louisa Chin was taken by an unmarked police car."

"Yes."

"Who told you that?"

"An eyewitness."

Rita is becoming very linear in her answers, as Rosco presses her. He is getting to her a bit. Nick and Sherri listen intently inside their squad.

Nick has a theory. "I think Chin is her primary source. If Commander Washington is listening, he may want to interview her. One officer already has."

Sherri is worried. "Jesus, she could identify us, don't you think?"

"Possibly. So, we have to have some kind of cover. Or, Commander Washington could press Rita to reveal her source. If that happens, she will dig in her heels and that will make her story bigger."

Sherri thinks a second or two. "Yes, but the Commander also doesn't want to get any of his cops in trouble. So, he may ignore the whole thing."

Silence in the squad.

Back in Rosco's studio, things are heating up. Rosco loves it. *Do you mind if we take some calls, Rita?"*

"Of course."

"Hello, you're on the Rosco Biggs Show with Rita Jackson."

"Hello Rosco and Rita. Rita, what does it matter where Tang and Martinez are? They're off the streets and isn't that what you want?"

"Yes, of course. But, if the law is broken by police officers, then they have to pay for that."

The caller persists. "Nothing else has worked to get the destructive gang members to stop ravaging our neighborhoods. So, why don't you drop it?"

Rosco picks it up. "This caller makes a good point. It could have been a legitimate undercover operation. And, undercover means undercover. Remember, a young man was killed by one of these savages. Let's not forget that, Rita. And, let's not forget the two little Rebald girls who died at the hands of these animals."

"I'm not forgetting that."

Rosco winds it up. "Got to take a break now. Thank you, Rita. We'll be reading your full article overnight in the 'Digital Defender.' Back with more calls and a special guest, after these messages. This is the Voice of Chicago."

From the farm comes a text from the Chief to all his Marine buddies. "Leathernecks: No way they'll discover our mission. Rita Jackson is guessing, and her sources are probably not credible."

Conor responds from Milwaukee. "I agree, Chief. But we have to be doubly careful from here on out."

And, from Gunny: "Fuck Rita Jackson. We faced more serious enemies together. Who's next?"

Nick responds. "I agree with all of you. Let's move ahead with caution and stay in close touch as we go after Budreau and whoever's taken over the Hellraisers from Martinez. Wonder who Biggs' special guest is?"

Back on the air with Rosco Biggs: "We're back. And, as I promised, we have a special guest. His Honor the mayor has joined us by phone. Mr. Mayor, thanks for taking the time to come on with me."

"Thank you, Rosco."

"Mr. Mayor, I assume you heard what Rita Jackson said. What do you say?"

"First of all, Rosco, my heart goes out to all of those who have been impacted by these recent killings, especially young Sammy, the two Rebald sisters, and Mrs. Tang. This is all so sad."

Rosco butts in. "I know, Mr. Mayor, but what about what Rita Jackson had to say this evening?"

"Well, Rosco, it's all speculation on her part. I know nothing about her sources. But, I do know that we've gotten two thugs off the street. That's a blessing."

Rosco presses. "Yes, I know, but what about Rita's accusations that it was an undercover police operation?"

"I can't comment on that, Rosco. But I can say that, like one of your callers said, undercover operations are extremely important in rooting out evil in this great city. We have an excellent police force in this city, with brave officers who put their lives on the line for our citizens every day and every night. And, we should appreciate that."

"Then why haven't you and the City Council provided more funds, as per Commander Washington's request for more Gang Unit officers on the force?"

"We're working on that, Rosco. I'm trying hard to find funds for that very purpose. But budgets are tight right now and we have a lot of other funding requests. Like for repairing streets and making sure that garbage is picked up in our wards."

Rosco has his fangs out on this one. "Mr. Mayor, I'm sure the people of Chicago would rather you spend money on picking up and prosecuting the gangs, rather than worrying about whether people's dirty diapers are picked up on time."

"We have to do all of it, Rosco. It's not easy balancing the books and satisfying our citizens, too. There's only so much money to go around."

"I appreciate that, Mr. Mayor. But I'm sure if you take a poll of the people who are threatened by this city's human garbage, they would prefer you do that, and let their disposable trash go for a week."

"I'm currently working on a special budget for the Gang Unit and I hope the Council will approve."

"In the meantime, Mr. Mayor, we'll be watching, because that's what we do. Thanks for taking the time to talk to us this evening.

"—Oh, and just one more thing." Rosco is always good at dropping the final bomb. "I have it on good authority that there is a Jihadist gang in the city. Can you confirm that?"

The mayor was taken back. *"Whoever your good authority is, has it totally wrong. The FBI anti-terrorist unit is quite competent in keeping track of Jihadist groups. And, I trust them."*

Rosco retorts. *"My good authority is usually right, Mr. Mayor."*

"Not this time, Rosco."

"Okay, Mr. Mayor, thank you for being with us tonight."

"You're welcome, Rosco."

CHAPTER 30
ALLAH AKBAR AND THE MAD ALBANIAN

East Lake College in Evanston has long been one of the premier institutions for the study of Islam in Africa. More recently, the university has expanded its focus to include Islam in the Middle East and South Asia, as well. Head of the Department is Abdul Al-Said, who came to East Lake five years ago from Saudi Arabia. Professor Al Said lives in an attractive apartment overlooking Lake Michigan in Evanston. This evening, the professor is hosting one of his graduate student dinners at his place. A small group of students is in attendance and they are honored to be in Al-Said's presence for a discussion around his living room.

Their conversation centers on the difference between Islamic Jihadists and peaceful Muslims and the roots of such differences. It is an interesting discourse. The meeting lasts only a couple of hours and as the students bid their host professor a good evening, he asks two of his guests to remain. They sit and look out over Lake Michigan as darkness falls.

"Are the plans in place?" asks Professor Al-Said.

"Yes, sir, Professor. Plans are set," replies the female guest.

"We have everything we need for the operation," exclaims the male student.

Professor Al-Said says in a passionate voice to the young students, "*Allah hu akbar* to the WAQF Warriors."

The students respond in unison, "*Allah hu akbar*," as they depart.

Nick and Sherri are still trying to figure out who now leads the Hellraisers, since their leader is holed up in his resort in Iowa. They also need to find out who's heading the Bad Tigers, now that Tang is inside Camp Keokuk and Chin is in the Skokie jail.

"An informant says that the person leading the Hellraisers is Sopra Rojas."

"We've got to find a way to get to Rojas, Chin, and Budreau to Camp Keokuk in one trip." Nick says.

Sherri has a thought. "It's one thing to capture all of them at once. But we also have to take into account that Conor's chopper won't carry three scum and the crew."

"Yeah, right."

They both stop talking for the moment as they cruise the West Side Englewood neighborhood in their beat-up car.

Nick is adamant. "Goddamnit, Sherri, we have to stay on mission. We have to get this Rojas, who allegedly has replaced Martinez as head of the Hellraisers, plus Chin and Budreau, in the next few days. I want to call another meeting of our team in the next twenty-four hours. I'm pulling over and texting now."

Sherri agrees and offers to drive while Nick communicates with the team. They change seats and Nick begins texting. *"Lady and gents. Suggest we meet at my place tomorrow night. We have a lot to go over and there's some urgency. Chief, you can join us by phone and you can too, Conor, if you can't get down here. Let me know ASAP."*

As Sherri winds her way through Englewood, the texts begin to come in.

Chief: *"I have a date, but just let me know what time."*

Gunny: *"Who is she? A nice fair-skinned farm girl or a beautiful squaw? I hope you score, Chief. I'll drive down. Tapas and margaritas gonna be there?"*

Emma: *"No problem."*

Conor: *"I'm in."*

Pete: *"You bet your ass Nick. Maria and your mom will send stuff with me."*

Nick: *"7:30 at my pad."* Nick is amazed, but not surprised, at the quick responses from his teammates and the barbs from Gunny.

Inside a small apartment in West Garfield Park, Nikalla Bushati is holding a meeting with the leaderless Bad Tigers, since Tang is at Camp Keokuk and Chin is locked up in a Skokie jail. Bushati is a Tang loyalist, recruited three years ago. She had always encouraged him to move out of his mom's basement and set up somewhere else. She and the men and women gathered around her are hurting, since Tang disappeared. Now, it's time to elect a new leader of the Bad Tigers and go after Tang's and Chin's abductors.

They all like and fear Bushati, who is tough, hardheaded, savage, and very good-looking with a beautiful complexion and dark eyes; a soft mixture of Italian and Greek features. No one ever crosses Bushati. She moved here with her family seven years ago from Tirana, Albania. Her father is now a taxi driver, but was a soldier during the heavy conflict and a redrawing of country borders after years of war among East Adriatic countries. Albanians have a reputation for being harsh, dangerous and unpleasant. That sure describes Bushati.

She is elected unanimously to take over Tang's position as leader of the Bad Tigers. She says she will take the position until Tang returns. She doesn't know that he's not coming back, at least not in this lifetime. She also wants to change headquarters. She has an idea.

Rita Jackson's article on the *Digital Defender* hasn't yielded much more information than what she revealed on the Rosco Biggs Show. There is one tidbit that Nick is worried about. In one of Rita's paragraphs, there is reference to a conversation she allegedly had with a "City Hall Operative," who told her he thinks, "the capture of Tang and Martinez was executed by some rogue cops."

Nick tells Sherri he'd like to know who Rita's source is, or if there really is one.

Sherri responds. "Unless Rita reveals her source, we won't know. And she's not about to do that. So, I think we need to stop worrying about it and stay steadfast to our mission."

"Good point," Nick says. "But we'll have to be ready with alibis."

"I agree, but we have a lot to do to get Chin, Rojas, and Budreau to the Camp ASAP."

"We also have to find out who's leading the Tangless Bad Tigers."

Nick ends the conversation. "We'll see what the team says at our meeting. We'll have to assign tasks."

Maria and Adoncia, in all their finery, enter the Little Bad Wolf restaurant on the north side in Andersonville shortly after noon. They are pretty damned good-looking middle-aged Hispanic women, each showing a little cleavage.

After Pete's description of Budreau and a picture of her from the FBI's Wanted List, they want to lay eyes on Sammy's murderer themselves in order to start and finish their mission. They enter and ask for a table in the window facing the street, but not far from where the bartender is busy serving his regular customers. The back of the bar is jammed with a huge variety of whiskies and a hundred beers; a drinker's paradise. The sisters order two glasses of white wine and some fried shrimp. They each keep a watchful eye on the street and the door.

"Maria, don't turn around now, but I think our Little Red Riding Hood has arrived. Do you have her picture?"

"I don't need a picture. It's burned into my soul."

It is Budreau. Maria and Adoncia try not to be conspicuous. But, their excitement over spotting Budreau makes it impossible not to watch her as she approaches the bar and orders a beer.

Maria whispers to her sister. "I wish I could hurt her now."

Adoncia calms her sister. *"Tené paciencia, querida. Nuestra tiempo vendra."*

The Marines, Sherri, and Pete are finishing the delicious tapas that Maria and Adoncia had prepared. Nick has also fixed his famous margaritas for the troops. The Chief is on the conference phone. "I'm having my cheeseburger and beer here on my front porch."

Gunny responds, "A fat Indian is not attractive, Chief."

"I'm thin, Gunny, but you're ugly."

Everyone chuckles.

Nick kicks off the meeting. "Ladies and gentlemen, we have a big agenda tonight. I'll set the stage. We must act as quickly as possible to capture Budreau, Sammy's killer, and this Rojas person, who allegedly replaced Martinez. We also have to find out who replaced Tang as head of the Bad Tigers, since Chin is still locked up in the Skokie jail. This is going to be tough to coordinate. But we've been here before."

Sherri says that one way or another, she will find out who replaced Tang.

Conor says, "Maybe we have to make two trips."

Pete is steadfast. "I want Budreau to be on the first flight out. I want that badly."

Gunny agrees. "I think Pete's right. We have to honor Sammy first."

Silence reigns as they ponder what Pete and Gunny have said.

Emma makes a suggestion. "Why don't we center on Budreau and Rojas for the first flight and then we pursue Chin and whoever is heading the Bad Tigers."

They all agree with Emma. Now what?

"How about this? Pete and Gunny go after Budreau and Sherri, Emma, and I can capture Rojas. We have to find a way to locate her. Sherri, see if you can use our neighborhood sources to find her. We can discover who replaced Tang later.

Gunny says, "The timing of the capture of both Budreau and Rojas has to be perfect in order to rendezvous at Palwaukee Airport and head toward Keokuk."

Nick closes the meeting as they take a final sip of their margaritas. "So let's go about this next round with close, confidential communications among us. *Semper Fi.*"

Professor Patricia Botkin works late on her observations of Tang and Martinez via the live video from Camp Keokuk. She observes that both men are running out of food. She will have to alert Sherri. But, for right now, she's watching for behavioral changes in the two captives. She notices that they both have moved into new cubicles closer to each other. She wonders what that means. There are no more words between the two, just ugly glances from time to time.

Then she notices something peculiar. Martinez has wetted his T-shirt in his sink. He walks slowly toward the high-voltage fence dividing the camp. As soon as he gets about six feet from the fence, he hurtles the wet shirt into the fence. Sparks fly, the fence sizzles, the lights dim, and the cameras flicker inside the camp. Then, darkness and quiet. Patricia picks up her cell phone and texts Sherri.

Got a problem at the Camp. She relays what she observed.

Sherri looks at the text and immediately calls Nick. "Nick, my mom just saw Martinez wet a T-shirt and throw it into the fence. Sparks flew and the fence sizzled, then the lights and cameras went black."

"Jesus, Sherri. These guys are really cagey. I'll alert Chief right now. Call you back. Thank your mom for this."

A sleepy Creed answers. "Nick, what's up?" When Chief hears the story, he immediately calls JJ to come over. It's about midnight. Creed and JJ meet in the barnyard. "What the fuck, JJ? Did we put the electric fence on a special circuit?"

"I think so, Chief. We can check it in the morning, but right now, I'll check the circuit breakers for all the electric stuff, including the fence."

Chief scratches his head. "Now, once we figure this out, how do we keep the filth from doing it again?"

Inside the Camp, for the first time since they arrived, Tang and Martinez laugh.

CHAPTER 31
MR. TANG HEADS BACK TO CHICAGO

At breakfast, Maria and Adoncia are telling Pete that they saw Budreau at the Little Bad Wolf restaurant yesterday.

"Nick assigned Budreau to me and Gunny. So, it looks like the same team as the night we captured Martinez, Tang, and Chin outside the Chinese restaurant."

"This team is the best," Maria exclaimed. "Should we use the same bag lady strategy?"

"I think so," Pete replies. I'll check it out with Gunny."

Adoncia adds, "It worked before, why wouldn't it work now?"

Pete cautions, "This time it will be in broad daylight. That's when Budreau has lunch."

The sisters sit back and think.

Gang Unit Commander William Washington and Homicide Commander Scott Green are meeting with Chicago FBI Head Ronald Bartelme and his terrorist specialist, Charlene Tibbs. They're going to discuss some new information about a Jihadist gang being formed.

Bartelme turns it over to Tibbs. "Gentlemen. We have it from a credible source that a young jihadist gang is gelling on the northwest side. According to our source, it's being led by a professor from either DePaul, Loyola, or East Lake College. We've got our team digging deeper to find out more."

Washington wants to know more. "Ms. Tibbs, can you be more specific about the general location of the new gang? Do you think we should keep an eye on the mosques?"

"We're not sure, Commander. I don't know if the mosques are involved or not. I don't know whether that would help. I have teams going through

DePaul, Loyola, and East Lake College curricula now to see if anything pops up. Something that would connect with radical Islam."

Special Agent Bartelme adds, "We have contacts with senior Muslim leaders we're following up with. These are good people who abhor the jihadist movement. They can possibly get us some leads."

Commander Green says, "We should probably brief the mayor."

Bartelme says that he and Tibbs will brief Mayor Kelly as soon as this meeting is over.

Commander Washington thanks the two FBI agents and asks, "Is there anything else we can do to help?"

"Yes," Bartelme says. "Just brief your officers to keep their eyes out for any activity that may connect to a Jihadist gang and let us know."

Sherri says that the Hellraisers' Rojas has not been located. She also says that she has a contact who is searching for who is heading up the Bad Tigers. "I'll keep pushing for more information," she promises.

"If we find out, that means we could leave Chin in the Skokie jail while we escort Rojas and Budreau and possibly the new Bad Tigers' leader to Camp Keokuk."

"Yes. We can deal with Chin at a later time.

On the farm, Creed, JJ, and JJ's friend Monte Mac have found a way to separate the circuits in the Camp after Martinez had caused a short in the entire system. But Creed wonders what would happen if the wet T-shirt trick were used again. Monte surmises that the fence would lose power, but the rest of the electrical systems in the building should work.

Creed worries about that. "That means when the women are dropped into the camp, Martinez could use the same tactic to shut down the fence. The scum could get through to the women if they had a way to cut the fence."

Monte says, "We can install a back-up generator that would kick in if that happens. It would run like that until circuit breakers on the main unit are reset. The same thing would happen again and again until your guest gets frustrated and stops."

Creed thanks Monte and tells him to install the generator.

"That should do it, boys, until the two shitbirds come up with another way to fuck things up."

In San Francisco, two plainclothes police detectives are now tracking Mr. Tang across the Bay Bridge. He's in the same black car as before, with a driver. He sits in the front passenger seat. They follow Mr. Tang's car to the Amtrak Station in Emeryville.

Mr. Tang exits the car, retrieves a large suitcase from the trunk, and heads into the station.

"If my hunch is right, he's heading for the *California Zephyr* for a trip to Chicago."

"You're probably right. If that's the case, should one of us also get on the train, or just notify Chicago PD?"

"I think we should just make sure he's on board and then contact our colleagues in Chicago."

"But what if he knows we're following him and gets off in Salt Lake or Denver?"

"Maybe we should contact Amtrak Security and have them keep track of him."

"Call the commander and recommend he do it."

The two detectives follow Mr. Tang into the station and watch him enter the first-class lounge for the Zephyr.

"Let's just wait until the train leaves, in case Mr. Tang tries to pull a fast one on us."

"We then can have the commander contact his counterparts in Chicago."

"And hopefully they can catch Mr. Tang red-handed in some kind of drug deal."

Sherri tells Nick she has additional information on Rojas. Her source says that Rojas and the Hellraisers had moved their headquarters to a new location on Homan and Arthington in East Garfield Park. It was a building that housed a product-testing lab when it was Sears Worldwide Headquarters.

"My source doesn't know the exact location in the building, but she'll find out soon."

"Good work, Sherri. You've become a great investigator."

"Thanks, Nick. That's important to me."

"Any word on who's leading the Bad Tigers?"

"Not yet, but soon."

"Shall we drive out to Homan and Arthington and scope out Rojas's building? I know a cool restaurant on South Sacramento called the Original Maxwell Street. Great Polish sausages, pork chops, and hamburgers."

"All low fat. Good idea. Let's go."

CHAPTER 32
TIGHTENING THE NOOSE--CLOSING IN

As Nick and Sherri drive their old beat-up squad through the Maxwell Street neighborhood of tattered buildings and abandoned cars, Nick gives his partner a short history lesson about Maxwell Street.

"Uncle Pete once told me the story of this area. Jewish immigrants set up a street market here in 1912 and it flourished with bargains; food like corned beef, clothes, and blues music emanating from the streets... It became famous, and other cities copied the Chicago experience. Pete's dad used to bring him here to shop. It was shut down in 1994 to make way for a Chicago campus of University of Illinois. The U of I claimed eminent domain and another historic scene was scrubbed from the colorful Chicago landscape."

"That's a shame, Nick. I think the city is poorer for that. Literally."

Nick thinks to himself: *Ironically, the prime contractor for the U of I campus was none other than Jon DiFrisco.*

Pete, Gunny, Maria, and Adoncia are having a planning dinner at Pete and Maria's home. They begin to formulate a plot for carrying out the capture of Budreau. Pete is pretty much in the lead. He wants this so badly. "It's all about the timing. We have to coordinate everything with Rojas' capture, so they can make the trip together to the Camp."

"That's right, Pete," Gunny says. "If timing is not quite exact, though, we can store Budreau some place until Nick and Sherri get their hands on Rojas."

"Do you think we can put her here until Rojas is ready?" asks Maria.

The foursome thinks for a minute as they sip a glass of red Spanish wine. Pete then responds. "I think it's a good idea, Maria. We just have to make sure no one sees or hears us when we bring her in. We have to do it in the dark of night and put her in the basement."

"That said, we have to take Budreau at lunchtime when she's at the Little Bad Wolf." Gunny says.

"Not if we just follow her home and take her late at night."

"That's a good point, Pete. Let's plan to do that, the four of us."

"The bag ladies can be making noise outside where she lives and hopefully, she will come out to see what the midnight commotion is and we can snatch her then."

"Unless the neighbors call the police first," Adoncia warns.

Pete has an idea. "Nick and Sherri could run interference as police officers."

They all toast the mission.

An Amtrak security officer reports back to the San Francisco police commander that his people are watching Mr. Tang and he's still on the Zephyr after leaving Denver. The commander alerts Commander Washington, his contact at the CPD, who then assigns two detectives to keep an eye on Mr. Tang when he arrives Union Station.

"We have to follow him to see where he goes. Hopefully he will lead us to Gerald Tang, or whoever replaced the guy as head of the Bad Tigers. I don't want him arrested, since we have nothing concrete yet. It's just curious why he's coming back to Chicago, since his wife is dead, and his son has disappeared. I wonder where Gerald is. Maybe he's still out there and the senior Tang will lead us to him."

One of the young detectives asks the commander a question. "Sir, do you think it was some rogue cops who took Tang? That's what Rita Jackson is implying."

"If Rita Jackson were running this police force, we would all be rogue. Tang is off the streets and that's all I care about. And so is his girlfriend, Louisa Chin. Wish I could spring her from the Skokie jail and bring her here. We'd get some real answers on the gangs. Let's just go to it and not worry about what some old, washed-up reporter says. Dismissed."

After lunch, Nick and Sherri drive to the old Sears Lab building on South Homan to find out more about where Rojas and the Hellraisers hang out. Railroad depot man Richard Sears and watch repairman Alva

Roebuck would be appalled at this—a street gang hanging out near their once-sacred ground.

Nick thinks one of them has to go undercover to find out where Rojas and the Hellraisers are inside the building.

"I'll do the recon, Nick. Do we have a picture or a description of her?"

"Not sure. I'll check. You sure you want to do this?"

"Never been more sure. How about tonight when we get off duty?"

"That will be fine."

FBI Chicago Director Ronald Bartelme and Agent Tibbs are just winding up their meeting with hizzoner. "Mr. Mayor, we'll keep you posted on what we find out about any jihadist group here in the city. We have resources on it now. We'll continue to look at Loyola, DePaul, and East Lake College."

"Thank you, Ron and thank you, Agent Tibbs. You've been a great help. I look forward to our next meeting."

As they get up and exit, the mayor can't help but think, *Agent Tibbs has a nice, firm ass*. The mayor is known for having a keen eye for good-looking women.

CHAPTER 33
PRESSURE'S ON GUNNY AND EMMA

Emma has ridden her Fat Boy up to Billy Mitchell Field to meet with Conor to go over last-minute details for their next flight of snakes to Camp Keokuk. Emma reports that she noticed an oil pressure problem when she started up the Ranger.

"I'm having it checked now to see if it's a gauge or a real problem with the oil cooling system."

"I'm not worried at all, Emma. You've always known what you're doing. In Iraq, you fixed a lot of problems with the Huey. There was nobody better."

"Thanks, Captain. I just want to make sure your bird is in tip-top condition when we get the signal to go. Hopefully soon."

"I'm glad the team has settled on just taking two gang leaders, Rojas and Budreau. Pete and Gunny are working on Budreau and Nick and Sherri are trying to find Rojas. Nick says they're getting close. As you know from Nick's text yesterday, Commander Washington says that Mr. Tang is on his way back to Chicago on the *California Zephyr*. He'll be tracked by two of Washington's detectives."

"I know, I saw that. I find it curious. And we still haven't found out yet who the new leader of the Bad Tigers is."

"Don't worry, we will."

Nick asks Emma and Gunny to join him and Sherri for dinner at his place. They sit for a linguini with clams dish that the police partners prepared. They sip on glasses of 2013 Sicilian Grillo and chat about the mission. Then Nick states his proposition. "Emma and Gunny, Commander Washington has gotten a budget approved to recruit some new members for the Gang Unit. Do you know anyone who can do this?"

Gunny replies first. "I'll have to think about it and maybe I can come up with some names. I'd like to help out some young Marines who are just ending their service in the Corps. I'll check with the guys at the Marine Lodge tomorrow."

Emma follows. "That's a good idea, Gunny. Nick, have you thought about some rookies from suburban departments who may want to change?"

"Yes, I have my feelers out now. But my sense is that we need to introduce some real tough former Marines, like you two, to Commander Washington."

Emma and Gunny stop eating and glance at each other, then at Nick.

"You're not seriously thinking of asking Gunny and me to join the Gang Unit, are you?"

"Yes, I'm very serious. You two have all the qualifications."

"Nick, you've always been a little untamed, but this takes the cake. We also have jobs."

"I know, but this is a great opportunity to serve together again."

"Nick, I may be too old. I'm 43."

"I don't think so, Gunny. You're in better shape than most Chicago police officers."

"I have a good job at United with good benefits, Nick."

"I know, Emma. But, if you resign now, would you still get a pension? Also, the CPD has good salaries and great benefits."

"This is crazy. Aren't Gunny and I already serving together on Operation Sammy?"

Sherri, who's been listening all this time, chimes in.

"The Gang Unit needs people like you two. Nick and I need you. The people of the neighborhoods need you on a regular basis. I don't think our secret mission to Camp Keokuk is enough. We need more trained officers on the streets. Please consider it."

There is silence around the table as they continue to share the pasta and wine.

Gunny breaks the silence. "I tell you what. I can't speak for Emma, but I will consider it. I have my Marine retirement money and just work part-time with the security company. My leaving won't be a problem. I just need a couple of days to think it through. If I do decide to do this, I think it would be best if Emma and I come in as a team."

"I agree, Gunny. But I can't force our good friend to do this against her wishes. No pressure, Emma."

"First of all, I'm honored that you think I can do the job. Makes me feel wanted. It would be great to work with you two and Gunny officially. This would be a serious move for me. I really have to think hard about it. Is the commander in a hurry?"

"I think he would like to do it soon, before the mayor and the city controller change their minds. In the meantime, we need to complete our second mission to Camp Keokuk with Rojas and Budreau."

Patricia Botkin is in her study again obsessed with the video of the day's activities inside Camp Keokuk. She's made copious notes about what she has observed since she agreed to take this on. Since she doesn't know much about the prisoners' backgrounds, she can only make some assumptions about their feelings from their behaviors, as they interact with each other. Then, she has to make the study relevant to finding some solutions to solving gang violence. That's going to be the hard part.

She sees that the two guests are running out of food and water and are sorting through last scraps from Cali's box lunches. They both have lost weight. Patricia assumes that Nick and Sherri are keeping watch via the video and are going to take some action.

Tang lies listlessly in his cubicle and Martinez is roaming around outside his. From time to time, he glances in Tang's direction to see if his rival is behaving. Patricia believes he may be thinking about another tactic like the wet T-shirt antic. He paces for a moment and then stares up at the moveable roof through which he and Tang were lowered into the Camp. Patricia, talking to her computer screen, says, *There's no way Martinez, there's no way. Creed and his friends have made the roof too high for you to tamper with.*

Tang exits his cubicle and stares at Martinez. "You thinking about flying up there, Superman?"

"You have any ideas, you Chink mothafuckah?"

"If we had some kind of shovel device, we could start digging a tunnel inside one of the cubicles."

"Where we gonna get a shovel, you stupid fuck?"

"Don't know, I'm thinking."

TIM CONNER

"I thought I smelled wood burning."

Patricia observes the two and their dialogue. There is some socialization, but their feelings toward each other are still hostile—Martinez's more aggressive than Tang's. He's still pissed that Tang killed his friend Gomez.

Patricia continues to observe while she calls Sherri to tell her that somebody has to get food to the Camp Keokuk dwellers. She also tells her about the tunnel discussion between Martinez and Tang

---

FBI Chicago Special Ron Bartelme has dispatched Specialist Tibbs to East Lake College to see if she can take a class in Islamic Studies. The Bureau is checking out all the city's universities based on a tip from a friend in the Muslim community. Agent Tibbs is posing as a prospective student and is asked to fill out a registration application. She tells the nice lady behind the counter that she's interested in Islamic Studies and has heard that Professor Al-Said is the best.

"Yes, Ms. Tibbs, he is well known, and his students love him."

"That's wonderful to hear."

The receptionist asks Tibbs to fill out the registration form and she will get it into the system for the fall semester, which starts in two weeks.

Tibbs lists her occupation as a hairdresser who wants to further her education.

The lady commends her for that and asks, "What makes you interested in Islamic Studies, young lady?"

Gibbs was ready. "Some of my friends are Muslim, and with what's going on in the world, I want to be better informed."

"That's very good."

"Thank you for your help, ma'am. I look forward to studying under Professor Al Said."

CHAPTER 34
MR. TANG GOES TO CHURCH

Two Chicago Gang Unit detectives watch as Mr. Tang exits Union Station after his trip on the *California Zephyr* from San Francisco. Tang, with suitcase in hand, enters the back of a town car. The detectives are curious about where Tang is going, and if it will give them some leads on where his son is, or if he's been replaced as the leader of the Bad Tigers.

Surprisingly, the town car stops in front of the St. Nicholas Albanian Orthodox Church on North Narragansett, just south of Diversey. From a block away, they see Mr. Tang get out, take his suitcase from the trunk, and enter the building next to the church, marked "St. Nicholas Banquets." The detectives report this to Commander Washington.

"Stay with him, boys. I'll think about how we get into the banquets building. We have to have an Albanian friend somewhere. I'm curious. That's not a gang area."

The detectives drive slowly around the building to see if there's a back door. One of the detectives says he'll get out and walk around.

One of Commander Washington's aides finds out that the St. Nicholas Church senior priest is Father Armand Carcani and also that the banquet hall is often rented out for weddings. The commander has an idea.

"What if we send a plainclothes officer there to find out about the place for a wedding for his niece?"

"I'll do it, Commander," offers one of his detectives. "I'll call the office now to set up an appointment."

"If there's funny business going on there, I don't want to tip our hand. Maybe we ought to have Matysiak do it now. He's already walking around the streets near the church and the banquet hall."

"That's better yet."

TIM CONNER

Officer Eric Matysiak enters the St. Nicholas Banquet Hall and is greeted by a pleasant nun.

"Hello, young man, can I help you?"

"Yes, Sister. I'm helping plan a wedding for my niece and someone said that your hall is a good place."

"I'm glad you've heard good things. When is the date for the wedding?"

"Late October, Sister. They'd like to have it on a Saturday."

"Let me look at the book."

"How many people will your hall accommodate?"

"It will seat 250 comfortably."

"We will probably have 150. Do we cater it or do you make those arrangements?"

"We can do it for you. Just let us know what kind of food you would like."

"And, can liquor be served?"

"What would a wedding be without spirits?"

"Thank you, Sister."

At that moment, an office door opens and out walk Mr. Tang and a good-looking young woman. They are talking to each other and barely notice the nun or Officer Matysiak. He tries not to be obvious about this discovery and keeps asking the sister questions about the wedding venue.

The young lady escorts Tang to the door and bids him goodbye. Matysiak notices that Tang no longer has his suitcase.

As the attractive young woman walks past Matysiak and the nun, she greets them and keeps walking.

"Have a good afternoon, Nikalla."

She smiles, "You too, Sister." The office door closes behind her.

"That's Nikalla Bushati. She's our wedding coordinator and I'll give her all your details."

Matysiak can't wait to get the hell out of here so he can report in and continue tracking Tang with his detective partner.

"Thank you, Sister, I will follow up with Ms. Bushati."

"Thank you, young man. Good luck."

Out on the street, he watches as the town car picks up Tang in front of the church. Matysiak lets the black limo pass and walks toward his partner's car.

They continue following Tang. Matysiak's on his cell now with Commander Washington reporting what he just saw.

"Jesus Christ, Commander. We hit pay dirt. I think we found the new leader of the Bad Tigers. Her name is Nikalla Bushati and she's posing as a wedding coordinator at the church banquet hall. She and Mr. Tang had a meeting in the office, and he left without his suitcase."

"Nice work, Eric. You are terrific. Now, we've got to send someone to track her."

"May not be necessary, Commander. I think the banquet hall is serving as the Bad Tiger's headquarters."

"A gang holed up in a church? What the hell is the world coming to? Can you give Detective Carbone a description of Bushati? I'll put him on. After that, I think you and Petri should be relieved of duty following Mr. Tang and get back to the church to keep an eye on Bushati, since you're the only one who can identify her."

"Okay, sir. But someone ought to get to the church now before we possibly lose Bushati. We have to see where Mr. Tang is going before we switch."

"Stay with Tang and let me know what's happening. I'll send two detectives to the church now."

―――――――――

Matysiak and Petri track Mr. Tang toward downtown. But they're surprised when the town car heads south on Canal Street and pulls up in front of Union Station.

"What the hell?" Matysiak exclaims to Petri. "He's going back into Union Station."

Matysiak and Petri park the unmarked squad and follow Mr. Tang into the station and to the *Zephyr's* first-class lounge.

"That son-of-a-bitch is going back to San Francisco. He delivered his package at the church and now he's going back," he says to Petri. He hits speed-dial on his cell phone. "Commander Washington, this is Matysiak. Tang is heading back to San Fran on the *Zephyr*. He's in the first-class lounge."

"Eric, I'm sending backup. Don't let him get on that fucking train. I want his ass back downtown. When backup gets there, arrest the bastard, read him his rights, and deliver him to me."

―――――――――

Commander Washington calls Nick to have him and Sherri pick up observation duty at the St. Nicholas Church and the banquet hall, watching for any signs of Bushati. He briefs them on the afternoon's activities there and gives them a description of Bushati, who is probably the new leader of the Bad Tigers. When they arrive, they watch as parishioners walk into the church for early evening prayers.

"Damn, I wanted Bushati for Camp Keokuk. Now, the Unit has tracked her here."

"Sherri, if we're going to take her, we have to do it fast. That means that we may have to hold up on Rojas and take Bushati and Budreau on our next trip. Pete and Gunny say they're ready to seize Budreau."

"Nick, we still haven't located Rojas's exact location on Homan. I've got to go there undercover. But this comes first."

Nick and Sherri spot a nun and a person fitting the description of Bushati carrying on a casual conversation outside the banquet hall.

"Nick, I wonder what Mr. Tang delivered in his suitcase?"

"A drug shipment, probably. The San Francisco Police report that Mr. Tang has been involved with a serious Asian drug ring for a long time. So, it makes sense that he's delivering stuff here to the Bad Tigers. Commander Washington has ordered Matysiak and Petri, with backup, to take Mr. Tang before he gets on the *Zephyr*."

"I hope they can get something out of the bastard."

"I hope this nun is not part of the Bad Tiger gang. That would be a shame."

At Union Station, Matysiak, Petri, and two backup detectives approach the *Zephyr's* first-class lounge. As they enter, they show their badges to the receptionist and tell her to stay where she is. They spot Mr. Tang over in one corner reading a newspaper. They approach him, show their badges, and order the other waiting passengers to stay put.

"Mr. Tang, you are under arrest for transporting drugs across state lines. Please stand up and come with us peacefully."

"I have transported nothing across state lines. This is absurd."

Petri reads Mr. Tang his rights, Petri pats him down, and they escort him out of the lounge and the station, past very curious bystanders.

"Commander, we have Mr. Tang in tow and should be there soon."

"Great, Eric. You guys do good work. See you soon."

Mr. Tang is still protesting as they stash him in the squad. People gawk at the police activity, all drawing their own conclusions.

Nick calls his Uncle Pete. "Hey, Unc. There's been some progress made on finding out who's leading the Bad Tigers. Sherri and I are on the northwest side, tracking the info. My question is, how soon are you and Gunny ready to get Budreau?"

"We're pretty much ready anytime. We have a plan. If we're not able to coordinate the exact timing with you, we will store Budreau until you're ready with Tang's replacement. What about Rojas?"

"We haven't been able to pinpoint exactly where she is. I think it's best to go after Budreau and the Bad Tiger leader first. We can get Rojas later. Unc, would you do me a favor and let the others know what's happening?"

"I will, Nick. Just keep us plugged in."

Commander Washington and two of his detectives have Mr. Tang at a table in one of their investigation rooms at headquarters.

"Mr. Tang, you are here because we believe you transported drugs from San Francisco to a person at the St. Nicholas Banquet Hall on the northwest side. Our officers tracked you there, saw you go in with a suitcase, and come out without it."

"I was delivering clothes for my son Gerald to a church charity that might be able to deliver them to him, wherever he is."

"Sir, I've been in this profession for a long time and have heard some big stories. This one is one of the biggest. Why did you pick St. Nicholas?"

"My son used to go to church there."

"Is your son Albanian?"

"No, but his friend used to go there."

"Sir, do you know a Nikalla Bushati?"

"No, I've never heard of her."

Commander Washington knows Tang is lying. He presses on. "You mean you came all the way from San Francisco to deliver clothes? Why didn't you just send some money so the sisters at the church could buy new clothes and hold them there for your son, if he shows up?"

"I just wanted to deliver them myself in case Gerald would be there."

Washington is losing his patience. One of his investigators steps in.

"Sir, Gerald is a violent young man who threatened neighborhoods and probably killed your wife and two innocent children in a horrible gunfight and fire. So, why don't you come clean with us? We know you delivered a suitcase to the banquet hall. We have it on good authority that you met Nikalla Bushati inside the building. Is she the new leader of the Bad Tigers?"

"I have no idea, and I don't know what Bad Tigers is."

Mr. Tang, I have your cell phone and for the past week or so, you've been calling a 312 number. Who was that to?"

"The church."

"Who at the church?

"A nun. I don't remember her name. I want a lawyer."

"No problem."

Commander Washington and his investigators depart the room, leaving Mr. Tang to cook for a while. Outside the room, they observe Mr. Tang through the one-way glass. He's Chinese stoic. "We have to find out what's in that suitcase, gentlemen. Let's get a warrant."

Nick and Sherri, still circling the church, get a call from the commander. He relates the Tang story and tells them that he's trying to get a search warrant to get inside the banquet hall to find the suitcase and hopefully take Bushati at the same time. Nick and Sherri must make a decision now to take her or let the Gang Unit have her. They know if their police colleagues get her first, she'll just operate her gang from her cell, just as her gang forefathers did.

"We have to operate under the cover of darkness, which is an hour or so away, Sherri. But we have to get in before the banquet hall closes."

"Do you think you can ask the commander to delay the warrant for a couple of hours so that we can go in and carry out our mission?" Sherri asks.

"I'll try. I have to think about why we're requesting a delay."

"How about telling him we think she may be leaving, and we have to track her?"

"I'll do that." Nick pulls out his cell phone.

Creed is busy cooking food in his farm kitchen to feed the two guests down in the Camp. Fried chicken, green beans, green salad, bread. Then, some bottles of water. That's all they deserve. Now, how to get it to them? He calls JJ. "JJ, it's Chief. I need you and Harvey tonight with the hook and ladder. Before these two slugs starve.

"No problem, Chief. I'll call Harvey and we should be over within the hour."

On the street near the St. Nicholas Banquet Hall, Sherri has an idea. "Nick, Eric said he posed as an uncle who wanted to check out the place for his niece's wedding. He met Bushati, who is supposedly the wedding coordinator. Why don't you go in and pose as the bride's father coming to check it out?"

"Good idea. Where will you be?"

"I'll drive the squad around back and we'll bring Bushati there."

"I'm on my way."

Nick enters the banquet hall and sees a nun at the desk. "Good evening, Sister."

"Good evening, young man. How may I help you?"

"My brother-in-law was here checking on your place for my daughter's wedding. I just want to visit it myself. He said that the wedding coordinator is Nikalla Bushati. Is she still here?"

"Yes, of course, she's always here. I'll get her." The nun goes back into the office and gets Bushati. When they come out, she introduces Nikalla to Nick.

"Good evening, sir. How may I help you?"

Nick is surprised by the firm handshake of the beautiful young woman. "Good evening, ma'am. I'm wondering if you could show me around. My brother-in-law says he likes the place for my daughter's wedding."

"Of course. Please follow me."

As Bushati escorts Nick around the hall, he sees a back door out of sight of the nun at the reception desk.

"This is very nice. I think my family and friends will like this. I guess the orchestra can park back here and load in from this door?"

"Yes, of course. It's very convenient."

Nick opens the door and looks outside. He sees Sherri parked a few yards away.

"Terrific." Nick taps his cell and calls Sherri. "Honey, I'm at the banquet hall and it looks terrific. I think she's going to like it. So will you and the family…Great, I'll talk to you later."

He leaves his cell phone open. Nick walks near the door and asks Bushati if there's any parking in back.

"Yes, there is some." As they come close to the door, Nick grabs Bushati from behind and clasps his strong hand over her mouth.

"I'm coming out," he says.

Sherri pulls the squad up to the door and Nick struggles to get the very tough Albanian into the backseat. Sherri scrambles to the backseat and pulls Bushati in by her hair as Nick pushes. Sherri notices the scent of *White Linen* perfume, the kind her grandmother used to wear.

"Put on the cuffs and tape her mouth, Sherri."

"I'm trying, but she's tough."

"So are you."

Nick kicks the powerful Albanian in the butt and closes the door to the squad. He then remembers to close the back door to the Hall before they drive away. Bushati is still kicking and squirming. Sherri manages to tape her mouth closed, hoping the nun hasn't heard anything.

"Now, we've got to find a place to store this bitch until Pete and Gunny get Budreau," Sherri says, panting a bit.

"Let's just drive away from here until we decide."

Commander Washington has acquired a search warrant. His men and a SWAT team pull up in front of the banquet hall and cautiously approach the door. The lights are still on. The team enters the building and heads toward the stunned nun at the desk.

"Ma'am, don't worry. I'm Officer Mark Cambria and we're here with a search warrant looking for a Ms. Nikalla Bushati. Is she here?"

"She's escorting a potential customer through the hall. What's going on, Officer?"

Cambria orders two of his men to search the office and others to look for Bushati in the hall. They all draw their weapons and proceed. A moment later, one of the officers shouts, "Eureka, we've found the suitcase full of cocaine."

From the banquet hall a voice comes, "There's no sign of Bushati."

Cambria approaches the scared nun. "Sister, where is Ms. Bushati?"

"I don't know, Officer. She was walking a customer through the facility just a few minutes ago."

Cambria goes over to join his men in the hall. He sees a back door.

"She may have fled out that door. I'll put out an APB." He comes back to the nun at the desk. "Did you hear anything back there, Sister?"

"Just talking."

"Did you know that this suitcase contains about $300,000 worth of cocaine?"

"Oh, my Lord, no. I just know that an Asian man dropped it off."

"Can you give me a description of the supposed wedding customer?"

"Just a well-dressed young man who was looking for a place to hold his daughter's wedding."

"Did he come back out this way?"

"No."

Cambria calls Commander Washington to inform him about what has happened. The commander's pleased about the suitcase but is furious that Bushati has fled. "I want that whole neighborhood searched. And, have someone stay at the hall with the nun. I'm not sure she's all that innocent."

"Yes, sir."

As Nick and Sherri cruise the Northwest Side with Bushati still making life miserable in the backseat, Nick calls his Uncle Pete. "Unc, we've got Bushati. We got her just in the nick of time before SWAT came."

"That's great, Nick. Now, we have to get the other half. Probably won't be until tomorrow when we can nab her after lunch."

"What do you think we can do with our cargo in the meantime? We can't drive around with her for 24 hours."

"Bring her here to the house, Nick. Wait for a couple of hours until it's really dark and bring her here."

"Are you sure, Uncle Pete? Is it okay with Aunt Maria?"

"I wear the pants around here, Officer Santos. Yes, I'm sure. Can Emma come to help us with Bushati until we get Budreau?"

"I'll call her now."

Commander Washington calls Nick. "Nick. Are you and Sherri willing to stay on the job for another shift?"

"Yes, of course, Commander. What's up?"

"Our SWAT raided the St. Nicholas Banquet Hall and it appears that Bushati has fled. We need you two to comb the northwest side. I thought you and Sherri were standing watch."

"She must have slipped out another exit, maybe through the church."

"Be careful, there are a lot of other officers combing the neighborhoods, too."

Nick and Sherri are silent as they drive endlessly through the neighborhoods working their way to Uncle Pete and Aunt Maria's with Bushati in hand. Emma says that she will meet them at the house at midnight. Their passenger has quieted down, but she's agitated. She stares at Sherri sitting in the seat beside her, big, dark eyes filled with fury.

Sherri gets in her face. "What the fuck are you wearing *White Linen* for? That's for old ladies like my grandma. You should try something more contemporary."

Nick wonders what the hell she's talking about.

Sherri begins to sing Merle Haggard's *Sing Me Back Home,* then growls, "Where you're going, you Albanian bitch, you're going to wish you were dead."

Nick loves the way Sherri has adopted Marine Corps language. He tunes in to Rosco Biggs, who's back on the air about to rant and rave again.

"Good evening, ladies and gentlemen. This is the Voice of Chicago, Rosco Biggs. A lot to cover tonight. It seems that the mayor has designated some funds for fighting the neighborhood gangs. Thank you, Mr. Mayor, for waking up. But we still have some unfinished business.

"Rita Jackson of the 'Defender' still believes that a band of rogue cops captured Gerald Tang and Sal Martinez. She says that her source confirms that. We've learned from our sources that her source may be Louisa Chin, who's locked up in a Skokie jail. She's the one who's a friend of Gerald Tang who led the Bad Tigers before his disappearance. Skokie police won't let us talk to her. What's going on with that?

"While we search for the truth, let's hear from a confidential source about the situation. Our source wants to stay anonymous, so we will filter the voice.

"Good evening. You're on the air with Rosco. Thanks for talking to us."

"Good evening," comes the intentionally manipulated voice on the other end of the line.

"Tell us, what information do you have that could be new? Something we don't already know."

"I can tell you this: There is a group of rogue cops who are capturing gang leaders and taking them to a farm in Michigan and stashing them in a secure barn."

"Where in Michigan?"

"Somewhere upstate."

"How are they getting them there?"

"Airplane."

"You mean to tell me that rogue Chicago policemen are taking fugitive gang leaders from the Chicago streets to a farm in Michigan and holding them prisoner?"

"Yes."

"Michigan is a large state. You can't tell me where?"

"Not exactly."

"Where are you getting your information?"

"From a reliable source."

"That's always what people say… Well, let us know when you find out more specifics.

"This is Rosco Biggs. Don't forget my podcast after the show tonight, where I'll ask the question about why the 'Chicago Defender' went digital. We'll be back in a moment after these messages."

Nick turns off the radio. He is dismayed and frightened at the prospect of a leak somewhere. He's praying that it's not one of his troops or friends. Sherri just stares at their captive, who seems to be curious about the news.

As they make their way to the West Side, Nick and Sherri notice a higher presence of police cars patrolling the streets. Nick is concerned that with so many patrols in the neighborhood, they may discover what he and Sherri are up to. He sees two patrol cars in the next block and tells Sherri to put Bushati on the floor. He then turns abruptly into an alley and exits on another street.

Commander Washington and his colleague Scott Green are pulling out the stops to try to find Bushati. If they only knew.

Pete calls Nick. "Nick, we're ready for your cargo. Emma is here and waiting in her car outside. We're gonna put your passenger in the basement until we get Budreau tomorrow. So, drive up the driveway to the basement door."

"Gotcha, Unc. We should be there around midnight. I'll call you when we're five minutes away."

Commander Washington, surrounded by Gang Unit officers, works late. He wants this woman badly, to the crowded room he says, "How could Nick and Sherri let Bushati escape? They're such good officers. She's a slippery one."

He also wants to talk to Father Armend Carcani at St. Nicholas Church.

"Should I call him now or go over in the morning?" one of the officers asks.

"I think we should find out where he lives and have him meet us at the church. One of our officers is still on stakeout there."

"Have him go into the church and see if he can find out how to reach the head priest."

"Right away, sir."

"Also, I want another meeting with Mr. Tang now. And, bring the suitcase full of cocaine to the interview room."

CHAPTER 35
MR. TANG MEETS THE GOOD FATHER

As Mr. Tang enters the interview room late in the evening, Commander Washington is sitting at the table with Tang's suitcase open. It reveals neat, clear plastic packages of white powder. Mr. Tang sits down near the suitcase and looks at Commander Washington.

"I told you, Commander, I want a lawyer. I'm not saying anything until I get one."

Washington is now in Tang's face. "I appreciate that, Mr. Tang, but you lied to me before. That pisses me off. Our team found this suitcase at the St. Nicholas Banquet Hall where you dropped it off and met with Nikalla Bushati."

Silence. Mr. Tang stares straight ahead.

"You'd better have a very good lawyer, Mr. Tang. But it's my guess you're going up the river. And, I don't mean the Yangtze."

Silence again. Mr. Tang shuffles in his chair.

"You want to tell me where your friend Bushati is?"

"I said I want a lawyer."

"Then why haven't you gotten one?"

"I do, but I can't reach him this late at night," Mr. Tang says.

"Then perhaps we'll sit at this table all night until he can join us."

Mr. Tang shows signs of agitation. The door to the interview room opens and a detective brings a note to the commander. He reads it and puts it in his pocket.

"Mr. Tang, do you know a Father Armend Carcani?"

"Who?"

"Father Armend Carcani, senior priest at St. Nicholas."

"No."

"You've never met him?"

"No."

Father Carcani stands behind the one-way glass with two detectives, peering in at Mr. Tang. The commander's men located him and brought him to the station. One of the detectives asks Father Carcani if he recognizes Mr. Tang.

"I sure don't. You say he dropped that suitcase of drugs off at my church?"

"Not exactly, Father. He turned it over to a young lady by the name of Nikalla Bushati at your banquet hall."

"It can't be. She's the wedding coordinator and one of my loyal parishioners."

"Sir, she's suspected of leading a violent street gang called the Bad Tigers, formerly headed by Mr. Tang's son before he disappeared. She may have been using the banquet hall as her headquarters. She's now on the run."

"Blessed Father, I can't believe this. Are you sure?"

"Yes, sir, we're sure. Do you know where she lives?"

"No, Officer, I don't. May I talk to this Mr. Tang?"

"I'll check with the commander." The detective picks up the phone and talks to Commander Washington, who approves of Father Carcani coming in to talk to Mr. Tang. Once seated, Father Carcani asks Mr. Tang some questions.

"Sir, is Nikalla Bushati the leader of a Chicago street gang?"

Silence. Mr. Tang avoids eye contact with the priest.

"Sir, did you deliver cocaine to my church?"

Mr. Tang doesn't flinch.

"Do you want me to pray for you?"

"No, I'm not Catholic. I'm Buddhist," Mr. Tang says in a defiant voice.

"I've prayed for Buddhists before."

Commander Washington watches this interchange with interest. *A whole different line of questioning,* he thinks.

Father Carcani goes on. "Mr. Tang, do you think young Buddhists should use drugs like LSD, Ecstasy, or cocaine?"

No response.

"Mr. Tang, do you think Buddha would approve of your delivering drugs to street gangs who sell them to teenagers and ruin their lives?"

Still no response.

"Mr. Tang, did Nikalla Bushati use my church as a headquarters for her street gang and sell drugs from there?"

Tang flinches. As he does, Father Carcani leaps from his chair across the table and strikes Mr. Tang in the face with his big fist. Blood spurts from Mr. Tang's nose as he falls from his chair and onto the floor. The strong Albanian priest is not through. Several detectives move in slowly to protect Tang, but not before the feisty churchman strikes him again and again. By the time Commander Washington's men rescue Tang from Father Carcani's fists, the Asian man is not in very good shape. The detectives carry Mr. Tang from the interview room. He'll need some stitches in his nose and lips.

Father Carcani and the commander sit alone in a bloody interview room looking at the open suitcase of cocaine.

"Is it all worth it?" the priest asks.

"You sure are one tough guy, Father. You a former soldier?"

"I was, when I was a boy in Albania. My dad was a warrior."

"It shows."

"Commander, I'm sorry I messed up your interview room. I hope Mr. Tang heals."

"He will, Father. I'll make sure he's healthy for his trial."

As Father Carcani leaves, he makes a promise to the commander. "I will keep my eyes peeled for Nikalla. If I find out anything, I'll let you know. She has violated the values of the church. She shamed us. Read Matthew 5:38, Commander. 'An eye for an eye.' But not 5:39."

"I will, Father. Thank you for coming tonight?"

"You're welcome to our church any time, Commander. Bring your family."

CHAPTER 36
ANOTHER SNAKE - ONE TO GO

Just before midnight, Nick and Sherri, with Bushati aboard, approach Uncle Pete's driveway. They see Emma parked in front. They pull the squad into the driveway next to the basement door. Emma joins them as they begin the process of unloading their passenger into the basement where Pete, Maria, and Adoncia are waiting. Emma grabs Bushati, pulls her from the car, and drags her down the short stairway, where Pete is waiting to thrust her into an old family chair. Bushati grunts under the silver tape and struggles to get the cuffs off. Her dark eyes stare coldly at Nick, who suggests they take the tape off her mouth, but keep the cuffs on. The woman continues to squirm and kicks at Emma.

"If she starts protesting, tape her up again. We should also give her some water."

"She's beautiful," Maria says. "Too bad she's such a bad girl. I wonder why."

"I guess Gerald Tang brainwashed her," Sherri says.

Emma agrees. "Yes, and who knows about her upbringing."

Adoncia brings some water and puts the glass to Nikalla's lips. She takes it willingly and thanks Adoncia. This seems to calm her.

"Are you hungry, dear?"

"No."

"Let me know when you are. I'll find something for you. And, you can sleep comfortably in that chair. It was my grandmother's. Of course, she wasn't wearing handcuffs."

Nick is amazed at what a little motherly love and a sense of humor can do. Emma pulls a chair up next to Bushati to keep watch. The rest of the team goes upstairs. They sit in the kitchen to discuss next steps over a glass of Cabernet.

Pete wants to talk about capturing Budreau, but he can't reveal the bag ladies' strategy to Nick. So, he talks around it. "Gunny and I will take Budreau tomorrow and bring her here. We'll have to follow her home from lunch and see where she lives, so we can take her under the cover of night."

Nick's cell rings. It's three in the morning.

"Commander?"

"Yes, Nick. You and Sherri still active?"

"We are, Commander. Just having coffee. You want us off the clock?"

"Good idea. Get some rest."

"You too, Commander. It's been a long day. Any eyes on Bushati yet?"

"No, but I had another long talk with Mr. Tang. I'll brief you later."

"Commander, could Sherri and I have off today and tonight, since we worked two shifts yesterday?"

"Of course. I'll see you when your shift starts tomorrow morning."

"Thanks, Commander." Nick breathes a sigh of relief. Now they can carry out their next flight to Camp Keokuk late tonight. "I suggest we all get some much-needed sleep. I'll relieve Emma in an hour or so."

"You can all sleep here," Nick's Aunt Maria says.

The morning comes fast. They all gather around the kitchen table. Maria and Adoncia have fixed a tasty breakfast of sweet pastries, small rolls with sausage inside, and espresso. Nick reports that their basement guest got some sleep and is behaving. Sherri relieved him at 5:30. Adoncia takes some breakfast to Bushati, who accepts it with a word of thanks.

After a second cup of strong coffee, Emma is back down in the basement keeping an eye on their houseguest. She takes the day off from her duties at United Airlines. Pete calls Gunny and tells him he'll pick him up and head for the Little Bad Wolf around noon.

"I've got a pair of bogus license plates I'll put on the Explorer."

Nick is against this. "Unc. I don't think that's wise. Can the plates be traced?"

"Not really."

"Since Sherri and I are free for the next twenty-four hours, we can help in the unmarked squad."

"I think it's best for you, Sherri, and Emma to stay here. Take turns watching Bushati and get ready to take her to Palwaukee. Gunny and I will handle Budreau as originally planned."

"Okay, Unc, I trust you and Gunny to carry out your plan. I'm just being extra cautious, since Rita Jackson and another confidential source are still claiming a rogue police operation. So, you're going to bring Budreau here after dark tonight?"

"Yes."

"And, I've got to remember to ask Emma to call Cali and order boxed food for the bad girls and for Tang and Martinez."

Pete confirms. "Then, if everything goes as planned, we should be heading for Palwaukee at around ten. Sunset's at eight."

"That's right. I'll call Chief and Conor and let them know our plan."

Nick and Sherri leave to go home to get some sleep before this evening's mission. Emma stays on watch in the basement. Pete, Maria and Adoncia are still at the table.

Maria is concerned. "How are we going to pull off the bag ladies act when Emma is here, and we have to get our costumes on?"

Pete thinks, as he sips his espresso and nibbles on a pastry. "I think we have to scrub the bag lady idea and let Gunny and me handle things after we follow Budreau home."

Maria is disappointed, but she knows it's probably best. "Damn, I was looking forward to it. Why do the guys have all the fun?"

Adoncia agrees. "We can also help Emma take care of Bushati. She'll need some relief."

At 12:30 midday, Pete arrives in the Explorer and parks across the street from the Little Bad Wolf. Gunny is riding shotgun. Pete remembers meeting Budreau here at the bar. "I'll never forget it. I can spot her a mile away."

"So we'll sit and wait, Pete." Gunny puts his seat back and lights up a Cuban.

After getting some sleep, Sherri gives her mom a call. "Hi, Mom. It's your baby daughter. Can you talk?"

"Sure, Honey, I'm between classes. What's up?"

"We're going tonight, Mom. The Ranger should be departing Palwaukee about eleven. Bushati is tucked away in Pete and Maria's basement. Emma is guarding her. Pete and Gunny are up on the North Side waiting to pick up Budreau after dark. Then they'll bring her to Pete and Maria's and we'll leave from there at around ten. Conor, Nick, Emma, and Gunny will fly out with the ladies and Pete and I will go home. I'll keep you posted as we go."

"All I ask is that you be as safe as possible."

"I will, Mom. Talk to you later and make sure you watch the live video tonight."

Emma is on her cell to Cali ordering food for tonight's flight. "Hi, Cali. Just calling to see if you can fix up some boxes for a pick-up at around 10:30 this evening. I think we're going to need enough for four people for a couple of weeks. Is that possible?"

"No problem, Emma. They'll be ready. Same meals as last time?"

"Yes, and I'll bring you a check for tonight's boxes and for the last ones, too."

"No problem, Emma. I know you're always good for it."

"Thanks, Cali. You're a real friend."

"Anything for a former woman Marine."

CHAPTER 37
THE BAG LADIES ARE BACK

Pete rolls down the windows on his Explorer. Gunny's Cuban is getting to him. Gunny isn't sympathetic. "You're Hispanic, Pete. You should love the aroma from these fine Cubans. I remember when we had to smuggle them in from Havana."

"I'm Dominican, Pete, not Cuban."

"Same difference."

Pete smiles and continues his vigilance. Not five minutes later, Pete alerts Gunny.

"There she is, Gunny. There's the bitch who ended my Sammy's beautiful life. She's entering the restaurant pretty much right on schedule."

"She's pretty tough-looking, Pete."

"Yeah, I know, but we can overpower her when the time comes, Marine."

Gunny loves a challenge. Always has.

Pete sees something across the street in front of the restaurant. "Jesus Christ, Gunny, do you see what I see?"

Gunny glances over and sees the two bag ladies outside the restaurant.

"Holy shit, Pete. I thought you told them that it was off. Their help isn't needed."

"I did, Gunny. They ignored it. Now, what the fuck do we do? They're going to screw things up big time."

They watch as the bag ladies stroll back and forth, pushing their grocery cart. The restaurant manager comes out to shoo them away from his door. The bag ladies move along down the street a few yards. Maria spots Pete and Gunny, but glances away.

"Is there any way to contact Maria or Adoncia?"

"Maria may have her bluetooth."

Gunny sits back and puffs on his Cuban. "Let me think a minute. Goddamnit! Women just won't listen." They wait as Gunny's cigar continues to cloud the air. Gunny comes up with something. "If you can reach Maria, tell her when she sees Budreau to follow her and harass her. Since you've met Budreau, you can come to her rescue and offer her a ride home. If she goes for it, we can just keep driving to your house to store her with Bushati until tonight. What do you think?"

"It's risky, Gunny, but it could work. I'll call Maria."

Maria's Bluetooth rings.

"Yes?"

"We have an idea since you two wouldn't listen."

"I'm listening now."

Pete tells her Gunny's idea.

"That should work. Let's try it."

The men wait patiently as the bag ladies continue to roam the street. A police car comes by and ignores the ladies.

Pete gets a call from Nick. "Hi, Nick. You get some sleep?"

"Yes, Unc. How are you and Gunny doing?"

Pete can't tell him about the appearance of the bag ladies. That would reveal their secret and upset him. "We're doing fine, Nick. Just waiting for Budreau."

"Okay, Unc. I'm going back to your house to relieve Emma. She'll need some sleep before tonight's mission."

Pete has to think fast.

"Your mom and Aunt Maria went to visit their old friend Gemma in Schaumburg. They'll be back later today."

"Okay, Unc. See you tonight. Good luck and be careful with that grouchy old gunnery sergeant at your side."

At 2 o'clock, Budreau leaves the restaurant. Pete alerts Maria. "She's on her way."

Budreau heads toward the bag ladies. As she gets near them, they begin to panhandle. She ignores and dodges them at first. Then after they've followed her for a block or two, she turns and asks them to get away from her.

"Just leave me alone."

"We just need a couple of bucks for some food."

"If I give you a couple of bucks, will you go away?"

"Yes."

Pete and Gunny are underway.

Budreau digs in her purse, pulls out some singles, and hands them to the bag ladies.

"Oh, thank you, nice lady."

As Budreau walks away, the bag ladies continue to dog her.

"You eat at a fine restaurant. Can't you afford more?"

"No, I can't. You said if I gave you money, you'd stop fucking with me. Now go away, or I'll call the police"

At that moment, Pete pulls up to the curb. "Alida, it's Pete. We met at the Little Bad Wolf bar a while back. Are these ladies bothering you? I can give you a ride home so they won't harass you anymore."

"Oh, hi, Pete. That would be nice of you. I'm only a few blocks away."

Pete opens the back door of the Explorer and lets Budreau in. The bag ladies continue to hassle her. Pete shoos them away. "Get the hell out of here, you two scags, and stop bothering my friend."

The bag ladies back off.

"Alida, this is my friend Andrew. I told you about him being sick when we were at the bar."

"Hope you feel better, Andrew. I'm just up here. You can turn right on Catalpa."

Gunny tells Pete to stop. "I've lost my wallet in the seat, Pete."

Gunny exits the passenger seat, enters the rear door of the Explorer and climbs in next to Budreau. He searches under the passenger seat for his wallet. And then, like a mongoose attacking a snake, he puts a blood choke on Budreau, a maneuver that cuts off the flow of blood through the carotid arteries. Budreau goes limp, temporarily unconsciscous. Gunny cuffs her and covers her mouth with silver tape.

Pete heads for home and calls Nick. "Nick, plans have changed. We have captured Budreau. Gunny put her out, then cuffed and taped her. We're about twenty minutes away. We'll come to the basement door. I'll call you when we're five minutes away."

Nick alerts the team. *"Bushati and Budreau in hand. Heading for Palwaukee at around 2200, as originally planned."*

Pete pulls the Explorer up next to the basement door. Emma comes out to help Gunny extract Budreau, who is now awake, but confused and groggy.

"Gonna join your new friend Bushati, you fucking kid-killer," Pete says gruffly.

Gunny and Emma put Budreau in a sturdy chair across the basement from the other bad girl. Pete stares back and forth at both of them. "You fine ladies had better get along. You're gonna spend a long time together. A long time."

Maria and Adoncia arrive home and shove their disguises into Maria's closet. Nick goes up to greet them. "Surprise downstairs. Pete and Gunny have captured Budreau and put her in the basement until the trip tonight. How's your friend, Gemma?"

"She's fine and sends her best to you. What time do you leave, Guapo?" his mom asks.

Nick is aware that the sisters know about the secret missions. Pete got permission to share the information, but Nick doesn't know they're the bag ladies.

"Ten."

Maria, as usual, wants to make sure everybody is fed. She and Adoncia head for the kitchen to prepare food. "We're going to have to feed the two captives, also."

In the basement, Emma keeps an eye on the two women. The silver tape is gone, but the cuffs are still on. She watches and listens to a conversation between the two bad girls.

Bushati is still angry as she sizes up Budreau. "I don't know what the fuck is going on here. I was abducted from my church and brought here."

Budreau responds sarcastically, "That sounds awful. That sounds un-Christian. I was taken off the street by that prick, Pete. He rescued me from two bag ladies and then I was choked by his buddy and brought here. Wonder where we're going."

"I haven't a fucking idea, but it can't be the Ritz-Carlton."

Emma thinks, *What bag ladies? Are these the same bag ladies that tazed Sal Martinez's goons down the street from the Chinese restaurant? That is curious.*

Conor lands the Ranger at Palwaukee and files a visual flight plan for Keokuk. His sleek, black bird is all fueled and parked out on the tarmac, just as it was on the first trip. He does a pre-flight walk-around, which he always does before a flight. Everything looks good. He alerts Nick that he's in place waiting for their arrival.

Everybody at Pete and Maria's has been fed. Maria has also taken food to the two outlaws in the basement. The team is making final preparations to depart. Pete will drive his Explorer with Gunny in the back guarding Budreau. Nick will drive the squad with Emma and Sherri in the back watching Bushati. They will pick up the food at Cali's on their way.

At 10 o'clock sharp, Budreau and Nikalla are loaded into the two cars. Maria and Adoncia watch from the kitchen window. "God bless them."

"*Si, Dios las bendiga.*"

CHAPTER 38
A FRIGHT IN FLIGHT

Pete is the first to approach the security gate at Palwaukee. After showing his ID, the Rent-a-cop points to the Ranger out on the tarmac and waves them through. A couple of minutes later, Nick pulls up to security. Emma jumps out, goes to the trunk, and retrieves a lunch box for the guard. He thanks her and signals that the second car can proceed.

Conor is waiting and helps them load the struggling Budreau and Bushati into the Ranger. He closes the door and climbs into the cockpit. Nick climbs into the right seat; Gunny and Emma restrain the two ladies in the back. Conor cranks up the two Pratt and Whitney engines and engages the main and tail rotors. They begin moving forward as Conor gives Sherri and Pete a thumbs up. The bird climbs into the night. Pete and Sherri head home.

It's midnight. Conor flies southwest to intercept the Mississippi River. The weather is partly cloudy, with no rain predicted. Visibility is about ten miles.

Creed, with remote in one hand and a beer in the other, waits on the farm with Chesty at his side.

They are flying about thirty miles northwest of Peoria when it happens. What every pilot fears: a bright-red warning light glows on the Ranger's instrument panel. Conor immediately throttles back and checks for secondary indications. He knows from experience that it could simply be an electrical problem. It could also mean real trouble. His passengers see it, too, and look at Conor.

"No problem, troopers, I'm checking it out." Then Conor sees the oil pressure drop and the engine temperature increase in the starboard engine. He knows it's not an electrical problem. He immediately throttles back more and begins to look around for a field to land in as he prepares to auto-rotate.

He tells his team that the bird will fly with one engine, but he's not going to take chances. He's going to shut down the engines, disengage them from the main rotor, and begin the auto-rotation process. This will allow the main rotor to continue to produce some lift as they head toward a landing and keep the helicopter from becoming a flying brick. Conor, as the late ESPN commentator Stuart Scott said, "is as cool as the other side of the pillow."

He tells Nick to look for a field without trees to land in. They had all been there before in Iraq. They know the drill.

Sly and Caroline Clevenger are sleeping after a long day getting everything ready for the soybean and corn harvest on their farm just south of the small town of Wyoming. Sly is awakened by a strange sound outside. A *whop, whop* and then a thud near the house. He gets up, pulls on his shirt and overalls, and heads out to see what's going on outside.

Walking to the barnyard, he sees the eerie silhouette of a large helicopter in a bean field just south of the house. Amazed, a bit frightened, and more than somewhat curious, he strides toward Conor's Ranger. The occupants are now exiting the Ranger and walking around, somewhat dazed. Sly approaches Nick.

"Everybody okay?"

"Yes, sir, we just had an engine problem and had to land. Hope we didn't ruin any of your beans."

"No problem, as long as you're all okay."

Nick shows Sly his police badge.

"We're transporting some fugitives to a place out west of here on the Mississippi."

"Can we do anything for you all?" Sly asks.

"No, sir, we'll be fine. Just need one of our colleagues to come from Chicago to continue transporting our cargo by land. We have a veteran mechanic with us. She'll begin troubleshooting the faulty engine."

"I can bring my tractor over to give her some light."

"That will be great, sir, if you don't mind."

Sly heads for the barnyard to get his red Massey-Ferguson.

As Emma starts her inspection, Nick calls Pete. "Uncle Pete. We've got a problem. The Ranger had engine problems and Conor had to land in a farmer's field a couple of miles south of Wyoming on Highway 90. We need you and Sherri to come fast to take Bushati and Budreau on to Camp Keokuk."

"Jesus Christ, Nick. Is everybody okay?"

"Yes, we're fine. A little shook up, but nothing serious. Gunny is keeping an eye on the trash and Emma and Conor are beginning to troubleshoot the bad engine."

"Okay, I'll call Sherri and we'll get underway right away. I'll keep you posted on our progress."

Caroline Clevenger, a slim, attractive, middle-aged woman with a farmer's tan, comes out into the night to see what's happening. She rides with Sly on the tractor to the Ranger. She gets off and approaches Nick.

"Good morning, I'm Caroline Clevenger. We don't normally get guests coming to see us in a helicopter in the middle of the night." She shakes hands with Nick.

"Good morning, ma'am. I'm Officer Nick Santos of the Chicago Police Department. I guess we woke you, huh?"

"No problem. Did Sly offer you any coffee? I make the best."

"That would be terrific, Mrs. Clevenger, if it's no problem. We'll probably be here for a while."

"I'll be back soon. I have some homemade cookies, too."

Nick is taken aback by the Clevenger's cool demeanor and their kindness.

Pete picks up Sherri and they head toward Wyoming and the broken Ranger. "I figure it will take about two and a half hours at seventy miles an hour. It means we should be there by 4am. Then, according to my GPS, it's another two and a half hours to the Camp. Maybe we can make it before it gets light."

"I wonder if they've contacted the Chief. I'll call Nick," Sherri says.

"Nick, we're on our way. Pete says we should be there around 4 o'clock. Then we need to get to Camp, hopefully before sunrise. Have you alerted the Chief?"

"I was about to call him. He has to find a new way to get Bushati and Budreau into their side of the camp."

With Pete's permission, Sherri turns on WCOU to listen to some country music to ease the stress. It's Willie Nelson singing *Blue Eyes Crying in the Rain*.

"I've heard that song before, Sherri. Willie Nelson, right?"

"Yes, but actually it was written by Fred Rose and first sung by Roy Acuff in 1945."

"You sure know your country music, Sherri."

"I love it, Pete."

"I prefer Sinatra."

Creed's waiting in the barnyard for the cargo to arrive. His cell rings.

"Nick?"

"Yeah, Chief, we've got a situation. We had engine problems and we're down in a farmer's field here in Illinois. Pete and Sherri are underway to pick up the ladies and deliver them to Camp by land."

"Holy shit, Nick. Are you guys OK?"

"Yeah, Chief, just a little shaken up. Emma and Conor are troubleshooting now and Gunny's watching the cargo. Can you begin making arrangements to get the girls into Camp by some other means?"

"No problem, brother. I'll start working on it now. Don't worry. We should be ready by the time Pete arrives. What's his ETA, do you think?"

"He thinks he'll be here at about 4am. It won't take us long to load the cargo into his Explorer. Then it's another two and a half hours to the farm."

"OK, I'll let you know what's going on."

"Thanks, Chief."

Caroline delivers hot coffee and cookies to the Marines. Gunny is still keeping the cargo inside the Ranger. Conor is discussing the engine problem with Emma, as Sly's Massey provides much-needed light. Emma's confidence is low as she goes about taking the engine apart, but she will keep working on it. She wonders if she missed anything during a routine maintenance check back at Mitchell Field.

Pete gives Nick a progress report. "Nick, we're about an hour out just past the Ogilsby exit on 80."

"You're making good time, Unc. Keep her coming. The Chief has been notified and he's working on a solution now. Has Sherri been listening to country music or is the station out of range?"

"She's giving me country music history lessons. Do you know who wrote *Blue Eye's Crying in the Rain?*"

"Of course. It was Willy Nelson."

"You flunked your first lesson, Nick. I'll tell you later."

"Drive careful, Uncle Pete."

The Chief reports to Nick that he's contacted JJ and his friend Harvey Swingley about the problem. As volunteer firefighters, they have decided to have the large hook-and-ladder truck at Camp when Pete and Gunny arrive with the new guests. It will be rigged to lift the prisoners one by one into their side of the Camp. The high-voltage fence will need to be shut off so that Bushati and Budreau don't get electrocuted before they have a chance to enjoy their new home. He will also have Deputy Jack Boyd on the road again.

Nick is constantly amazed at the Chief's problem-solving abilities. He hopes they can get everything done before it gets too light.

Patricia Botkin is fast asleep when her cell phone rings.

"Sherri, what's wrong? It's 3 o'clock."

"Nothing serious, Mom. Just a small glitch. The team had a helicopter problem and had to land in a farmer's field about halfway to Camp. Everybody's okay, but Pete and I are driving to pick up the cargo and drive them to Camp."

"Jesus, Sherri. This is a very dangerous turn of events. Are you going to the Camp with the prisoners?"

"Don't know yet, Mom. Nick will decide that when Pete and I get to the downed 'copter."

"I don't want anything happening to you."

"It won't, Mom. I'm in good company. I'll keep you posted. Our estimated time of arrival at Camp is around 6am. Get some more sleep and then tune in the cameras."

"Be careful, Sweetheart."

At 4am sharp, Pete and Sherri pull into the Clevenger's barnyard. They see lights in the field illuminating the downed Ranger. They make their way to the team around the 'copter. Caroline and Sly greet the two and offer them coffee and cookies.

"Welcome to the Clevenger farm," Sly says warmly.

"Thank you, sir," Sherri says, showing her badge. "I bet you never planned to have an airport on your place, did you?"

"No, ma'am. But, it's okay. Nice to have company out here. Hope you can stay and help us pick corn and soybeans today. We feed the farmhands very well."

"Not a bad idea," Sherri replies.

The other members of the team greet the newcomers. Nick hugs both Pete and Sherri. "Uncle Pete, I think you, Gunny, and Sherri should escort Bushati and Budreau to the Camp. Chief says he will be ready by the time you get there. Where's Gunny?"

They all look around for Gunny. Conor spots him sitting out in the soybean field with his head in his hands. Conor goes out to see if he's okay. He sits down next to his old friend.

"You okay, Gunny?"

"I'll be alright, Captain. Just need a minute."

"Don't worry, Gunny. You don't have to fly in the bird again tonight."

Gunny and Conor return to the downed bird. Nick takes over. "Okay, troops, let's start loading the fucking precious cargo into the Explorer."

Sly and Caroline Clevenger are amazed at what's happening in the middle of the night in their soybean field. This is a story they will tell for a long time.

"Okay, girls, here we go," Gunny says, as they unload the two "scum" from the Ranger. Both women have their mouths closed with silver tape and are wide-eyed as they look around at what's happening. Budreau has anger in her eyes as she mutters something foul beneath the tape.

"Get in the fucking car," Gunny shouts at them, as he and Pete hoist the two into the back of Pete's Explorer. Then Sherri loads Cali's lunch boxes in behind them.

At that moment, a Stark County sheriff's squad car pulls into the barnyard. Sly goes to greet the night deputy.

"You okay, Sly?"

"Yeah, we're okay, Jerry. Helicopter with two fugitives being transported by Chicago police had engine problems and landed in the field. They're gonna take their human cargo on by land."

"Mind if I take a look?" Sly and the county deputy walk to the field. Nick introduces himself to the deputy and thinks to himself, *This is all we need. Damn.*

"You guys and gals need anything from the sheriff's department?"

"Not right now, but we appreciate your offer. Three of us are going to stay here to see if we can get the chopper working again, while our colleagues carry the cargo to their destination by land."

"I'll be happy to escort them through the county if they want to expedite their travel."

"That would be very helpful, Deputy."

"Then, I'm ready when they are. Incidentally, what kind of crime did these two commit?"

"They're both from Chicago street gangs who threaten the neighborhoods and commit murder."

"Hope you're taking them to a very secure place."

"We are, Deputy, we are. They won't bother innocent people again."

Caroline offers Jerry coffee and cookies as Pete, Gunny, and Sherri pull to the driveway for their departure.

"Thank you, Caroline. You always bake the best cookies. You spoil Sly."

Pete tells the deputy that they're headed to Keokuk. The deputy pulls in front of Pete, turns on his red flashing lights and they head out in the early morning darkness. Destination: Camp Keokuk.

In the darkness, JJ and Harvey steer the huge, red hook-and-ladder into Creed's barnyard. Creed and Chesty are waiting with coffee. Deputy Jack Boyd is parked on the road. He says, "Can't thank you enough guys. Cargo should be here by six or so. Should we rig this thing up and see if it's going to work?"

Creed takes Jack some coffee. "Thanks, Jack."

"You owe me a beer, Chief."

"I owe you a few six packs, Jack."

JJ and Harvey move the hook-and-ladder into position. They raise the huge ladder up to the top of the Camp and swing it over the movable roof, which Creed has opened with his remote. JJ is satisfied that it will work.

"I think it's going to be fine, Chief. We just have to do it in three loads, one for each of the guests and one for the food.

"We have to find a way to lower them in and drop them."

Harvey says it can be done.

"I'll rig a quick release to do the job when we get them five feet from the floor."

They go to work on the rigging and release mechanism. It won't be as good as the one on Conor's Ranger, but it will do.

Creed calls Pete. "Pete. How are you guys coming along?"

"Doing fine, Chief. A county deputy is escorting us quickly through Stark County."

"Good. Sunrise is at 6:20, Pete. I'd like to get it done and closed up before that."

"That's going to be tough, Chief. I calculate we should be there at around 6:30. After the deputy stops leading us, we won't be able to keep these speeds. I don't want to get picked up."

"You think the deputy could get permission to bring you all the way?"

"We could ask but we don't want him near the Camp, do we?"

"I guess not, unless we take him into our confidence, and he doesn't have to report it."

"Maybe he could go off the clock and we could pay him to do it privately. But that doesn't solve the problem of his knowing what we're doing."

"Pete, if we don't want to risk any of that, we could store the cargo in the barn until tonight and have JJ and Harvey come back with the hook-and-ladder. They're here now testing it to see how we can do this, and it looks good."

"That might be a better solution, Chief. That way we don't have to rush now to try to beat the light."

"Let's do it. I'll brief JJ and Harvey. You want to call Nick and advise him of our new plan?"

"No problem. We'll talk shortly before we arrive."

At the Stark County line, the deputy pulls over and waves Pete on.

Back at the Clevenger Farm, Conor and Nick watch as Emma continues to examine the starboard engine. She has it partly dismantled. Conor tells his partners that he woke up the Bell Helicopter service rep. in Chicago. He's on his way. Chief has briefed Nick on the new plan for putting the cargo into the Camp.

As Pete nears the mighty Mississippi, Sherri calls her mom to tell her about the new plan. "Mom, sorry to wake you, but the plans have changed again. We can't get the cargo to the Camp before light. So we'll stash them in the barn until tonight after dark. Chief has a way of using a fire truck to lift them into Camp. Go back to sleep."

"I can't sleep. Been up for hours waiting and watching the live video from inside the camp. They're both sleeping. I'll have some coffee and get ready for class. Oh, by the way, did I tell you I'm using Camp Keokuk as a hypothetical case study in my graduate class? They love it and have some thoughtful ideas. Of course, everything is anonymous. Thanks for keeping me posted."

"That's great, Mom. I'll call you later."

CHAPTER 39
HOMEMADE BUSCUITS AND GRAVY

As the sun breaks the horizon and begins to cast a golden glow on the soybean and corn fields, Nick, Emma, and Conor are invited into the Clevenger home for breakfast. Caroline is fixing homemade biscuits with sausage gravy, orange juice, and coffee. She also has baked a new batch of cookies, just hot out of the oven. The five of them sit around a kitchen booth that Sly rebuilt when he rescued it from his aunt's restaurant in Wyoming. It is a fine piece of work and could probably tell a lot of stories.

Nick thinks, *What a strange and wonderful morning. A bent helicopter in a farmer's field somewhere in Illinois and being served breakfast by a delightful farm couple. Their graciousness is remarkable, but not unlike my urban family back home.* He says, "Sly and Caroline, on behalf of my colleagues and myself, I'd like to thank you for your kind hospitality. Not only did we frighten you in the middle of the night, we also messed up your bean field and kept you from getting a good night's sleep. We thank you and will remember this for a long time to come."

Sly asks them all to bow their heads and hold hands while he says a blessing. "Lord, thanks for this food from your bounty and thanks for keeping the police officers out of harm's way along their worthwhile journey. We know that you helped them land their helicopter safely in our field. We are blessed to have come to their side to support them in their dangerous mission. And, we know that you will bless them as they continue to rid the earth of evil. Amen."

Everyone echoes. "Amen."

Caroline brings more helpings of her appetizing breakfast. "You eat up now before you go back to work. Sly and I have to get started on our farm chores for the day. Corn and beans have to be harvested so we can get them to market. That's how we make a living. If any of you want to get some rest, we have two guest rooms upstairs. They won't be used until Thanksgiving when the kids come home."

Nick speaks for the team. "Thank you, Caroline. We appreciate that."

CHAPTER 40
CREED BRING'S SAMMY'S KILLER TO TEARS

Pete pulls the black Explorer into Creed's barnyard with Gunny, Sherri, and the two snakes aboard. Creed, with Chesty at his feet, is there to greet them. He tells Pete to pull the car into the barn. He has everything ready and has piled two stacks of hay inside cattle stalls on different sides of the barn. As they unload Budreau and Bushati, Creed can't keep his mouth shut.

"What dirt do we have here? Two of the finest creatures on the earth. Which one killed Sammy, Pete?"

"This one, Chief." Pete points to Budreau.

Creed approaches Budreau, who's now lying in her haystack. He stares at her for a moment. He then walks over to another side of the barn and takes a full Native American warrior costume off a hook: a headdress, feathered cape, a leather shield, a pair of moccasins, a wooden hatchet, and a drum. He carefully dons the costume, then starts beating the drum and chanting as he circles Budreau. Pete, Gunny, and Sherri look on, surprised at this spectacle. Budreau's eyes are wider than saucers and her breathing turns to wheezing. She doesn't know whether she'll live through this.

"*Ah nana, nana, renana nana….la nahana..hey yo neho hey ho yana ye ha nan, ah,*" chants the Chief, as he continues to orbit Budreau and beat on his drum faster and faster, and more frantically. He shakes his hatchet at Budreau. "*Yo he yah, yah hey, hey, yeah ha yah, yah nah, nah.*" He goes on for five minutes, remembering every step his elders taught him when he was a boy. Soon tears begin to stream down Budreau's cheeks. Fear overcomes her. She hides her face in the haystack. Chief stops his dance, walks over to the hook, takes off his costume, and hangs up his drum.

"That was for Sammy, Pete."

"Thanks, Chief."

The team exits the barn and heads for the house, where Creed has prepared a country breakfast for them.

The Bell Helicopter rep is now in the Clevenger's bean field examining the Ranger engine with Emma and Conor. He's brought all kinds of testing equipment and has further dismantled the engine. It would be a while, he tells Emma.

Conor informs WTMJ-TV that his bird is down and he won't be able to do the traffic reports until it's fixed. Emma takes another day off from United and Nick informs Commander Washington that Sherri is sick and he doesn't feel so good either. They'll come in tomorrow. The Commander is patient and approves. He asks Nick if he has any candidates for the Gang Unit.

"I'm working on it, Commander. I have a couple of prime candidates. They're supposed to give me an answer soon. I think you'll like them."

Creed takes two plates of food to the barn to feed the guests. Gunny uncuffs them, as Pete and Sherri look on. Budreau is still afraid that the Chief is going to hurt her. Bushati stares blankly up at the hayloft. After the two ladies are fed, led to the restroom in the corner of the barn, and recuffed, the team goes outside to talk about tonight.

Creed calls Nick. "JJ and Harvey are bringing the hook-and-ladder at 8pm, just after sunset. Deputy Boyd will be on the road. The boys have rigged the hook-and-ladder to lift the two in one at a time and then the food. I also have to remember to turn off the high-voltage fence before we start the operation."

"Thanks, Chief."

Gunny, back to himself again after his PTSD spell, is sarcastic as always. "No, we wouldn't want the hags to fry, would we?"

"Don't worry. I'll take care of that and use my laptop to guide the operation."

"I want to watch the live video as we go. I especially want to watch Tang and Martinez's faces. Priceless. My mom will also be observing from her home in Hyde Park," Sherri says with a grin.

Sly delivers the *Chicago Tribune* to Nick at the site of the downed Ranger. Nick looks and is startled by the headline: **SORIANO TO RUN AGAINST KELLY!**

"Jesus Christ, Conor, the alderman is going to give it a shot against the Kelly machine. This ought to be interesting."

"I wonder if that serves us or not. Our angel, Jon DiFrisco, is a close friend of the mayor's."

"But Soriano wants to spend more funds on cleaning up the street gangs, and the people of his ward will surely turn out for him."

"That's true, but Jon gets a lot of city jobs through the mayor, which helps our secret funding," Conor reminds Nick.

"True."

"The Kelly machine has a lot of money to put behind his reelection."

"It's an uphill fight for Soriano. But, he could do it."

"The *Defender* will support Soriano. Don't know about the *Trib* and the *Sun-Times*."

Emma steps from behind the Ranger. "You two reading the comics?"

"And the baseball scores."

"Rep says he's got to get new engine parts, Conor. He's going to put a rush on them, but probably won't be until tomorrow."

"Christ. Can you get off for another day?" Conor asks.

"No problem. I've got a lot of vacation time. What about you two?"

Nick thinks. "I should probably get back. The Commander's been very patient. And Sherri's stuck at the Camp."

"I'm okay. WTMJ's got another chopper and pilot."

"I guess what I should do is get a driver to pick up Sherri at the Camp, and then come and pick me up here so we can get back. Gunny, Pete, and Chief can take care of the insertion mission," Nick says.

Conor has an idea. "Why don't you call the Chief and ask him if Sherri can borrow a car and come pick you up? He has his Corvette, his dad's old Plymouth, and his Ram. We can get it back to him in a couple of days."

"I'll call him now and ask him if he would do that."

CHAPTER 41
SHERRI LAYS RUBBER AND MEETS A TROOPER

Creed, Pete, Gunny, and Sherri are sitting on the front porch. They're having a beer and Gunny is smoking a Cuban when Creed gets the call from Nick.

"Nick." He listens. "That's a damned good idea, Nick. We can handle things here. I'll get her underway."

"That was Nick, Sherri. He thinks that you and he should get back to work. You need to get underway to the Clevenger farm to pick up Nick and head back to Chicago. I'll get the keys to the Corvette and you can get it back to me whenever."

"Jesus, Chief, is it manual or automatic?"

"It's automatic, so you can handle it. Just don't go over 120."

"You sure, Chief?"

"I'm damned sure. We'll handle things here. It has a GPS, so just plug in Wyoming, Illinois."

They all walk to the barnyard to see Sherri off. As she climbs into the beautifully kept silver Corvette and adjusts the seat, Creed has some final words. "You look beautiful in that car. Put the top down and head out. Have you driven a Corvette before?"

"Never. But I can handle it. My dad had a Mustang."

"Not even close, Sherri."

"Thanks, Chief. I'll keep you posted on my progress." As she rips onto the road and lays a little rubber, the guys chuckle.

Pete comments as they watch her speed out of sight, the Corvette's 638-horsepower engine emitting a beautiful voice. "Nick's a lucky guy."

"Nick, Sherri is on her way in the Corvette. She should be there in a couple of hours."

"Thanks, Chief. The Gunny was wrong when he said you weren't worth a shit."

"I never paid much attention to that burly bastard."

"Yeah, sure."

Caroline walks through the bean field to where Conor, Emma, Nick, and the Bell rep are still working on the Ranger engine. She's carrying a picnic basket full of sandwiches and cookies, as well as homemade lemonade.

"You all are working so hard, you need nourishment."

"Thanks once again for your kindness, Caroline."

The Bell rep is also thankful. "Thank you, ma'am. I've never been treated this well working on a broken helicopter. You and your husband are very nice people."

"Thank you. That's all we know how to be out here."

Sherri crosses the Mississippi River at Burlington, Iowa, home of actor William Frawley and NFL quarterback Kurt Warner. She finds an open stretch of road and mashes down on the accelerator. The Corvette's powerful engine comes to life. 80, 90, 100, 110. She enjoys the exhilaration of cutting through the country air on such a beautiful day in a magnificent machine. The corn and bean fields on each side of the silver 'Vette are a blur. Her hair blows back like a Bose Speaker TV commercial. Sherri sings along with a Tanya Tucker song at the top of her voice, as the Corvette purrs through the countryside.

"Tanya, you are one beautiful babe!!" At 120, she backs off. In her rear-view mirror, she sees flashing red lights. "Oh, shit. I've been nabbed." She slows down and finds a place to pull over as the state police car approaches. The tall, young Illinois State Trooper gets out and walks to her car.

"Good afternoon, ma'am. Hope you're having a nice day. Sure is a beautiful car. And fast too. But so is my Mustang."

"Thank you, Officer. Just airing it out a bit."

"Yes, at 120. That's quite a bit over the speed limit. Can I see your license and registration, please?"

Sherri takes out the registration from the glove compartment, pulls her license and badge from her purse, and gives them to the officer.

"Officer Botkin. What are you doing way out here?"

"Visited my friend in Keokuk and heading home."

"The car is registered to a Creed Tsoodle. Is that your friend?"

"Yes, sir. He's letting me borrow it for a couple of days."

The officer hands the registration, driver's license, and badge back to Sherri. "Do you think he can afford to pay for a speeding ticket?"

"No, I'll take care of that."

"Out of professional courtesy and with a promise from you that you'll obey the speed limit, I won't give you a ticket."

"Thank you, Officer, I appreciate that and promise to drive the speed limit."

"Farmers cross these roads on their tractors and wagons. At 120, that could be lights out for you. Your friend Tsoodle is a lucky guy. I hope he treats you well. And, I hope the Chicago Police Department does, too.

"They do. Thank you for the compliment and the pass."

"I have an aunt in Chicago. I go to visit her from time to time. Would you be up for a lunch or dinner sometime?"

"That would be nice, Officer. What's your name?"

"Corporal Robert Watson."

"You can reach me through the department, Robert. I'm in the Street Gang Unit."

"I'll do that, thanks. Gang Unit. You must be brave. Have a nice day, Officer Botkin." As the trooper heads back to his patrol car, Sherri notices in her rearview mirror that he's in very good physical shape. Or, as Mayor Kelly would say, *"Nice ass."*

At City Hall, Mayor Kelly is meeting with his election campaign staff. He's anxious as he paces the room. "Ladies and gentlemen, is Alderman Sariano a threat?"

Sarah Krakowiak, the mayor's campaign director, reassures him. "Sir, I don't think the alderman can sustain a campaign, let alone win the election."

"He got a lot of publicity when he lit into me at the City Council meeting and asked for more funds for the Police Gang Unit."

"Yes, but the blight is in his neighborhood, not the middle-class neighborhoods. The middle and upper demographics are ours."

"I always make sure that the garbage is picked up and the snow is removed throughout the city."

"Yes, sir, but we can't lie back. The current controversy over street gangs may be much worse than banks of snow."

"Always the optimist, Sarah."

"Just realistic, Mr. Mayor."

Sherri turns the Corvette into the Clevenger's driveway, parks it in the barnyard, and walks over to the Ranger. "Man, that was some ride!" she says to her friends.

"Your hair is a little bit windblown. Was it fun?"

"It was fantastic. I've never driven anything like it."

"Did you wring it out?"

"I hit 120 and then a statey got my ass."

"You're shitting me?"

"No, but he gave me a pass when I showed him my badge."

"You're lucky you're a cop."

"He was cute, too," Sherri grins.

"Well, so are you. Now, we better get underway, so we can get some rest and get back to work tomorrow morning."

Nick and Sherri say goodbye to Conor, Emma, and the Clevengers and head out for Chicago with Sherri at the wheel and Nick holding on with white knuckles. Sly and Caroline know that the Ranger will be in their bean field for some time while the Bell rep gets the parts and fixes the problem.

Caroline approaches the group still working on the engine. "You all are working so hard to fix things. We have that happen to our equipment and it's a real pain and slows things down."

Emma stops to talk to Caroline. "You're so right, Caroline. We'll be out of your hair soon, so you and Sly don't have to bother with us anymore."

"Don't you worry about that, Honey. We're glad to have you. Most exciting thing that's happened around here since a tornado blew the door off the Methodist church."

"Did anybody get hurt?"

"No. Luckily it was not on a Sunday morning. During Pastor Lindsey's sermon the following Sunday, he said, "The wind can blow the door off our church, but it can't blow Jesus away."

Emma looks kindly at Caroline. "You truly live in a wonderful world."

"We do, and we're blessed. I came out to tell you that we would like to share our blessings with you three tonight. We'd like to invite you to have supper with us and have bedrooms all made up for you to stay the night so you can get some deserved rest. We would like you to accept our invitation."

Emma steps forward to give the farmer's wife a gentle hug. "Caroline, I'm touched by your invitation. Strange as it may seem, I'm glad we had engine problems, so we got the opportunity to meet such wonderful folks as you and Sly."

———————————

CHAPTER 42
IN GO THE GIRL SNAKES

At 8pm sharp, JJ and Harvey pull the giant hook-and-ladder into Creed's barnyard. Creed, Gunny, and Pete watch as Creed's two friends maneuver the fire engine into place near the Camp wall. Jack Boyd is parked on the road.

JJ and Harvey show Gunny and Pete the contraption they've constructed to strap the guests into and then the release mechanism when they're close to the Camp floor.

The plan is for Gunny and Pete to take one of the girls at a time from the barn, fasten her into the harness, and then JJ and Harvey will hoist her into her side of the Camp. After both girl snakes are in, they will drop in the boxes of food. Creed will turn off the high-voltage fence and guide them by watching the live video on his computer.

They will wait to start the operation until it's dark

Professor Botkin sits in her den tuned into the Camp video to watch the operation and observe the behavior of subjects of her study, as well as the new guests. She has her logbook next to the computer ready to be filled in with this new chapter in her study. Her cell rings. "Sherri?"

"Yes, Mom, Nick and I are back in Chicago. We have to work tomorrow."

"How did you get there?"

"The Chief let me borrow his Corvette."

"Where are you now?"

"Nick and I are having dinner at Twin Anchors and then we'll get some sleep."

"You sound tired, Sweetheart."

"I am, Mom. It's been quite a journey."

"Who's going to drop Budreau and Bushati?"

"Pete, Gunny, Chief, and two of his friends."

"I'm already tuned in and ready to watch the proceedings. I hope everything goes as planned. What about Conor and Emma?"

"They're still with the broken bird. But the farm couple is taking good care of them and the Bell rep."

"Good. Have a nice dinner and I'll talk to you in the morning. I love you."

"Love you too, Mom."

As Nick and Sherri enjoy fall-off-the-bone ribs, onion rings, a cold Bud, and a glass of Merlot, they talk about the operation tonight at Camp Keokuk. "I know we're tired, Nick, but we have to watch the operation live. I won't be able to sleep."

"I think you're right. You want to watch it at my place? You can have the guest bedroom."

"That's a nice invitation. I'll accept. I'll have to get up early in the morning to go home and get ready for work."

"I'll pick you up at 7am and we'll hit the bricks. You have a safe place to park the Chief's 'Vette?"

"Yes. It'll be safe in the parking garage."

"Okay. Let's enjoy our meal. Here's to the drop team tonight."

"*Semper Fidelis.*"

It's dark on Creed's farm and time for the operation to begin. JJ starts the powerful engine of the big hook-and-ladder. Gunny and Pete bring Bushati from the barn. As they struggle to put her in the harness, she screams and swears. "You motherfuckers will pay for this. I'll turn the Bad Tigers loose on all of you. What the fuck are you doing? Unstrap me, you fucking pigs!"

Gunny stares her in the face as JJ finishes clamping her in. "You bitch. You're gonna join your friend Tang in the resort. So hang on for your sad life."

JJ starts the long ladder toward the open roof, lifting Bushati skyward into the night, as Chief monitors his live video. She's still screaming. There's no one to hear her cries for help, except maybe Deputy Boyd on the road.

Creed turns off the high-voltage fence.

Patricia Botkin watches from her study. She looks for any reaction from Tang and Martinez.

Nick and Sherri watch from Nick's apartment. "This is so cool. These guys are terrific," Nick says to Sherri.

Sherri watches in amazement. "I would never dream I'd be part of such a mission."

Conor and Emma watch on their computers at the Clevenger farm.

JJ begins to lower Bushati through the roof. The Chief is at his side to let him know when she's about five feet from the floor. "Slowly, JJ, slowly. It's going fine. Just a little bit to your left."

Tang and Martinez exit their cubicles to see what is going on. Tang watches as his Bad Tiger successor is being lowered into the camp on the other side of the high-voltage fence. "Nikalla, is that you?"

"Yes, Gerald! Help me!"

"I can't help you. That fence is high-voltage. I can't do anything."

"Where are we?"

"I don't have any fucking idea. I just know we're being held captive."

Bushati is still screaming.

Martinez watches from his end of the camp. "Tang, who is this bitch?"

"She's my friend and second in command of the Bad Tigers, my organization."

"Not no more she ain't."

Creed tells JJ that she's just about five feet from the floor.

"Okay, Harvey, let her go." Harvey flips the release switch and Bushati falls to the floor. She's dazed but manages to get to her feet.

"What the fuck?!" she screams.

"Don't go near the fence, Nikalla," Tang warns. "It's high-voltage. Go over to one of the cubicles."

Bushati yells. "They're bringing in another prisoner."

"Who is it?"

"She's some scag from a North Side gang."

Patricia Botkin is taking copious notes as she watches the feelings and behaviors of all three.

Gunny and Pete go back to the barn to get Budreau. She is furious, her eyes filled with hatred. She just grunts as the two men haul her to the harness for the trip into the Camp. They maneuver her into position as she struggles. Gunny has news for her. "If you don't settle down, I'll hook this into your ugly nose ring."

"You bastard. If I ever get out of this, I'll kill you."

Pete responds. "Just like you killed my son?"

"I don't know what the fuck you're talking about, you Spic."

"You know goddamned well what I'm talking about. And, you'll never hurt anyone again, unless you want to kill your camp mate."

Gunny and Pete finally get her strapped in and give JJ and Harvey the signal to begin the lift.

"Up you go, bitch," the Chief says.

"You fuckers, you'll pay for this," as she dangles in the harness, feet kicking.

Bushati, Tang, and Martinez look up at the roof as Budreau is lowered to the floor on the girls' side of the fence.

"Where you from and what's your name?" Tang yells up at her as she comes closer to the floor.

"None of your fucking business, you Chink."

Creed signals Harvey to release her. Harvey complies and Budreau falls to the floor. Bushati greets her. "Welcome to our little home. We'd better like each other or one of us isn't going to survive."

Budreau just stares at her, and at Tang and Martinez through the fence. She then walks slowly toward a cubicle away from Bushati.

As JJ lifts the harness back through the roof, Gunny and Pete retrieve Cali's lunches from the barn. JJ puts half the boxes of food in a net and hoists it toward the open roof. Once over the roof, he empties the net over the men's section with help from the Chief on his computer. Then he brings the net down to load the other half. Up goes the second. He dumps this load on the women's side. Then, as he brings the big ladder down, the Chief turns on the high-voltage fence. Chief clicks his remote and the roof closes, leaving the four to fend for themselves.

"Mission number two is done," the Chief exclaims to his brothers.

Patricia Botkin observes the entire operation via live video. She is writing in her logbook.

Feelings: Aggression, anger, fear, mistrust. All present.

As she writes, she wonders about commonalities among the group of four. What is it that made them end up this way? Were their backgrounds similar? Did they have a decent upbringing? Were they from single parent homes? Were they led to this point by peer pressure? Was it in their genes? All of these questions factor into Patricia's study. She would discuss it with her graduate school students. They might have some insights.

Gunny, Pete, Creed, JJ, and Harvey rest on Creed's front porch having a late-night beer and some beef sandwiches after their exhausting and successful operation.

Gunny asks Creed, "Why can't you have some PBR, instead of this river swill?"

"This is good beer, not like PBR. Drink and enjoy it, and don't be picky."

The Chief then commends them on a great job. "You gentlemen did it. We have two more brutal snakes out of the neighborhoods of Chicago."

"We couldn't have done it without you and your good friends, Chief," Pete says. "Getting Budreau to the Camp means a lot to Maria and me. I thank you all."

Gunny reminds them. "We still have a lot of work to do, gentlemen. There are more heads of snakes to be chopped off. We have to remain committed to our continuing mission."

All agree.

Chief's cell phone buzzes. "Nick?"

"Hi, Chief. You guys fucking amaze me! What a super job you did tonight getting the two new guests into the Camp. I could hardly believe my eyes the way you did it. I'm thankful for all of you."

"You too, Nick. And, for Conor, Emma, and Sherri also. I'll put Pete and Gunny up for the night and they'll head back in the morning. Gunny says he wants to stop by the Clevenger Farm on the way back to see how Conor and Emma are doing with the bird."

"Chief, I'd like to have a meeting at my place in the next two days or so, whenever the Ranger's fixed and everybody's back. We need to tie up some loose ends and discuss next steps. It would be great if you could be there in person. Do you think you can make it?" Nick asks.

"I'll try my best, Nick. But there's a lot to do around here and I'm behind. Besides that, Sherri has stolen my 'Vette."

"Okay, let me know. Thanks again for everything you've done. And, by the way, was that rip in your Corvette fender before Sherri took it?"

"There was no rip anywhere on that beautiful machine. What the hell did Sherri do?"

Nick chuckles out loud.

"That's not funny, Nick, you son-of-a-bitch."

Early the next morning, Pete and Gunny head out for the Clevenger Farm and Nick and Sherri check in at work, ready to hit the streets again in the neighborhoods. Conor, Emma, and the Bell service rep are back in the bean field after a great home-cooked dinner and a good night's sleep in the Clevenger farmhouse. The parts for the broken engine are to arrive this morning.

Maria and Adoncia are having breakfast on Maria and Pete's back porch. They were up late watching the video of the activities at the Camp.

"That was truly a remarkable operation last night," Adoncia says, as she sips her espresso and nibbles on a cookie.

"Those men did a great job of getting Bushati and Budreau into the Camp. I'm proud of all of them. And, I'm happy Pete got to be a part of getting Sammy's killer out of society for good."

"And, don't forget the role the bag ladies played in capturing her."

"I'll never forget. Although, Pete wasn't too happy that we didn't stay away."

"He'll get over it, sister. He knows he and Gunny couldn't have done it without us, let alone what we did down the street from the Chinese restaurant."

"*Seguro, hermana.*"

CHAPTER 43
PROFESSOR BOTKIN GETS SOME HELP

Patricia Botkin enters her graduate school social psychology class at the University of Chicago.

"Good morning. Today, I'm going to ask you for your help with our hypothetical scenario of street gangs in isolation, and what caused them to get to that point in the first place. The scenario now includes two women gang leaders who have been placed in isolation near the two male gang members already there. I observed aggression, fear, anger, and mistrust. I don't have any information on their backgrounds, except that they haven't turned out well as model citizens. What else would you consider?"

"Doctor Botkin. If any of us were grabbed from the street and thrust into isolation next to our adversaries, wouldn't we also be aggressive, angry, afraid, and mistrustful?

"I think that's right. What I'm after beyond that is something deeper. They apparently had some of those feelings already to end up in violent street gangs, don't you think?"

"I suppose so. But how do we separate the two—behavior and feelings on the street and behavior and feelings in isolation?"

"These men and women are violent individuals," Professor Botkin said. "Even psychotic. They are, or were, leaders of violent street gangs. So, I'm assuming that their behavioral patterns are continuing in isolation. Is it family environment, genetics, peer pressure, or what? Let's just eliminate afraid and angry. That leaves aggressive and mistrustful."

"Professor Botkin, do you think they were aggressive and mistrustful on the street, maybe, because they grew up in an awful ghetto?"

"That's a possibility. And, that's what I'm trying to decipher, so that we can make recommendations on what can be done to stop the violence before it begins."

"This is tough, Professor. I think it's a combination of factors: Upbringing, peer pressure, genetics. Now, is it possible that each person is so different that we'll never find commonalities? And, your sample in the hypothetical scenario is only four people. Is it possible to expand the sample?"

"Yes, I can do that over the next few weeks."

"Professor Botkin. I wonder if we could widen the sample by going back and taking a look at the behaviors of some of the old gang members?"

"I think that's a good idea, Sandra. So, why don't we make that the assignment for our next class? See what you come up with. In the meantime, I want to remind you as budding social psychologists, what your mission is: the scientific study of how people's thoughts, feelings, and behaviors are influenced the by the actual, imagined, or implied presence of others. This includes all psychological variables that are measurable in human beings."

"Professor Botkin, I've been thinking. I wonder if the leaders of the violent street gangs can be considered serial killers, like the doctor in *The Devil in the White City* by Erik Larson. Maybe we could study the psychological make-up of some famous serial killers."

Patricia is amazed at the student's clever thinking. "That is something that would be worthwhile to look into. Would you take that on as a project, Judy?"

"Yes, Professor. I will."

"In the meantime, as we go forward, I want you to think about how all of this applies to our hypothetical scenario of gang violence. I'll take your thoughts in our next class. Thank you."

When Pete and Gunny pull into the Clevenger Farm, they see a lot of activity around the Ranger. There's a Bell Helicopter van parked near the bird.

Sly and Caroline meet them with a mid-morning snack of coffee and cookies.

"Welcome back, you two. We missed you. Hope our deputy friend was helpful getting you through the county?"

"Yes, he was. And, we appreciate the help," Pete replies.

"Did you deliver your bad people to a secure place?"

"We did, and they won't be a threat to anybody ever again."

Caroline is biblical about it. "Our Maker will give them justice when they get to Heaven. They'll only be there a short time."

As they all stand in the Clevenger bean field drinking coffee and munching on homemade oatmeal cookies, Conor and Emma are assured by the Bell rep that the Ranger will be as good as new and flyable by this afternoon. Sly waves and smiles at them as he moves through the field on his green soybean harvester.

Conor wonders if they should pay the Clevengers for their hospitality and ruining some of their bean field. The other three agree that they should offer.

Conor approaches Caroline. "Caroline, we think we should compensate you and Sly for your kindness and ruining some of the soybean field."

Caroline pauses and looks intently into Conor's eyes. "Conor, we thank you for that offer, but kindness and hospitality have no price tag. And the damage to the field is minimal. God has given us a good crop this year. And we're blessed by that. And God blessed us with your visit. It was His will that you found our field."

The four team members look at Caroline with admiration.

Conor hugs Caroline. "I wish that more people in the world were like you and Sly."

"There are many, Conor. You and your friends are some of them. You're doing God's work by ridding the earth of evil."

Conor tells Emma that he can handle the rest of the engine job with the Bell service rep and that she should go back to Chicago with Pete and Gunny to get back to work.

"I didn't abandon you in Iraq and I won't do it now. I'll stay until the job is done. We'll fly back together. Isn't that what *Semper Fi* means? I just want to get back, strap on my leather, and straddle my Fat Boy."

Caroline is shocked at this seemingly sexual comment.

Conor chuckles and intercedes. "It's her Harley Davidson motorcycle, Caroline."

Caroline sighs. "Oh, that makes me feel better,"

Pete and Gunny bid them goodbye and wave to Sly in the field. Sly pulls the harvester up near the Ranger and shuts it down. He climbs off and approaches Pete and Gunny.

"Have a safe trip, fellas. I hope you'll come and see us again. You're always welcome. You can land in the bean field again, or just drive out and see us. We should have a reunion someday."

Pete thanks Sly. "We'll do that, Sly. It would be a joy to see you two again."

"Come for Thanksgiving. The kids will be home and I'd like them to meet you."

"Thanks, Sly."

Pete and Gunny climb into the Explorer and head home.

―――――――――――

That afternoon, the Bell service rep tells Conor that the problem is solved and the Ranger is airworthy.

After hugs for the Clevengers, Conor does a walk-around and then slips into the cockpit of his Ranger. Emma straps herself into the right seat. The Bell rep and the Clevengers stand back as Conor starts the two Pratt and Whitneys. Conor checks all the instruments and gives the rep a thumbs up. They wave at Sly and Caroline as Conor powers up and engages the rotors. The bird moves forward and then up and across the soybean field. Conor does a 180-degree turn and makes a low pass over the Clevengers and the Bell rep. They wave as Conor and Emma zoom by, heading for Palwaukee Airport.

―――――――――――

CHAPTER 44
DEBRIEFING AND THE BAG LADIES

Two days later, Conor picks up Creed at the farm and flies him to Palwaukee, where Pete is waiting with his Explorer. They head to Nick's place for the meeting.

A delicious spread is once again laid out on the dining room table. The whole team is here, this time including Sherri's mom. Nick thought it important to have her meet the team in person, and to hear what she has found so far in her study of the activities inside the Camp.

"Thank you all for taking the time to come to this important briefing. And, we're happy to finally meet Sherri's mom, Patricia. Also, I'd like to thank the Chief for coming here to be with us. Now we can stare at his ugly face and not just hear his voice.

"I'd first like to congratulate all of you for carrying out the second sortie to Camp Keokuk. It was almost flawless, except for a faulty engine. Apparently, Emma didn't do preventative maintenance."

"Thanks a lot, Nick," Emma scowls.

"We did meet some wonderful farm folks. Let's toast and *Semper Fi*." They hold up their glasses of margaritas.

"*Semper Fi*."

"We have a lot to discuss tonight. There are quite a few loose ends." At that moment, comes a knock on the door. Nick is surprised. "Who the fuck is that? Everybody's here."

Sherri stands up, unholsters her weapon, and follows Nick to the door. When he opens the door, there stand two ugly bag ladies. Sherri recognizes them as the two she had to shoo away from in front of the Chinese restaurant on their first mission.

"Can we come in for dinner?"

"No, you can't. It's a private meeting. How did you get past security?"

"We bribed him."

Just then Pete gets up and comes to the door. He's not sure what to do. Nobody's supposed to know who they are.

"You'd better let them in, Nick. I know them."

"Jesus, Uncle Pete, you know them?"

"Yes."

As the bag ladies enter, Maria and Adoncia start shedding their disguises.

Nick is shocked. "Jesus, Aunt Maria and Mom! What the hell?"

"Hello, Guapo, can we come in and join the party?" As they enter, everyone just stares at them from the dining room table. Adoncia tries to give Nick a hug.

"Mom. You and Aunt Maria are too beautiful to be this ugly."

Pete and Gunny now have to reveal the truth about the bag ladies. "They're our secret weapon, Nick. We tried to keep it from you, but now you know."

"Jesus Christ, you two. You could have been hurt. Gunny, Uncle Pete, this is crazy."

Gunny weighs in. "Yeah, we know, Nick, but it's also effective guerrilla warfare. They were key to both operations."

Adoncia compliments Sherri. "Sherri, dear, you were so sweet to us bag ladies that night on the street in front of the Chinese restaurant. Thank you, and I'm glad you're Nick's partner." The rest of the team members are speechless as they watch this spectacle unfold before their eyes. Gunny takes a big sip of his margarita.

"Mom, you and Aunt Maria finish taking off those ugly get-ups and join us at the table."

As they settle down, Nick offers the two former bag ladies a margarita and introduces the Chief and Patricia Botkin.

"Once again, let's toast the mission and our two new bag lady guests."

"*Semper Fi.*"

"Now we can really get down to business. For our next mission, we have to nab Rojas and Chin. Sherri is in the process of finding the exact location for Rojas and we know where Chin is. She's still in the Skokie jail. That one is complicated and we have to give it some extra thought."

Emma is concerned about the media, especially Rita Jackson and Rosco Biggs. "We also have to keep tabs on both Rita and Rosco as we go forward. There's a mole somewhere."

"In addition, we have to keep an eye on what FBI Special Agent Tibbs finds out in her class with the Islamic history professor at East Lake College."

"Nick, if we don't get Rojas and Chin in due time, I will keep an eye on the food and water situation inside the camp."

"Thanks, Chief."

Pete asks about Alderman Sariano's chances against Kelly in the upcoming mayoral election.

"I will campaign for him. He went to bat for us in the City Council meeting. But I don't know if he can beat the machine."

Gunny supports his friend. "I'm with Pete. I'll also campaign for the alderman. I can't vote since I don't live in the city, but I can help."

"Don't worry, Gunny. Even dead people vote in this city."

Adoncia and Maria are also supportive of the alderman. "We can do some, what they call, grassroots work," Adoncia says.

Maria follows her sister. "We can go over to Sariano's office and ask if they have any flyers. He knows us."

Nick continues. "We also have the issue of Mr. Tang being held in our jail."

"It's not our issue, Nick," says Sherri. "We can't do anything about him. The Commander is on top of that one. We just have to watch, as it develops."

"Right."

Nick turns to Sherri's mom. "Dr. Botkin, how are you doing with your study?"

"It's very interesting and thank you for including me. I observe the live video every evening and even between classes. And I take a lot of notes. It's still early, but there are some interesting dynamics among the four Camp Keokuk guests. I've created a hypothetical scenario for my graduate social psychology class. My students have some interesting observations about gang members being isolated. Most interesting observation at this point comes from a very astute young lady. She says that gang members may be considered serial killers. She's going to research the psychological profiles of some of the more famous serial killers and get back to the class."

Emma is intrigued. "I would never have thought of that. That young lady may be right. They are serial killers. I hope you'll share the findings with us when she reports back."

"I will be happy to. I'll snail-mail it to all of you, if you'd like."

"Thank you Dr. Botkin. And one more thing. You have a wonderful, brave daughter."

"Thank you, Emma. We'll keep her."

Nick wants to bring up something else. "The Gang Unit has received some additional funding to recruit new members and Commander Washington has asked Sherri and me to give him some names. I hope Gunny and Emma don't mind, but we've asked them to interview with Commander Washington. We think they'll be excellent Gang Unit members.

In unison, everyone says, "*Semper Fi, Semper Fi, Semper Fi.*"

"They haven't accepted yet, but I'm expecting a decision soon."

The Chief chimes in. "You mean you truly think that an over-the-hill Marine gunnery sergeant can hack it?"

Gunny looks up from his margarita. "Listen, Tonto, I can whip your ass anytime. Let's arm wrestle right now and see who's fittest. I notice that Nick and Sherri didn't ask you to be a member."

"Is that discrimination against Native Americans?"

"I hope so, Chief."

Nick brings things to order again. "Don't let this worry you, Doctor Botkin. This has been going on for years."

"Maybe I should do a social psychology study on this group."

Conor responds. "I don't think you want to do that, Professor. No one will believe it. Besides, I can tell you a lot about their psychological make-up, and how they get along with others after serving with them in the Marine Corps. You can just interview me."

"That's a deal."

Sherri makes one last appeal to her mom and her friends.

"We can't forget Woody Archibald at the U of I and his mission to help kids get back on track. We need to find him an office space and some funding. I ask all of you to think about what we can do for him."

Nick also reminds them to pray for Mrs. Rebald. "Our police department Family Notification Team is helping her out."

Nick closes the meeting. "I think that just about covers everything. We have lot to do and we need to be very diligent as we move forward. Once again, thank you all. Let's toast Sammy."

"To Sammy."

"Conor, you and the Chief can stay here tonight. I'd appreciate it if you could fly the Chief back to the farm in the morning. That okay?" Nick asks.

"Of course."

"Uncle Pete, can you drive them to Palwaukee?"

"Yes, as long as they pay for breakfast."

———

CHAPTER 45
BACK ON THE FARM & AT GERT'S

The next day, Conor drops Creed off in the barnyard. He salutes Conor as the Ranger lifts off, blowing dirt all over the place. Chesty dashes around in circles. The Ranger disappears over the trees. Creed takes a deep breath of the fall country air and heads to Gert's for a late breakfast.

As he enters, the same old group of friends is there. They all smile at Creed as he sits down at the round table. He's glad to be back home away from the city.

Creed orders ham and eggs with cottage fries, as only Gert can cook them. "Thanks, Gert. I don't care what Hop says about you, I think you're terrific."

"I don't give a shit what that old flea-bitten, has-been says."

"You know you love me, Gert. You always have, even in high school," Hop grins.

"That's bullshit, Hop. And, you know it."

Chuckles, as usual, around the table. They all love this time of year, when the crops are almost in and the temperature is getting cooler. They now hope for a mild winter, especially those who have to milk the cows twice a day. That has to happen 365 days a year, no break. There's also the same old complaining, which farmers do as a pastime.

"I tried to get an insurance claim from the Federal Crop Insurance Program and the bastards gave me a load of shit," Whitey Hartley exclaims.

"What's the claim for, Whitey?" Hop asks.

"It's for an overdose of fertilizer that burnt five acres of beans."

"Who is the asshole who put too much fertilizer on the beans?"

"It was me, Chief. But I followed the instructions on the bag."

Bobby Ruble, who most of the time just sits and chortles, responds. "I didn't know you could read, Whitey. Did the bag have pictures?"

"You got a lot of nerve, Bobby. I remember two years ago you planted too late and lost a whole field of corn."

"I don't remember that, Whitey."

"I do. And so does everybody around this table."

Gert approaches the table to refresh everybody's coffee. Chief looks up at her and asks, "When are you gonna get a liquor license, Gert?"

"Do you really think I'd serve alcohol to you and your buddies? You guys would never go home, and I'd have irritated farm wives in here looking for you all. No way, Chief, no way."

"How about just beer?"

"No alcohol, Chief. You turkeys can drink at home or go to Paddy's. I'll consider getting a liquor license when you get a girlfriend."

"You're no fun, Gert." The conversation continues into the afternoon. It will resume tomorrow with the same old characters. There's something comforting about that.

Creed heads home to get ready for tomorrow's picking and storage. He will observe the inside of Camp Keokuk on his computer tonight at supper. He can't wait to watch the four guests on either side of the high voltage fence, and for the next mission.

As Creed sips a couple of beers on his front porch, there's a cool breeze and the night is serene, except for the constant croaking of the tree frogs. The air is pleasant with an assortment of sweet country aromas, just as it was when he was a kid. It brings back warm memories when he and his dad fished on Cedar Creek at midnight to the flickering glow of a campfire and tribal family stories. He thinks to himself, *I wouldn't change a thing, except to go fishing with my dad again.*

ACKNOWLEDGMENTS

Elaine Conner for her beautiful cover design.

Michelle Levy, my first editor, who set me on the right track from the beginning.

Neil Geary, a wonderful writer and novelist, who helped me make my story richer and even more compelling.

Kira Henschel, who was bold enough to publish my first work of fiction.

ABOUT THE AUTHOR

Tim Conner has combined his vast, global adventures with his fertile imagination to craft this inventive, compelling saga. His Marine Corps fighter pilot days and experience as a Chicago TV reporter were fuel for this socially relevant journey, full of bold action, surprising twists and turns, including an engaging contrast between urban and rural life. His career spans over four decades as a TV journalist, advertising and public relations executive and well-known communications consultant. Tim co-authored the non-fiction book, *Who Goes to the Door and Then What?: Guidelines for those who may face the daunting task of notifying and supporting families if there is a workplace serious injury or death.*

Contact: connermarine@gmail.com